LANDS OF FIRE

RAIN TRUEAX

CHAPTER 1

June 1902 Tucson Arizona

Walking into the cool of the house from a morning spent in the growing heat of her yard was one of life's small pleasures. Lily Jacobs put her oil paints, palette and brushes on their shelves, cleaned her fingers with turpentine, followed by soap and a rose lotion before pouring herself a cold lemonade.

Sitting at the table in the small kitchen, she appreciated again, how much she loved the little home she had purchased from her sister. The Rose cottage, as it had come to be called, had such a wonderful energy —not the least of which was a garden filled with flowers, most of which flourished despite the heat of a Southern Arizona summer. She had met Rose, the creator of all that beauty. She knew her better through the rich, fragrant garden.

She smiled as she thought of all the ways her life had changed in positive ways. She missed nothing about Chicago, even though her home there had been a mansion. Mansions could be cold places to live. Her family's certainly had been. When Holly suggested she move to Tucson, she had packed paints, canvases, a few clothes, and taken the next train south. The six months she had lived in this cottage had been the happiest of her life.

She sighed as she knew her joy and relief in being in Tucson hadn't just been being closer to her sister. It also wasn't only the cottage. No, she had escaped a most obnoxious suitor, Harold Brooks. Wealthy, attractive, used to getting his own way, he had not been willing to take no for an answer to his proposals.

Far away from his insistency, she told herself that his unwelcome attentions hadn't truly been threatening. Yet, they had felt that way. With few friends in Chicago for support, having lived a somewhat cloistered life, keeping Harold Brooks away had become a daily nightmare.

When her father had died, sad as death always was, it had freed her on many levels—some economic. At first, she hadn't known what to do with the new options. The invitation to move to Tucson had changed her world.

She had told no one that she was leaving—let alone where she would go. She supposed Harold could find out if he wanted to enough. She hoped he would not.

The tap at her door and its opening had her smiling more broadly. "Holly," she said as her sister entered. "Lemonade?"

"Definitely. It's a hot day out there."

'You said thunderstorms are likely?" She reached back into the refrigerator for the pitcher, pouring the drink and handing it to her sister who sat across from her at the table.

"By the end of the month more probably." She took a sip of the lemonade and smiled. "You made it just right—not too sweet. I came to tell you that Vince and I will be out of town for possibly a month."

"Another exploration?"

Holly shook her head. "Not of the archaeological sort. We are taking the train to San Francisco for what will combine a very belated honeymoon and a buying trip."

"Furniture for your new home?"

She shook her head. "No, we found most of what we wanted right here in Tucson. This is to discuss with buyers what their interests might be regarding the finest of Indian crafts. You remember it's what he did before I came into his life."

"I had forgotten."

"It works well with my archaeology—not that we are selling prehistoric goods, but the influence from the past, on the current creators, can prove inspirational as it has on some of your paintings."

"That is true. It would be a shame though if you didn't do more archaeology."

Holly smiled. "Vince is too hooked on it to give it up. We can do explorations when the weather permits, but with the monsoons almost upon us, this is not a good time. This is the right time for him to reconnect with his buyers. And I'd love to see the city by the bay. I never have been."

"I was to the Pacific Ocean once but not San Francisco."

"I am excited to see it, the restaurants, the shops, but am I deserting you? Will you be all right with us gone?"

"Of course. You have introduced me to your friends. I can contact James Angus for any legal problems that arise." She didn't expect there to be any.

"He's an attractive man, isn't he," Holly suggested as she sipped her lemonade with what seemed to Lily a bit of a sly look.

"I suppose. I hadn't noticed. He is though competent and has given me good advice on investments." Although Holly had been given the control over their father's estate when he died, she had quickly liquidated as many of the assets as she could, made sure Lily had her own accounts, and evenly divided it all. From being under the thumb of her father, Lily had become a woman of independent means. She had been wise enough to recognize she needed outside wisdom not to make mistakes. Holly had set her on the right course for that.

Lily remembered when she had been jealous and resented her older sister. She had come to realize that her father had fomented that as a way to control both his daughters—just as he had once pushed their mother to the background as of no consequence. Where their home had not been physically abusive, it had provided no example of how a loving one might be. With both parents gone, she and Holly had finally come to know each other in a new, healthier way.

"I was hoping you'd take the riding lessons from Ollie as I suggested."

As an older sister, Holly did have a tendency to think she knew what was best for Lily. "I will when it's too hot to paint," Lily said with a teasing smile. She felt more affectionate at the dictates, than she had when she had first arrived in Tucson.

"You are addicted to painting, little sister."

"I am and glad of it. Want to see my latest?"

"I always like to see your work."

They walked into the backyard where the large canvas was secured to a big, wooden easel. It was full of vibrant colors that Lily felt captured the flowers but even more the energy of the garden, which juxtapositioned intense colors. The relief from the bursts of energy came from the many shades of green and lavender shadows.

"I love it, but I love everything you paint," Holly said as she studied it from several angles. "If I didn't want to see you have a showing, I'd covet this one for our parlor. It would be wonderful over the stone fireplace."

"You know you can have it."

"I want Tucson to see what you do. I just wish I could take some with me to San Francisco. Galleries there would love these. They are so southwestern and yet with an energy almost of the Far East. You are amazing."

Lily glowed with pleasure. "You really think so?"

"I would not say it if I didn't. When will you share them with others? You must have at least twenty now, from just since you got to Tucson. And I know you stored more in Chicago that we could ship out here."

"I'll think about it." She had been reluctant to share her work out of a fear it would be torn apart by critics who would not be so loving.

Holly went to the small porch where a wooden support allowed the divided canvases to dry. "Do you mind if I look at your others?"

"Of course not, your encouragement has meant more than you know."

Holly brought out each one, taking her time as she studied the shapes and lines that often told more of the story than even the broader swatches of color. "A person would never believe you hadn't been trained in the fine arts. They really are magnificent. And I don't say that because you are my sister. If it was just that, I'd smile and say how nice." She grinned.

"Thank you. I think my lack of training though will hurt me with galleries, when I do finally look for places to show them. I have been thinking of taking some lessons." And having her work critiqued in the process. "I read in the Citizen that Patrick Jamison has arrived to spend a few months. He does workshops."

"I never heard of him."

"He studied in Europe under the Neo-Impressionists. He knew personally painters like Camille Pissarro, Paul Gauguin, Henri Matisse, Henri de Toulouse-Lautrec and Paul Signac."

"Well, at least I have heard of them."

"I am sure that Mr. Jamison won't see my work as impressive as you do, but perhaps he could instruct me in ways to do a better job in getting across the vision in my head."

"Of course, you should do what makes you happy. I just hope you don't let a teacher take away your own unique vibrancy. I love what you bring to the canvas. It's so free flowing and just oozes energy." She pulled out the last one and laughed. "You didn't tell me you were painting me."

Lily smiled. "It was from memory. I could do better if you sometime pose for me."

Holly stared at it for a long while. "As much as you capture the energy of flowers and nature, you appear to have a genuine gift for painting people. I didn't know that."

"I haven't done many. Mostly when I am inspired as I was by my beautiful sister."

They walked back in and finished their lemonade. "Please talk to Ollie about learning to ride," Holly insisted. "It is something you might need someday."

"You know automobiles are the coming thing, don't you-- even here in Tucson."

Holly giggled. "You think that'd be safer?"

"Maybe not."

"Even if they are someday, a horse is a backup and besides, it's an enjoyable activity with the right one. Ollie said he's had Jesse training just that horse for you."

"I've heard you talk about Vince's little brother, but all the time I have lived here, I have yet to meet him. You sure he exists?"

Holly laughed. "Oh yes, he exists—and although he's the youngest brother, he's definitely not the little one."

"I'll believe it when I see him."

"You met Cole."

"Briefly. He was not here long."

"He is busy, working cattle and then I don't know what. I wish he'd live closer as we see too little of him."

"Well Jesse is nearby and I've yet to see him. Maybe he's avoiding me."

"With Jesse, it's not about you. When given a choice, he avoids us too. He's... well, I guess the word is reclusive. Vince is going out there though today to tell him we'll be gone."

"Out there? He doesn't live with their father?"

Holly shook her head. "He has a home to the northwest of Tucson beyond the mines. He works for a ranch out there, the XY. They didn't need someone all the time, and although they pay him some, the home is part of his wage. Most would not like living so much on the desert, so far from people, but it suits him."

"He doesn't like people?"

Holly considered a moment before she replied. "Jesse is... different, and it's what has led to his avoiding people, I think."

"What do you mean different? Crazy?"

"No, no, nothing like that—just, well... slow. How do I describe it? He functions in the world and has coordination that amazes me. When he slides onto a horse, it's as though he is one with it. But he was born slow to reason and speak. People have not always been kind to him. His parents kept him out of school. I think he's just found it easier to avoid humans." She smiled. "He prefers animals."

"Didn't you earlier say he worked for Ollie?"

"He does jobs for him. He trains horses and then this gelding for you. Vince told him what he wanted for you. Ollie had the right horse, and Jesse took him out to his place to work with. He was only green broke when Vince bought him. He liked his temperament though and..."

"Wait, what is green broke?"

"He could be ridden but not trained to be dependable and know how to do the things a rider needs. Jesse has had him now for six months and says he's ready when you are."

"Six months? That's when I came."

Holly smiled. "I knew I wanted you to have your own horse. I kept mine in a stable nearby before Vince and I married and decided to build our own home with a barn."

"What is this horse's name and when do I get to meet him?"

"That was the other thing Vince was talking to Jesse about— bringing him to Ollie's. For this to work well, you will need lessons to feel confident in handling him. His name is Jethro."

"Jethro? Who named him?"

"I think Jesse. His own horse is called Judas."

"You can't be serious."

"I am. These boys were raised on the Bible, remember."

"Still, Judas was a betrayer."

Holly laughed. "Maybe it suits the horse's personality."

"If so, why would Jesse want to ride him?"

"Ask him."

"If I ever meet him." She was skeptical about that. It appeared the youngest of the Taggert brothers had little interest in meeting her.

CHAPTER 2

J esse sat on the front stoop of his adobe, sipping tepid beer. His gaze followed the rider coming at a gallop. The sun was not quite down, with the air cooling. Still, it was hotter than most men would choose riding so fast. "Must be Vince," he told Bear, a mixed breed dog, who had come to him as a stray. Some would say Bear was a big dog. He suited Jesse, who stood six foot six in his stocking feet— when he had stockings.

Vince put his horse in the corral with Jesse's two, and walked to where he waited. "Beer's not cold," Jesse said as he rose to get him one from the outdoor cooler. It was a primitive system comprised of a sack, which when kept wet, as it evaporated, helped to keep food relatively cool-- for a while.

"Sounds good anyway."

In moments, the brothers were watching the sun sink, with the colors of the sky turning brilliant red, orange, gold and purple.

"What's up?" Jesse asked after giving his brother time to finish off the tepid beer.

"Holly and I are taking the train to San Francisco."

"And you want?"

"Just to tell you."

"Need me to look after your place?"

"No, it's fine. Pa will be around. Ollie will feed the horses."

"Then?" Jesse didn't want to try and figure it out. He wasn't good at that. He could handle any horse out there and the same with cattle. Bear had seemed to like him. The two had formed a kind of friendship

—loosely anyway. But people, they weren't for him—not even his brothers.

"Two things. When will Jethro be ready for Lily to ride?"

"Take him with you." Jesse pulled out a cigarette and lit it.

"Safe for someone who hasn't ridden before?" Vince lit one of his own.

"I didn't say that."

"Holly thinks she should ride. I agree. Ollie can teach her, but you could do even better at it. You know horses like nobody I know."

"Maybe horses. Not women. Let Ollie." He glanced over to see Vince's reaction to that.

He was smiling. "You have to meet her sometime," he said.

"Why?"

"She's family, Jesse."

"Yours not mine."

Vince chuckled. "Actually that's not so. She's your sister by law since I, your brother, married her sister."

Jesse just stared into the growing darkness. Vince would never understand.

"All right," Vince said, "forget it. I understand you are afraid of people."

Jesse turned and glared at him. "Didn't say I was afraid."

"You think you can't teach her?"

He was slow but not stupid. He knew what Vince as up to.

Vince put his hand onto Jesse's shoulder. "I am sorry. I was trying to prod you. This business of being a big brother is new to me. Do what is best for you. I appreciate you training the horse for her. I know you will have done a good job on him."

Vince rose, but before he could turn to leave, Jesse said, "I'll do it."

"Not if you don't want to."

"I said I'd do it." When Vince looked back, Jesse stood and managed a smile. He didn't want to do it, but he also understood this mattered to his brother.

Vince pulled Jesse into a hug. "You take care of you while I'm gone," he said.

"Sure. Have a good trip," Jesse said. He knew he had pleased his brother as he watched him ride off into the growing dark.

Jesse had not done much for Vince. Well, with Vince leaving home at fourteen, when Jesse was eight, they hadn't had much chance to know each other until they had come back together in a violent way with the end result one of four brothers dead, leaving the other three trying to figure out whether they had any relationship possible, considering their outlaw heritage.

Jesse had never met his grandfather, Josiah-- shot dead by his own brother; however, he knew the stories of the family's road agent history, their time riding with Quantrill, the dangerous men his great uncles had been. Shortly after his Josiah's murder, his son, Jeremiah, had been convinced by his wife to take their small son, Vince, and leave Kansas for Utah. The hope was it would be different there. From the time Jesse had been born, four years later, he had seen no example that it ever worked out that way. Humans took with them who they were.

With dark settling around him and the moon not quite up over the distant Tortolitas, Jesse walked down to the corral to lean on the top rail and look at the gelding he had trained for a woman he had never met. That wasn't the whole truth. He hadn't met her, but he had seen her. He had ridden into Tucson for supplies, about a month after she had come to live in a cottage, which he had lived in for a while before Holly had married Vince.

Riding down the road that day, his thoughts hadn't gone beyond remembering the supplies he needed. Without knowing how to read or write, he memorized what he needed. Concentrating on that, his gaze caught first a glimpse and then a better look at the woman walking down the road before she turned into the gate of what everyone called the Rose Cottage. Their eyes had never met as she had been looking only toward the house, but he had seen her and knew who she had to be. She looked so much like Holly with the same fine bones in her face, wide lips, big eyes, with the exception being her hair was brown where Holly's was blonde.

He had ridden on, forgotten everything he needed but fought his way to getting most of it by walking around the store. What had been impossible to get out of his memory was that beautiful face. Lily. He had known that was her name. Beautiful name for a woman as beautiful as a lily. He remembered the many shades of her hair, the curls that escaped what looked like a bun. He remembered too much about her. From then on, he made sure that any invitation that might involve her, he wasn't there.

The one thing Jesse had known from childhood was that women, at least the kind he'd want, were not for him. It wasn't even just his inability to think fast like others. It was what he had been told about his being stupid and never daring to pass that onto another child. Given the horrors of his own childhood, he'd stayed away from temptation. Mostly it had been easy. Most women he felt no urge to be with. Probably it would be that way with Lily, if he got closer to her, except he'd never seen a woman who drew him so strongly.

Even if he'd been smart, Jesse knew he had nothing to offer any woman. He barely kept himself, his horse, and Bear fed. His kind of work paid little, but it was what he could do and was rewarding. He especially liked training horses. Helping a horse to communicate with humans was his gift. He could talk to horses-- well maybe not exactly talk but understand them and have them understand him. With no human would that be possible, not with his limited ability to speak his mind—such mind as he had.

Sitting on his porch, Bear again sidled up to him. He guessed the dog had been abandoned and forced to find his own food. In the desert, rabbits were plentiful, maybe an occasional lizard, or even a snake. Most likely, he was a mix of husky, shepherd and something unfamiliar to Jesse. He was a big dog. Good for a dog to be big, with the coyotes hanging around always looking for something easy to grab.

Lighting a cigarette, he didn't bother with a lantern. A waxing moon was high enough in the sky to light the desert with a soft glow. Something rustled the rabbitbrush to Jesse's right. Far in the distance, he heard the howl of a coyote and another answered from not far beyond his shed.

Until Jesse had come, this place had been theirs. Now, with him living in the adobe, putting a door back on it, his work on the corral, and increasing the size of the livestock lean-to, they had been pushed back. They didn't like it. He didn't blame them.

Bear growled. "Shhh boy," he said, "I hear it." He reached for his revolver on the barrel behind him. He never was far from a gun.

"You got any food, señor?" a man's voice asked from the shadows.

Jesse rose. "Come closer where I can see you."

"Your dog looks mean." The voice was old.

"He is. So mind your business. Come out where the moonlight hits you." A bearded old man, wearing a poncho walked slowly forward.

"Don't hurt me, compadre."

"Who are you?"

"Jose. I was gathering saguaro fruit. I got lost."

The gathering part was possible—the accent not so much. "You have family nearby?"

"I do. They will be looking for me."

"Jose, you are a liar."

The old man edged closer as he nervously watched Bear. "He's big. He bite?" he asked.

"Not if you stay where you are." Jesse edged back in the adobe and brought out a lantern, which he set on the table and lit. "Come up here now and let me get a look at you."

The old man came forward. "I did lie, but not about being hungry."

"Why are you out here then? This is not near any villages. You have no horse."

"I had a burro. She got away from me. You see her?"

Jesse smiled. "You really are a liar, aren't you? And a poor one. What's your real name? You aren't Spanish, not with that accent, and don't look Indian."

When the man smiled, he revealed a mouth with few teeth. "What you doing out here, son?"

"Me first."

"I thought I could find Silver Bell. I got lost."

"Why would you want that hell-hole?"

The old man cocked his head to look up at Jesse. "You are a tall one, son."

Jesse tried to reason it out. It made no sense. Silver Bell was no place for a white-bearded old man who couldn't work hard or handle trouble when it came. "You got family there?" he asked as nothing else made sense.

"A son."

Jesse shook his head at the obvious lie. This old-timer's story would muddy what little sense he had. He ducked into the adobe, took two biscuits from the shelf and came back out, handing them to the old one, who took them in grubby hands and ate them hungrily, washing them down with the bottle of beer Jesse handed him next.

"Thank you, son."

"Now tell me the truth. You're on the wrong side of the hills from Silver Bell."

"Nobody used to live here. I figured I could stay overnight, head on tomorrow."

"Where are you headed?"

"I told you."

"Now the truth." Jesse might not be smart with words, but he was good at reading people. This old man was lying to him. The question is why would he be out this far?

"What's your dog's name?"

"Bear."

"Good name. He kinda looks like a bear. How's about me spending the night in your lean-to?"

"You aren't carrying water. It disappear with your mule?"

The old man smiled slyly. "How'd you know it wasn't a burro?"

"Lucky guess."

"You are a smart one, ain't you?"

"Doesn't take smarts for that."

"Yeah, she took off, likely dead now. Damnitall. I loved her, and she left me. Just like a female," he mumbled.

"She'll show up here. This spring is the closest water from the way you came. You knew that though, didn't you?"

The old man cocked his head again. "Sarie is her name if she shows up."

"Fine."

"Your dog might kill her."

"Not likely. Mules kick...if that's what you really have."

The old man chuckled. "You don't trust me much."

"I don't trust anybody much."

"Why you out here-- young, good looking fella like you?"

"I work for the XY and this comes with the deal."

"They ain't runnin' many cattle anymore. Headquarters a long way to the east."

"You know a lot for an old man claims he's lost."

The old man smiled again. "My name is Sam. What's yours?"

"Jesse."

"Got a last name."

"Yeah." He went into the adobe and came out with a blanket. "See you in the morning if you're still around."

The old man chuckled but took the blanket.

Jesse didn't always, but he took Bear inside to sleep. He didn't feel the old man was a danger. On the other hand, he didn't know he wasn't.

Just before first light, Jesse came outside, shirtless but with jeans, boots and wearing his cartridge belt and revolver. It was another thing he didn't always do—wear his gun to fix breakfast, but one stranger could mean more. He went to the oven he had built out of bricks and adobe and fired it up. When the flames were high, he put the fry pan on the grill with bacon in it. On the other side, he set a coffee pot.

Lighting a cigarette, he looked toward the animal walking down from the spring. The mule looked as old as the man. She was staring back at him.

"Lost?" he asked blowing out the smoke.

The mule came toward him. "Sarie?" he asked sure it had to be her. He felt her energy. She was nicer than her owner. "You put up with a lot from him?"

"I never mistreat her, not never. Don't believe what she tells ya," the old man said coming from the shed.

"Animals never lie."

"Unlike humans, huh?" The old man chuckled but clearly in a better mood at seeing his mule. He asked no more questions as he took the coffee Jesse offered and then biscuits and bacon to eat at the plain outdoor table.

"You are a quiet one," the old-timer said finally.

"Your name really Sam?"

He shook his head. "Charlie Provo."

"I'm Jesse Taggert."

The old man had been looking at his coffee, but at that his head shot up and he stared at Jesse. "Yeah," he said after awhile. "Guess you would be."

"You knew some Taggerts then?"

He nodded. "Jackson and Jerome. They maybe your uncles?"

"Great uncles. My grandfather's brothers."

"Mean as snakes them two."

"It tends to go with the name."

The old man smiled, his expression considering. "You like that too?"

"What do you think?"

"Something different about you. What in blue blazes is it?"

"Look, I fed you. You can fill your canteens, then get."

"Where'd I go?"

"You said Silver Bell."

The sly smirk appeared even through the dirty beard. "I lied."

"So this was where you were heading." He had had little doubt of it.

"For a time. Vacant. I like empty cabins, but now you are here, and you take up a big space, son."

"I work to live here."

"I would too."

Jesse smiled with disbelief.

"I prospect some. Any gold I find, we split if you let me stay. These hills are full of metal."

"Most of it legally claimed."

The sly smile returned. "Not all though."

"Charlie, I figure, if I let you stay, when I wake up some morning, my horses and anything you could steal would be gone."

The oldster chuckled. "Wal, might be I'd do that to some... but not to you, son."

"Why not?"

"Don't know. Just wouldn't."

"I will be gone most of the day. You can stay for a bit... but if anything is missing and you're gone, you better be a long way gone." Jesse smiled the one he had seen on his father's face more than a time or two. He knew it was intimidating especially given his size.

"Nope, won't take nothin'. Want supper ready when ya come back? I got some food on my packs, flour. I cook. I like the looks of that outside oven, hot like it is these days."

"I'll be back before dark. And I'll see how good you cook."

Jesse went in, put on his shirt and chaps, added spurs although Judas rarely needed them, and finally came out with his carbine.

"You taking your dog?"

"Uh huh."

"Good."

Jesse rode the desert looking for the signs of where cattle had been. He had a section to look after, and it meant a lot of riding where the desert didn't make it easy with claws reaching out to grab anything that got too close. The chaps protected his legs, but it was too hot for a coat and he just tried to stay away from mesquite or cacti. His shirt showed that he often wasn't successful.

As he found the cow-calf pairs, he started them moving back to the main ranch. He'd seen their tracks mostly at the waterhole not far from his adobe. He had a good idea where he'd find them chewing their cuds. The only bad surprise had been the eleventh. He found her bloated and dead.

He dismounted and looked for tracks. Predators had been at her too long, leaving only their tracks for evidence. With the bloat, he couldn't be sure, but it looked as though she had died with the calf still inside. Where she lay was on the other side of the butte from his adobe, which explained why he hadn't seen the buzzards that were now eager to get back to their meal. Something human had cut off her hindquarter. If she had been shot, the scavengers had torn away the evidence.

Rustling happened now and again in remote areas like this. He looked more carefully for any tracks from horses... or mules. He saw nothing as he drove the cattle into the XY corrals.

"Lost one," he told the foreman, Rasmussen.

"How?" the older man lit a cigarette and studied him. Jesse didn't like the expression but couldn't say why. Rasmussen had come onto the job five months earlier and seemed never satisfied with what Jesse did.

"Couldn't tell. She was bloated but not likely dead more than two days. Buzzards and predators had been at the carcass."

"And you never saw the buzzards?"

"No." He didn't try to explain. If Rasmussen wanted to blame him. Let him. He'd miss staying in the adobe. He liked being far away from people, but he'd find something else.

"So you're saying there was no way to know how she died?"

"Only guesses." He decided not to mention the missing hindquarter. If he'd trusted Rasmussen, he might've, but as it was, it'd stir up trouble where there was no way to be sure there was cause.

"No tracks?" Rasmussen asked still probing.

"Coyotes and buzzards is all."

"All right. Good on bringing in the rest. Be here Thursday as we'll be castrating and branding."

It would be a good excuse for not going to Ollie's, but he could not put that off forever. He'd given his word. Maybe if he got lucky, Ollie would have been teaching Miss Lily to ride and he'd not be needed. Maybe.

The sun was ready to set when he got back to the adobe and unsaddled Judas, noting Jethro was still there and Sarie had joined him the corral. They seemed to get along fine.

"I see you found the hay," he said. Having Sarie around wouldn't be cheap.

"Sarie said thank you. Set at the table, and I'll dish you up some of the best stew you had."

"I have to wash up." He didn't like the sounds of that. Best stew. Where had Charlie gotten the meat?

At the spring, he hung his shirt and cartridge belt over a branch and splashed water on his chest and arms. Using the soap he had hanging from a cord in a mesquite, he finished off by taking a half bucket of water, walking away from the spring and pouring it over himself.

He didn't bother with the shirt but did belt back on the holster before he came back to where Charlie was bustling around whistling something off tune. He sat at his table and looked at the tin plate Charlie set in front of him. Looked like beef, potatoes and maybe some carrots. "Where'd the beef come from?" he asked before taking a bite.

"Ain't beef. It's venison." Charlie grinned that toothless smile. "Tender as can be, it is."

Jesse ate, but it tasted like beef to him. He could not have someone staying with him who was killing cattle. He though didn't have proof Charlie had done it. Given the direction he'd come from, it was possible.

"Son, what'd you do to your arm?" Charlie looked at the long scratch Jesse had been ignoring.

"Hung up on a mesquite. No problem." Other than what it did to one of his few shirts.

"Can't ignore a thing like that," the oldster said as he went to where he'd put his pack and came back with a brown bottle. "Witch hazel, best thing for what ails ya. Don't drink it, o' course." Jesse didn't argue with him or try to stop him from pouring it over the sore scratch. It stung but not for long. "Take the infection away if ya catch it soon enough. I swear by it."

"Thanks."

"All right," Charlie said as he walked back to his possibles and returned with a bottle of whiskey. "I can't lie to you son. It was beef. I come across a dead cow comin' here. She hadn't been gone long but coyotes already got the soft parts. I sawed off the hind quarter. Waste not-- want not." He smiled again.

It could be true. Or might not.

"If it wasn't dead when you got there, no killing stock if you stay awhile. If it happens again, I'll turn you into the XY. Got it?

16

Rasmussen, their foreman, he's not a friendly man to rustlers." Or anybody for that matter.

Charlie smiled with that sly look. "Your hound likes the meat."

"Easier than running down a rabbit, and he's tired from keeping up with Judas," Jesse said. Nodding when Charlie held up the whiskey bottle.

Sipping the strong liquor, he wasn't thrilled to have someone on his place, but for now, it might be all right. Just for now.

Jesse needed a lot of time alone, more than most. Some was due to his mental limitations, but it wasn't just that. He wasn't a people person. He also though wasn't a man to turn another out. At least, not unless he had to do it. He'd see how this went with Charlie. Maybe the old man would travel on before he was faced with that decision.

CHAPTER 3

A t the knock, Lily walked to the door. She had telephoned Patrick Jamison's hotel, been fortunate enough to speak with him. He had been interested in meeting her and seeing her paintings. Never having met a famous painter, she had spent some time trying to decide on the proper dress. Finally, she chose a gray cotton with a bit of white trim at the wrist and neck. She had done her best with pinning her hair into a tidy bun. Its natural curl made orderliness a constant struggle.

She placed her hand over her heart to still her breathing. June's weather was stifling, with a humidity that seemed to suck the energy from the room. Even though the Rose Cottage had thick walls, late afternoon was sweltering. She would be relieved when she could change or better yet be nude when she finally was free of company and could draw the drapes.

On the porch, was a distinguished looking gentleman, probably in his mid-forties with a full head of hair turning gunmetal gray. His mustache was perfectly trimmed. It framed what appeared to be a well-shaped mouth. She had seen his photo in the paper but in person, he was more attractive than she had expected.

"Miss Jacobs," he said with a smile.

"I am so pleased you could come, Mr. Jamison."

"Please, make it Patrick. May I call you Lily?"

She nodded and ushered him into her parlor. "Would you like lemonade?"

"Lovely."

18

She brought it out with a plate of scones. When she sat on the chair opposite the sofa, she said, "I first would like to tell you that I had seen your paintings in the Chalice Gallery in Chicago."

"I must ask if you liked them or not?" He smiled a confident smile.

She had to force her own smile. "I admired them very much. Your work reminded me of Matisse and yet it had your own vision. I thought you brought a force to the subject. It flowed through all of them and went beyond color, lines or shapes." His paintings had led her to expect the same energy from him. Perhaps she was too quickly assessing that.

His smile widened to show a full mouth of white teeth. "Then you have had art training yourself?"

"No, I am self-taught, I am afraid."

"Never apologize for that, sweet Lily. It means you have your own voice."

She felt repulsed and had to struggle for polite words. "I never quite seem to achieve what I hope." That at least was the truth.

"It takes time and patience. I look forward to seeing your work."

"I have some in the kitchen when you are ready."

He picked up his glass and smiled. "I am always ready to see new work."

She led the way into the kitchen where she had placed her paintings on the counters. She had chosen four that she hoped best exemplified what she was attempting to do. Three were of the flowers in Rose's garden but the fourth was a street scene of Tucson with burros, wagons and tradesman. A woman hurried along a boardwalk.

He stood without words for long enough that she felt nervous. Before she could say anything, he shook his head and smiled. "I am so surprised to see such insightful work from such a beautiful woman."

She ignored her irritation at the supposed compliment. "You see promise?"

"More than promise, my dear. I see a genuine gift. The colors, the way you have laid one against another with such verve. I especially like the ones of the gardens. Simply delightful."

Before she could respond, there was a knock at the backdoor. It was Rose Oliver—her saving grace.

"Rose, please come in."

"Oh I am sorry, I am interrupting you."

"Not at all. Patrick Jamison, this is Rose Oliver. She and her husband run a horse ranch out in the hills."

"How lovely," he said putting out his hand.

"I didn't mean to interrupt your company," Rose said shaking his hand and her head. "I just wanted to be sure you stayed for supper after your riding lesson on Friday."

"I would love that."

Rose then looked around the counters at all the paintings. "Oh, my god, Lily. Are these all yours?"

She nodded.

"Beautiful. I just love them. I had no idea you had such a talent. Oh my, that one of the plaza, it takes me right there."

"Thank you."

Rose then looked at Patrick. "Your face is familiar. Do I know you or should I know you?"

"I was in your local newspaper."

"Of course, that would be where. Welcome to Tucson."

"I am sure I'll love my time here."

"Rose created the garden you see out the window, the one I try to paint so often," Lily said. "The heat doesn't seem to suck the life from her flowers as it does everything else this time of year."

Patrick walked to the window and looked out. "It's like Monet's garden in Paris. I was fortunate to be there once." Lily felt unbelievably annoyed at his pomposity. She tried to restrain her irritation.

"I am grateful," Rose said, "that Lily has tended it so faithfully."

"You set it up to be easy to do. Would you like lemonade?"

"Thank you, but no, I have to get home and get supper started." She smiled again at them both and left.

"What a sweet lady," Patrick said as Lily closed the door.

"It was she, who first owned what is now my home. She was widowed but married recently to a wonderful man. Ollie Oliver. He trains horses and riders—like me." She smiled, knowing she was forcing it. Patrick Jamison was annoying her, and it made no sense. She fought the feelings.

"And you are learning to ride."

"My sister insists I should."

"I enjoy it myself when I have time. Does he have a stable for people to rent horses and go for a ride in the desert?"

"I could ask, but I don't think so. I don't know a lot about what is available in Tucson. I have only been here since January. I have been caught up in settling in and then painting."

They talked another half an hour but she was relieved when Patrick rose. "I really should go. Would you have dinner with me tonight?"

"No, I'm sorry, but I'm quite tired."

"Alas, well, I have an interview with your newspaper to discuss my showing. I do though want to encourage you in your work. You truly have promise, my dear. Keep it up" He put out a fist and threw it in the air in some sort of gesture of encouragement, she supposed.

"Thank you. I did think it was mentioned in the paper that you were going to be giving some private instruction while in Tucson. I wondered if you might consider taking me as a student." She asked because she had planned it. Shockingly, she hoped he would say no.

"I would like that. Perhaps we can even paint together. How would you feel about it being in your lovely garden?" He gestured toward it.

"Of course, that would be perfect." She was lying and hated it.

"On Saturday morning I committed to a workshop with some local artists. May we all come?"

She felt more enthusiasm at that. "I would like that very much. I will have lots of lemonade on hand." She let him take her hand and kiss it but quickly pulled it away.

At last alone, she walked into the parlor and tried to think what she was feeling. She had wanted to meet him. He was a handsome man, interested in what she was. Except. She forced the thoughts from her. Silly. It would be different when he returned. He'd seem less stuffy then.

Then she thought about the riding lesson. She was frightened at the idea of getting up on a horse. They were so tall. So unpredictable. She forced that thought from her also. She would do it. She had promised Holly. Now it combined a dinner invitation with the opportunity to get to know Rose better. Yes, she would do it. Maybe she'd see something there also to paint. She smiled at that thought.

As she undressed for bed and freed her hair from the deteriorating bun, the heat was stifling. The small fan helped a bit as she lay on the bed and assessed her day. She had to be honest. Patrick Jamison had bored her. Beyond bored her. She wasn't sure what she had expected but not a pompous fellow, very into himself. Now she had committed herself to more time with him. At least he'd be bringing others along. She hoped that would be enough to make him more tolerable. Painting with a group would be good for her—or so she told herself as she fell asleep.

Walking away from the newspaper office, Patrick pondered his wasted hour. The rube reporter had been less impressed with his resume than he had expected. Nothing that boob wrote would make it into newspapers beyond Tucson's. Annoyed, he headed for the Pedrales, the most respectable bar in Tucson and ordered a whiskey to sit in a corner and sulk.

Aggravated, he looked up and saw the day worsening. His brother came through the doors. The last person he wanted to see was Rupert. No way to avoid it and soon Rupert was at his table with a beer and his usual sarcasm. "What's got your tail in a twist?"

"That is a crude expression."

Rupert chuckled. "Answer it anyway."

"None of your business," he snapped and took another sip of whiskey.

"I am your big brother, am I not?"

"To my chagrin. It is not as though I am proud to have a brother who carouses with miscreants."

Rupert chuckled. "Mighty big words, little brother."

"I am not the only one who came from Connecticut. You know the same words."

"Don't need to use them though to put down others." He smirked.

"The interview did not go well."

"So?"

"What if the nosey reporter goes looking into my background and finds you?"

"He might find it of interest but so what?"

"Having an outlaw family will not help my painting career."

Rupert slugged his beer, went back for another before answering. "You didn't mind the money that paid for that fancy education."

Patrick gave a low growl.

"An education which has not paid off for either of us, dear brother. The money you make on the few you sell, in those fancy galleries, won't even keep you in the suits you like so much."

"It will in time." Not that he believed it. The art world was persnickety. European galleries and artists had looked down their aristocratic noses at him. Neither his paintings nor his background was acceptable. He had no rich patron to promote his work. It hadn't even been about his brother, about whom they'd had no way to know. It had not helped that he had no prestigious galleries behind him. The only gallery he'd managed to interest in Chicago had required a bribe.

"What about the gal you visited? Her family is rich, ain't it?"

"Why do you talk like that, Rupert. You know better grammar."

"Which would work so well with the men with whom I work."'

"You call it work?"

"I call it making money. What about the lady? Her family is rich. Marry her and be set for life. Paint your little hearts out."

He wasn't about to admit Lily's lack of interest in him, which had been another negative part of his day. He did though have the promise of another chance when he brought his students. Maybe it would yet pay off.

"That's no reason to marry someone." Besides Lily's lack of interest in him, he couldn't really say he had any real interest in her either. Maybe he only liked those who admired him. While she did have a gift for art, he felt some jealousy regarding it. She had more gift than he did. Women though never reached the pinnacles of the art world. Maybe he could pick up some of her natural genius and improve his own work.

"There are other ways to make it pay off with a woman like that," Rupert said forcing his thoughts back to his brother. "Some I can help with."

"What are you talking about?"

"I'll tell you if you find out you can't marry her… or don't want to." Rupert snickered as he rose and walked from the bar.

Friday came before Lily was ready. Holly had told her to wear boy's trousers for her first riding lesson. That alone was shocking. She had never put on a pair of britches. Holly had bought them for her. No excuses. She pulled them on and felt a shocking sense of freedom. She hadn't realized how heavy, long skirts were hampering her movement. She put on her chemise and a lightweight cotton shirt. The hat Holly had bought her was straw. She tucked her unruly hair up into it and looked at herself in the mirror.

Before she could change her mind, she ran down the stairs. She had arranged for a buggy to pick her up at three in the afternoon. She was relieved it had a canvas top. The sun was daunting as it poured its heat onto the land.

"How you liking it in Tucson?" the driver asked as he helped her up. If he was surprised at her garb, he said nothing. She supposed he'd seen more peculiar.

"It's beautiful but this is certainly hot."

"It'll improve some when the monsoons hit." He gestured off to the south. "See the buildup there. Won't likely bring a storm today but soon. The big ones will hit with lightning bolts, thunder enough to deafen a person, and all the rain the land can hold and then some."

"You describe it beautifully."

"Beautiful it is, ma'am, but dangerous. When they hit, get yoreself under cover, and I don't mean by a tree. They're the first thing the lightning hits."

"We had thunderstorms in Chicago."

"I heerd that. You folks get tornadoes too, dontcha?"

"I never saw one where I lived, but they say they do."

"Chicago? Ain't that the city what burned to the ground?"

"Before I was born."

He kept up a steady chatter as he headed first north and then east toward the Catalinas. She supposed talking helped him forget the sticky heat that had her sweating through her shirt before they'd left Tucson proper.

As they drove up to Rose and Ollie's home, she saw men by the corrals with the horses. The driver took her to the house where Rose came out and gave her a hug. "Do you remember Grace?" she asked. Lily looked and saw a beautiful dark-haired woman on the porch with a toddler hanging to her skirt.

"Yes, I do. Hello again."

"So today you learn to ride," Grace said, smiling as they all looked toward the corrals. Ollie was sitting on the railing with his grandson beside him. On the other side was a little older boy. They were all looking at the action in the corral where a man was on a horse, making it ride in circles, back up, and then even jump a small log. When he dismounted in one fluid movement, the other men laughed and came to him, patting the horse on the neck. She recognized one of them as being Grace's Yaqui husband, handsome, dark skinned, and with that kind of easy confidence around animals that she envied. All three were clearly horsemen of the type she'd never known before Tucson.

She looked more closely at the man who had been putting the horse through its paces. He wore a black hat that he pushed back as he talked. Handsome went beyond saying with dark hair, eyes that seemed piercing as he looked from one man to the other and then down to the older boy she recognized as Rafe's son, Danny.

The tall man wasn't smiling, but he had a kind of gentleness to his face that she both recognized and found surprising in someone with such rugged features. It explained how the horse had been so willing to do his bidding. The horse recognized authority.

"The horse he was riding is yours," Grace said coming to stand beside her.

"Oh my, I could never make a horse do all that or need it to."

"You never know," Grace said. "Life can throw you some surprises."

Easy for her to say. Holly had written her how envious she was of Grace's natural ability with a horse. Lily had no desire to be an equestrian, just staying on would satisfy her.

"He'll make you a good mount, Lily," Grace said. "Conformation, legs, and that gait. He should be wonderful for you to learn on."

"It looks like a nice horse." She knew nothing about horses although she could see it was a beautiful animal, kind of a tan color with a black mane. He would make a beautiful painting.

She should be looking at the horse, but she found her gaze drawn again to the man. He was talking to the others, as he easily lifted the hoof of the horse to show them something. She had no idea how tall he must be, but his eyes were above Rafe and Ollie, who were both tall. She only realized how much she had been staring when he looked up, and his gaze met hers.

"I will help Rose finish dinner," Grace said with a smile and left her.

Lily had heard of instant attractions but this went beyond anything she had experienced or imagined. When the others saw where he was looking, they turned also. Ollie chuckled and took the tall man's arm. They came out of the corral and walked up to where Lily stood, unable to make herself move. She had to shake her head to find a smile as they came to her.

"Lily Jacobs, this is Jesse Taggert," Ollie said with a broad grin. "He's the fella who trained the buckskin you just saw going through his paces-- your horse."

Still stunned, not at the horse, but at the man, she put out her hand. "I am glad to meet you."

When he reached for her hand, the impact of the touch was as shocking as when she had first met his gaze. "Thank you... so much," she said, stumbling over the words. She forced herself to release his hand. It had been rough on the palm, a strong, large hand. She looked down at it, liking the shape of his long, blunt fingers.

"He's Jethro. Change his name if you want," Jesse said, his voice

even and deep, forcing her attention back to his face. She was unsure
what was safe to look at with him.

"Did you name him?"

He nodded.

"I like the name fine. I know nothing about horses, but I guess
Ollie will have told you that."

"Yes."

Well, he didn't talk much. "I admit being afraid of them."

"You'll get over that," Rafe said before he, Ollie, and the boys
headed for back of the house to wash up, leaving Lily alone with Jesse.

"You have a gift with horses, I hear," she said trying to find something to say that didn't leave her feeling like a fool. That wasn't it.

"Some," he said. He was looking down at her. Being so close to
him made her even more aware of how very tall he was. She'd never
been near a man that big and muscular. It was strangely intimidating
and spellbinding at the same time.

"You think you can teach me to ride?" That was another dumb
comment. She was furious with herself for having lost her wits.

"If you want."

"I should want." Again, she was annoyed at what she was saying.
Of course, how could she instead say he was the most gorgeous man
she had ever seen, and would he pose for her?

"Ma'am, the horse will know what you do."

"Oh, you mean if I don't want to ride him, he will sense it?"

He nodded. "They feel you. You need to feel him too. Then it
will work."

"How do I do that?"

"Come." He turned and led her back down to the corral. Jethro had
come to the rails as soon as he saw him. Jesse reached out and stroked
the horse's forehead. Or she guessed they called it that.

Jesse turned back to her. "Put out your hand."

"He won't bite me?"

His smile softened as he shook his head. She didn't know why she
knew she could trust him, but she did. She held out her hand and let
the soft nose of the horse sniff of it.

"Good," Jesse said. "Now pet his nose."

She liked the feel of the horse. He seemed not to mind her touch. "I
thought he might be as afraid of me as I am of him."

Jesse smiled. "That's why you let him sniff of you. He knows you
don't mean bad by him."

"They can tell?"

"More than most humans."

She looked up at him. His smile was a little crooked, faint as before, but it seemed warm. He liked being with the horse. She felt their united energy, and it was beautiful.

"I might as well tell you now, ma'am," he said then.

She stopped stroking Jethro. "What?"

"I am dumb. You will figure it out sooner or later. I do better with horses than people."

"But you can speak."

"Stupid."

She remembered then what Holly had told her. 'Jesse is... slow in how he thinks.' So, he saw that as stupid. "You don't seem stupid to me," she said.

"Not yet, but I will."

"Why?" She could not believe any of this, not after seeing him with the horse, and then looking up into his eyes. They were intelligent and seemed to speak without words.

"I can't reason, lady, not like you." He shut his mouth, and she saw the muscle jump in his cheek. He was clenching his jaw. Clearly, he hadn't wanted to say what he had. Why had he?

He smiled then. "Because we will be working together on the... horse."

"You read minds?" She smiled then feeling finally relaxed as she reached out again to pat Jethro's nose.

"Sometimes."

"Hey, you two, food's on the table. Wash up out back," Ollie yelled from the door.

Without a word, Jesse headed for the back, and she followed. He pumped water into the large barrel and then stood back. "You first," he said.

She only had to wash her hands and did it quickly with the bar of soap that had been left on a bench. She dried her hands and waited as he rolled up his sleeves and dipped his forearms and hands into the bucket, sudsing up the bar and then washing his face. She held out the towel. He took it and dried his arms and face, his gaze on her all the time. "You are very pretty, ma'am," he said.

"You think so?"

"I always say what I think."

"Really?"

He shook his head. "No, but if I say it, it's what I think."

She laughed then. "I will count on that. How about when I am seeming stupid to you for how I handle the horse."

"You won't be stupid then." He smiled.

"I won't?"

"No, just ignorant."

She laughed again. "I am that where it comes to horses. I will count on you to tell me what I need to know."

"I can do that."

She looked up then amazed again at his physical beauty. She had met some who were considered mentally slow, but none had looked like Jesse. If he hadn't told her, she'd never have guessed he wasn't quite like others. She wondered then how much of that had come from his biology and how much from how he'd been treated. Maybe she'd find out. She smiled again.

"Jesse," she said just before they went into the house.

"Yes?"

"Would you let me paint you?"

She heard him suck in a shocked breath as she went into the house. He might not right away agree to pose, but he would. She knew he would.

CHAPTER 4

After eating the delicious meal Rose had prepared, they all went outside to watch the sunset. "You have a wonderful view here," Lily said. From the home, they could watch the Tucson Mountains turn lavender and then purple as the sky above went crimson to multiple colors of orange and purple.

"Ollie picked it for that view," Rose said. Holly noted she had begun planting flowers around the house of the sort that would withstand being on the desert and having less water.

"I need to phone the man who brought me. He said he'd come back for me." She felt somewhat relieved she hadn't had to get on the horse.

"No need," Jesse said. "Ride Jethro back."

"I can't do that."

He smiled. "It won't go easier to put it off."

"But..."

He just looked at her. She had worn pants to be able to do this. She knew probably Grace and Rafe would have taken her home. She had noted they brought their buggy for their children, but it would be out of their way. Maybe this was best. Finally, she nodded.

"Come again soon," Ollie said as they walked out the door and down to the corrals.

"Do you know how to mount?" he asked as he brought Jethro out and tightened the cinch before throwing the stirrup back down.

"I've seen it done." She put her left foot in the stirrup and stepped up, finally getting herself situated in the saddle. "Like this?"

"Lift your foot out of the stirrup." He adjusted some straps, then had her try it again as he did the same thing on the other side. "Toe in the stirrup, heel down." He looked up then. "Don't hold onto the pommel."

"Why not?" He handed the reins to her right hand.

He smiled up at her. "Trust me in this?"

"All right, but is there a reason?"

"Yes." He tightened the cinch on his mount and was up in one fluid movement. "Balance," he said finally. "Staying on horse means using your knees and balancing in the saddle." He studied her for a moment and then smiled. "Let's go."

"How do I make him go?"

"Nudge in the side with your heel."

"No spurs?"

"I only use them when working cattle."

"Why?"

"You ask a lot of questions, lady."

She smiled. "I do."

"Moving cattle needs faster turns. A light touch of the spurs is easier on him than using the boot."

A moment later, Jethro had begun walking slowly down the road. At first, she felt uneasy, but with Jesse alongside, she began to relax. "If you want to go faster," he said as they moved out onto the main road from Oracle, "just nudge him again. To slow or stop, pull lightly on the reins and lean back a little. He wants to do what you want."

She looked at his horse's head. "Your bridle is not the same as mine."

"I used one with a bit for you because you're new to it. Horses don't much like the bit. He's trained to hackamore like Judas. You'll use one too when you get more at ease."

"Did you name your horse Judas?"

He smiled and nodded. "When I got him, it was his reputation. I should change it. Maybe Jude now."

"You took a horse that had problems?" She was trying to understand him.

"He had the wrong hand with him."

She smiled then. She was beginning to get a feel for this man, who called himself dumb—but was anything but. By the time they reached her cottage, she felt secure at being able to stop Jethro. She was comfortable at a walking pace. Faster would be more debatable.

He was off his horse almost as soon as they stopped. "I'll take care of Jethro this time, but you will have to find a place to stable him and learn that too," he said as he walked her to her door but stopped as she went in.

"Won't you come in for tea... or something?"

"No."

"When do you have time for my next lesson?"

He considered a moment as he moved back to her steps. "Monday. Does that work for you?"

"Shall I come up to Ollie's?"

"I'll bring Jethro here. What time?"

"Morning would be cooler."

He nodded and smiled, that soft little smile, before he took her walk in three strides and leaped on his horse. Taking Jethro's reins, he nudged the horses into a trot, which quickly broke into a gallop. She watched until he disappeared and only then closed the door.

Instead of taking Jethro to Ollie's, Jesse headed back to his adobe. He felt edgy at having left Bear with the old man. Maybe Charlie was what he claimed, but he still hadn't made up his mind.

It was dark as he reached his place, but the moon was up and made it easy to avoid holes or obstacles. He heard Bear's warning bark and felt relief. In the corral was Sarie, which meant Charlie was also still around. He unsaddled his horses and put them in with the mule before heading for the adobe. There was a candle burning, and the old man was sitting on a bench.

"Where'd that come from?" he asked, as there'd been no bench when he'd left that morning.

"You had some old wood behind the shed. Do you mind?"

"No." It was a good idea. He went into the house long enough to take off his shirt. He pulled the cigarettes from a pocket and came back out, putting his cartridge belt and Colt onto the barrel alongside the bench.

"Want a drink?" Charlie asked holding out the whiskey bottle.

He shook his head and sat on the bench. Lighting one of his cigarettes, he leaned back against the adobe. The night air felt like velvet. He had noted that in the distance thunderheads were building. The moonlight accented them. Overhead stars were still visible, but soon clouds would cover them.

"You got a purty place here, son," Charlie said sipping from the bottle.

"Wish it was mine."

"Nobody else wants it."

"Someday they will."

"Gotta admit you're right. Living like I do, and it looks like you, we never have nothing we can really count on... Other than them." He nudged his chin toward the corral.

Jesse couldn't argue about that. He hadn't thought it mattered. Living with his pa, he'd wanted to stay away from the family. Maybe he should have left home as Vince had done. Not being able to read or write, his choices were more limited. He had stayed around but worked at what he knew—animals. He'd made little money, but it hadn't mattered.

Now he had no way even to permanently keep what he had in animals. Bear was safe if he stayed around the cabin. Anywhere else, death awaited dogs like him-- because they didn't belong to anybody. The tough part was what he had only recently come to realize—all that he really loved in this world were Bear and Judas.

He should have loved his pa, but he wasn't sure he even knew what love was. Maybe whatever was wrong with his brain had blocked love in the fullest sense. He knew only one thing. Animals were easier to love.

He only visited his pa when he had to. It was hard to forgive the hard years or the pressure he'd been under to do what he couldn't. Asa, who had been killed trying to murder Vince, had been the worst of his brothers, cruel and mean, but the truth was he didn't know either Cole or Vince. When he thought about it, he had nothing. It had seemed the best way to be.

He knew why he was thinking about it. It was her-- with her questions. He wished that was all it was, but there was more. She was so beautiful. He had only imagined how beautiful when he'd seen her on the street. Talking to her, hearing her laugh, seeing her with Rose and Grace, thinking what his friends had, that he never would, opened something that he wanted closed off.

Why the hell did she have to come so near to his world? It wasn't as if he was meant to have a woman like her. He wasn't meant to have any woman. He didn't have anything to give a woman. No love, no objects, nothing. He hadn't thought of it that way before but...

"You're thinking deep, son," Charlie said interrupting his thoughts. "Something go wrong today? I seen the horse come back."

"No."

Charlie cackled. It was the only way to describe his laugh. "You sure did throw that out like one of them spears. Want to close off the subject, dontcha?"

Jesse smoked and stared into the blackness. Off in the distance he heard the coyotes, this time it sounded like a small pack, maybe the mama and her pups. She would be teaching them to hunt about now. Bear growled. "Shush," he said. "Leave them be."

"What went wrong today, son?" Charlie asked, not letting up on it.

"Old man, if you want to stay around awhile, you have to learn to keep your mouth shut."

Charlie chuckled again. "You're a good man, but you got some things to learn."

Jesse snorted. Oh, he had that one right. A lot of things. He felt one of his headaches coming on. It'd been a month. He always hoped they wouldn't return, but it was here-- and with a fierceness that told him it'd be a bad one. He drew on the cigarette hoping it would go away.

"I could teach you what I know, what I've learned."

He had to struggle to remember what had gotten this all started with Charlie. "You've done so well with your life, haven't you?"

"Lived it as I wanted. You doin' that, son?"

He had thought he had. Maybe he had convinced himself he had. It was easier not to think. He needed a distraction from the pain surging through his head, feeling as though this time it would finally consume him. "You read much, Charlie?" he asked biting out the words.

"Haven't owned books, but I know how."

Jesse's mother had tried to teach him. She had finally given up with exasperation. "You could if you tried," she had said with as much anger in her voice as he ever heard from her. "I can't, Mama," he had cried with tears running down his cheeks.

God, he hated remembering anything about his mother, about any of those years, not the least of which when she had been murdered by Asa. If he had known in time, he would have saved her. Would she then have respected him, thought well of him? He rubbed his forehead. It wasn't helping.

I do think well of you, my beautiful boy. He heard the voice, but he knew it was not real. She had never even said she loved him when she was alive. Always it was wanting more from him than he could give, and there was the fear in her voice when she saw he couldn't do it.

"Don't press him," his pa had said. "You want them to come find him?"

"No, of course not," she had said. As a child, he'd never understood who they were, but clearly it meant he had to hide. They were dangerous. He had learned to stay away from them. He had given up on anything but the animals.

"You read, son?" Charlie asked interrupting his memories and barely getting past the pain.

"No." He took a long drag on the cigarette and looked at the old man.

"You want to learn?"

"No."

"I could teach you."

"No."

It was better things stayed as they were. He would teach her to ride. He'd do that for her, but it was all. He had shut the world away. He felt it pushing against him, but he could block it. He knew he could.

"Son, do you know a man named Rance Evans?"

Just when he had thought things could not get worse, they did.

Saturday morning Lily fixed several pitchers of lemonade with no idea how many painters might come with Patrick Jamison. The one thing she knew for sure about the whole morning—she was not looking forward to it. Until this happened, she had no idea how much freedom she had had with her art. She could sketch, paint, choose her subjects, and nobody looked over her shoulder or found fault. She didn't know what to expect from other Tucson artists. Maybe they'd be like Patrick Jamison with his pomposity.

On the wooden table, she set a tray with glasses. Her own easel was set up with a blank canvas, smaller than she generally used. With the possibility that not all of the artists would have easels, she had left her two extra easels empty. Finally, she sat in a chair and studied her garden with no idea what she would like to paint when they came.

Until she had come to Arizona and lived in the Rose Cottage, Lily had known little about flowers. In her father's home, a gardener had come to deal with the grounds. It was only here with this wonderful garden, shaded with cottonwoods that she had seen how colors could be brought together in ways that might seem garish and yet in nature, they worked. Surprisingly, they also then did on the canvas.

When she had expressed an interest, Rose had been delighted to teach their names to Lily. Poppies, devil's claw, chinchweed, trailing four-o'clock, desert marigolds, fairy duster, sacred datura with a backdrop of burrow weed, desert broom, and desert senna. Planted together in rich combinations, they bloomed lushly through even the heat of the summer. All it took was water and not always a lot. Rose had mixed together native plants with other perennials and created what felt to Lily as though it was a secret garden, hidden from the street and lush with fragrances, birds, butterflies, and bees. She was now about to share it with strangers, which she knew was probably what Rose would have loved, but Lily realized she was now reluctant to do. Would they appreciate this creation as she had? Would their energy reduce its? Well, the last was a foolish worry.

At the gate, the bell rang and six of them trooped in with Patrick Jamison in the lead. They each had bags over their shoulders. Patrick smiled and introduced Lily as they stood and studied the grounds.

"Lily Jacobs is our generous hostess. Lily, this is Robert Prince, perhaps you have seen his work. He paints more representational but with much verve." Again he made that gesture with his fist to encourage. Robert was short, balding but didn't appear to be much older than Lily. He smiled shyly.

"Frank Cutler runs the new mercantile and has been painting since a youngster." Frank was taller than the others, slim and looked away from Lily as soon as he could.

"Jessica Mason is the daughter of Reverend Mason. She has never painted but is enthusiastic to learn." Jessica was round of build, blonde of hair, and smiled almost as much as Patrick Jamison.

"John Ferris has painted all his life. I felt his work was quite exceptional, rather like my own actually." John appeared the oldest and most taken with the garden, if his expression was any indicator.

"And finally last but not least, Fanny Rogers. She began painting when her husband died, didn't you, Fanny?" She smiled at him and nodded. She was attractive and hardly seemed old enough to be a widow. But then, accidents happened.

Patrick turned back to Lily. "We thank you very much for allowing us to use your garden as inspiration for our paintings."

"I am glad you could come," she said looking from one face to another. The friendliest seemed to be Jessica Mason who helped her pour and serve the lemonade. She brought out a plate of sugar cookies that she had earlier bought from the bakery. The artists drank their lemonade as they walked around the garden studying various angles.

"Ladies and gentlemen," Patrick said, "I will set up my own easel here." He took it off his back and quickly put it together. "I will paint with you today and we can discuss our work later for those who so wish. Otherwise, I have nothing more to say as I must try to capture this lovely oasis with my own paints as you all will, I am sure. I will take some breaks and observe your work if you so wish. Otherwise, just paint." With that he did exactly what he had said and began squeezing oils onto his palette.

Lily moved her easel to where she could paint the gate with its little bell and soon was lost in colors and shapes forgetting for awhile that she was working with others. Whether they enjoyed the garden or not no longer mattered as she was caught in the same fervor she always felt in trying to make the paint bend to her will.

She had only realized someone was watching over her shoulder when she heard a feminine sigh. She looked back and saw Jessica looking at her painting. "I hope someday I can learn to do something anywhere near like this."

The painting had the gate open just a bit with the climbing rose still blooming over the trellis above it. The old bell added an interesting shape that she might never have thought of painting had she not wanted to leave the flower garden for the others. There was only room for so many easels at the best viewpoints.

"Thank you," she said. "Where is your painting?"

"I was overwhelmed by all the colors and sketched instead." Jessica held up a sketchpad with a finely drawn sketch of the cottonwood and the desert senna below it.

"That's lovely," Lily said. "And yes, the colors can be overpowering when first looking at them."

"I would love to come back someday perhaps when I have gotten a better idea how to use the paints."

"That would be fine. I will give you my phone number before you leave."

Jessica smiled.

An hour later, Lily went back inside and brought out the cold tea she had made the night before. This time she also had a plate of croissants. The painters were mostly eager to stop and cleaned their fingers before drinking and eating.

Patrick walked around with his glass as he studied each student's work. "Very good," he said to Robert. "I like the intensity of the colors."

Mostly he was careful to find something positive about each of the paintings. When he saw Jessica's sketch, he said, "I wish you had tried paints, my dear."

She frowned but forced a smile. "I will next time." Lily recognized the expression. It had doubtless been on her face many times when she wanted to please and, at the same time, felt annoyed at the expectation.

"I thought her sketch was very good," she said knowing it would likely annoy Patrick.

"It is," Patrick surprisingly agreed. "I just would love to see how she would deal with color." He went back to John Ferris' painting. "This is truly exceptional." Not surprising to Lily since he had said the man's work was most like his.

He then turned to her gate painting. She waited for the criticism. "I am envious," he said as he smiled at her. "You created a masterpiece, my dear. The gate says so much about life. It is options. The gate being just a bit ajar makes it uncertain if it's to protect or allow freedom. The bell though, that is the perfect touch about an announcement, the alerting to life. Look at how you captured its aging." Smiling, he shook his head. "I love this."

She felt pleased and yet strangely uneasy with his praise. As the others trooped back through the gate, he stopped. "I would like you to have dinner with me Monday night. I would make it sooner, but I have been committed for tonight and tomorrow."

Lily smiled. She remembered the riding lesson. It would not prevent her having dinner with Patrick. "I'm sorry," she said. "I have made other plans."

"Another night then?"

"I can't commit to that right now."

He left then, and she felt freed. She began to think about what she would prepare for dinner when she invited Jesse to stay after their ride. He would not want to stay. She already knew him well enough to know that much. She would convince him. She did not know why, but she knew she wanted more time with him. She wondered if she could convince him to pose for her. She smiled then as she thought of possible ways she might do that. She wished she had more feminine wiles. She needed to talk to someone who might. Better yet, someone who could teach her to cook—fast.

CHAPTER 5

A t the Plaza, Patrick met with Rupert even though he still preferred
they not speak in public. Connecting himself to his roughly dressed
brother was not going to help him-- even with Tucson's plebian citizens.
Still, if he didn't show up as agreed, Rupert would find him. He could not
have that happening. The vague hope his brother might not show up was
dashed when he saw him sitting on a bench looking annoyed.

"How did it go with her?" Rupert asked.

"Not going."

"Why not?"

"It's just not."

"All right. That's how it will be then. What about blackmail?
Anything she might be hiding, and we can find out?"

Patrick shook his head. "Are you insane?"

"I am practical. So tell me."

"I doubt it. From what I learned, she took care of her father before
he died. She's been rather cloistered to be honest."

"She has a rich sister. Kidnapping go too far and damage your delicate East Coast sensibilities?"

"Don't be ridiculous."

"It's not ridiculous. It's simply a way to gain the resources some
have, which we do not."

"It's a foolish idea. You and I are not capable of kidnapping a
woman even if I was so inclined—and I am not."

"Someone is coming who could."

"One of your outlaw cohorts?"

"Not with a poster out on him, but yeah, he walks the other side. He's free as a bird now. Did his time."

"Time for what?"

Rupert shrugged. "It's nothing to me or you. You don't ask some men questions. Likely, though bank robbery. It was his specialty.

"I don't like the sound of any of this. Count me out."

"Too late. You are already in."

Patrick sighed feeling sick at the machinations possible in a situation like his. A love of the fine things but no way to get them without... "You knew about Lily before you talked me into coming here, didn't you?"

"And if I did?"

"You hoped I could court her?"

Rupert shrugged. "It was one possibility. I wasn't sure."

"Not sure? You asked me to come."

"I was told to bring you but not why."

Patrick didn't like the sound of that. Asked? Asked by who? "I should never have come."

"You had no choice. He wanted you here, and you depend on my sending you money to live, do you not?"

Patrick let out a breath but nodded. "Who was it who wanted me?" He should have asked more questions before he had come—though had he ever had a choice?

"You'll find out when it matters."

"Is this crooked dealings?"

Rupert twisted his hand from side to side. "Possibly... Some anyway."

"Rupert, are you good at being an outlaw?"

His brother looked at him in surprise. "What do you mean by that?"

"Just it doesn't seem you are making much sense, and shouldn't an outlaw have good plans before he can carry them out?"

"What do you know about being an outlaw?"

"I read."

Rupert chortled. "Those dime books about Wild Bill, Jesse James, Masterson?" Irritatingly he laughed even louder. "You think those are guidebooks to being an outlaw?"

"Some could be."

"None tell the truth of life, brother—at least as I've understood it to be. The real deal is often stupid, operating with luck, where accidents determine more than planning."

"Why then do you do it?"

"I try to make my plans make sense."

"Well, on this one, you haven't yet."

His brother gave a low growl. "You want the kind of beating I used to give you when we were children?"

"Is this your answer to questions that make you think?"

"There are times you have to make the best of the cards you were dealt. We had a father who gambled poorly with his business and in the end cost us both any real future. You have chosen to ignore that. I have chosen to deal with it as best I can."

"Tell me then what you have offered to do."

"I was told to bring a few of men to Tucson."

"Outlaws?"

"Men with certain skills."

"And mine was supposed to be?"

"I didn't ask."

"Shouldn't you have?"

Rupert's face turned red with anger. "I have worked for him before. I had no real choice about this job. Asking questions would be futile if I had no choice—other than maybe looking for side options."

"Like Lily?"

"She might've been one or maybe…"

"Maybe what?"

"Forget it. And quit asking. A man can end up dead asking questions of the wrong person."

"You could kill me?"

"Not me."

"The one you work for."

"Look, shut up. Just listen for once. I got Billy Evans to come here by telling him his pa had cheated him on a job. Billy is mean as a snake, but not real bright. Then I got the word to Rance that his son was after him and Jeremiah Taggert and he better run for it. I knew he'd run straight for Taggert."

"And you wanted him here too?"

"To get Billy."

"God, Rupert, this is beginning to sound like a horrible mess. If you have the money for train fare, we should both leave town."

"We can't-- not 'til we get this done."

"This? Words might help me understand what in heaven's name you are speaking of," Patrick said.

"I can tell you a few things. You heard of Billy Evans, of course."

"He's an artist?"

Rupert shook his head with obvious frustration. "You ever read a newspaper?"

"A few sections."

"He's like Billy the Kid."

"Billy the Kid ended up dead."

"I said like. Billy is good with a gun and has little concern for how he uses it-- if he's paid enough. He has men to come with him, which saved me looking for the necessary crew."

"This has a reasonable point, I hope?"

"Give me time," Rupert said impatiently. "The man I am working for wanted someone with Evans' skills."

"Why trick him then? Why not just pay for him to come as you did me?"

Rupert sneered. "Why would I do that if I don't have to?"

"So you are cheating the man for which you work, who you said is dangerous?"

"Not cheating exactly. Besides, he won't have to know, will he?"

"If he's as dangerous as you said, he probably will know." Patrick felt beyond confused. "We should have met at the Pedrales. A drink might've helped this to make sense." Although he doubted it. "You really did all this without knowing what this man wanted?"

"I knew the skills, not how they would be used. I wasn't sure about you either though he asked for you."

"He knew I was your brother?"

"He's a man who is always a step ahead."

"I don't like it relating to Lily."

"I don't know exactly that it does. Once I got to Tucson, I did think maybe you being a painter and her being a painter… Well, perhaps he wanted you to court her, but he didn't say that."

Patrick knew he was being foolish to try and make any of this make sense but he felt unable to give up the attempt. "So, this person, who wanted me here and also wanted some outlaws, might have hoped Lily would marry me? Or was the kidnapping what he wanted?"

"I told you. I don't know it all. It was just an idle thought on my end. Actually if you married her, you and I would have her money. It might have protected her."

Patrick snorted. "I know it's being foolish of me, but let me repeat what you have said and you see if it makes sense."

Rupert growled but Patrick didn't let it stop him. "You bring an outlaw here with lies. You bring me here with no idea why I'd be wanted. You suggest I court Lily and if that doesn't work, that we kidnap her with no idea that's what this man you work for would want. Does any of this seem smart to you, Rupert."

His brother was silent, but Patrick waited. His head was still spinning with the complexities, the dangers, and all he wanted to do was paint. Why had he ever come to Tucson?

"We are in it, like it or not," Rupert said finally.

"Why don't we get a ticket on the next train and leave Tucson?"

"Some men have wide tentacles."

"And this man does. The one you say you are cheating? My God, Rupert, you sound insane. What has been your job up until now?"

"I told you."

"I mean before. What does he hold over you?"

"It doesn't matter what it was. It is there, and I will do what he tells me. You can leave though. Maybe you should."

Patrick considered that. "Would the man then be angry at you?"

"Probably."

"How sure are you that it involves Lily?"

"Only that why else would he want you? Maybe he hoped you would gain her trust for other reasons."

Patrick sucked in a breath. Making sense of this was impossible. "I don't want her hurt. She is a nice young woman and doesn't deserve anyone using her."

"You are soft, aren't you?"

"I am not hard if that means being a criminal."

"Your soft life has been possible because of what I've done."

"I never asked."

"Didn't you ever wonder?"

"I guess I should have. I will stay. I have no idea what any of this means but I will stay. You are my brother, but Rupert, you are going to end up getting us killed or ending up in prison."

"I will protect you."

"If you can. One other thing. You said Evans is a dangerous man. What happens when he finds out you lied to him?"

Rupert smiled. "He should not."

"But if he does?"

"I'm dangerous too."

"What about this boss?"

Rupert's smile disappeared. "In his own way, he's more dangerous."

Saturday after he finished his work for the XY and dealt with the obnoxious Rasmussen, without punching him in the mouth, Jesse rode to his father's home on the edge of Tucson. He hadn't been there for a month. He expected to hear the usual lament at that. He would have to put up with that. He needed to know what his father was doing. Rance Evans was a name from the past, one he had hoped never to hear again.

He pulled Judas up in front of his father's small home and dismounted, tying the reins to the railing. He looked toward the house but stopped to light a cigarette. Delaying tactics. It was still strange to imagine his old man living in a town, not being a blackguard... or was he still one and this was the proof-- Rance coming to Tucson where they hoped to put together the old gang.

Any such activity would ruin any chance for Jesse or even Vince to live here. Normally, he'd have let Vince take care of this. He could talk anybody into anything. Vince wasn't there. It was up to Jesse to do his best.

When the door opened, his father came onto the small porch. "Been awhile," he said as he leaned on a post and studied Jesse. "Got lost, did ya?"

"Been busy." He took a delaying drag on the cigarette.

"Maybe find me dead sometime when ya come."

"Could be." Jesse recognized his father's usual maneuvering.

"So what brings ya? Since it ain't love for your pa."

"What's Rance Evans doing in town?" he asked the cigarette dangling from his lips.

His pa looked at him. "How ya know he is?"

"Charlie saw him on the road, talked to him a little. Charlie knew Jerome, Jericho... and you." He watched his father maneuver through what lie he wanted to tell. Not much changed with that old man.

"Charlie who?"

"And that matters why?"

"You getting mean, boy?"

"Could be. Now what is Evans doing here?"

Another old timer came out of the house to lean on the opposite post. He was grizzled, bearded and looked nothing like he had the last time Jesse had seen him. "You shore got yourself a big 'un there with that son," he said as he grinned.

"He's big, and he's simple." Jeremiah turned back to Jesse with that mean look that was so familiar to him.

"Now that we got that out of the way. What's he doing here?" Jesse asked narrowing his eyes and tightening his mouth. He tried to think what he could do to change things, short of killing both old men and ending up hung.

"I'm on the run. That's the long and short of it," Rance said.

"From the law?"

He shook his head. "Nah, my son. He's out to kill me and won't care how he does it. Me and your pa too if that matters to ya, which maybe it don't."

"Why would he want to do that?"

"Thought you said he was simple," Rance said looking at Jeremiah. Jeremiah smirked. "Not stupid... simple... Sees things that way. Makes it easier, don't it, boy?"

Nothing had been easy in Jesse's life. That didn't look likely to change soon. "I'm waiting for the answer."

"Can we go inside and drink some coffee over it?" Jeremiah asked. "It's a long story."

"True or not?" Jesse asked but threw his cigarette down and ground it out, before following the old-timers through the door.

Jeremiah had a nice little home, not fancy but comfortable and that surprised Jesse. He hadn't been inside since he'd told his father he'd not live with him.

"I see you're surprised it's as nice as it is. Wal, Holly done it for me. She's real good with furniture and such."

Jesse followed him into the kitchen, hoping he was not making a mistake in hearing a long story that he might be unable to follow. In a moment, he had a cup of black coffee and straddled a chair. "Now," he said, let's hear it. And if either of you lie, you won't like how this kitchen ends up looking."

Jeremiah chortled. "Glad you ain't lost your sweet nature, son." He chuckled again.

"Here's the truth of it," Rance said. "My boy, Billy, he's mad at me and Jeremiah over a little deal that went south five years ago. He thought we held out on him."

"The problem," Jeremiah said, "is there wasn't no haul. Nothing

44

like he was told."

"Who told him that?"

"I don't know. This come out of nowhere. Maybe Asa in one of his moods. I should've killed him years before Vince did it," Jeremiah said adding a string of obscenities. "I'd still have Valerie. Should have strangled him the day he was born. If it's him, he'd know we never cheated a pard. He would've just been talking in his beer or out to get rid of me by getting someone else to do it."

"So what do you expect from Billy?" Jesse pulled out a cigarette, looked toward his father for permission and after the nod, lit it.

"For him to show up here, with his pards, demand the money, then when we ain't got it, kill us," Rance said. "He's more like Asa than not. That's the plain truth. We never cheated him, but he'd believe we would-- because he cheats."

Jesse smoked as he considered the possibilities. One that they had cheated Billy. Neither of these two were known for their honesty. It was also possible that the old scoundrels were telling the truth. Either way, from what he knew of Evans' reputation, he might not care and would shoot them anyway. He was surprised to realize that he didn't want his father killed. But what could he do about it?

"Now back to what I wanted to know," Jeremiah asked. "Lot of men knew Jerome and Jackson. Who is this Charlie?"

"If he knew you. You know him."

Jeremiah gave him a look, which Jesse ignored. "Provo," Rance said.

"You got him with you?" Jeremiah asked.

"For now."

His father's eyes went sly. "You got something going on you ain't told me? Last I remember hearing about Charlie, he was into finding gold. That changed?"

"I wouldn't know. If so, he's not making much at it."

"What are you doing?"

"What I was last time we talked-- working at the XY two days a week and training horses for Ollie the rest of the time. As for Charlie, he ended up at my adobe. Expected it to be empty."

Looking at Rance, Jesse tried to reason through what he'd been told. "I still don't see why you'd come here, Evans. People in Tucson know Jeremiah lives here. Seems it'd make it easy for your son to track you right to him."

"He's the only one I knew who'd stand up with me in a fight.

45

That's why. Ain't you ever had a good friend like that, Jesse?" Rance asked.

"No." He didn't know much about that word friend. It had been safer that way. His brothers hadn't been ones growing up. Vince left as soon as he could and before Jesse knew him. The year since he'd met up with him again had him thinking he might be a friend, but was he just hoping? Asa had been brutal and nobody could call him a friend. As for Cole, a year older than Jesse, he had probably learned to hide what he thought as much as Jesse had.

He smoked as he tried to reason it through. There was what he'd been told and then what had not been said. One way or the other, Billy Evans and those who rode with him would be in Tucson and looking for Jeremiah and Rance.

"We need to know if he's already here," Jeremiah said. "He wouldn't recognize you-- being so much bigger than the rest of us, face shape different too, just the dark hair but lots of men got dark hair."

"How would I know them?"

"Billy is short," Rance said. "Bout this tall." He put his hand to Jesse's chest. "He's blond and likes his hair longer, curling, then a goatee and mustache trimmed always. Ever seen a photograph of that Custer who got killed at the Little Big Horn?"

He shook his head.

"Too bad. Wal, like him. Slick and even wearing buckskins when it's not too hot. If you see him, you'll know him."

"So I go there and try to kill him?" He wasn't sure how far his father wanted to take it.

"No," Jeremiah said quickly. "God, don't get yourself into that. Just let us know if he's there and how many with him."

"Unless he recognizes me as a Taggert," Jesse said understanding his father wouldn't mind making him a sacrificial lamb, any more than Abraham in the Bible had minded using his son. The Bible, which Mama had read to her boys every night, was full of stories like that. He'd been teethed on them, and it wasn't a good feeling to know how they could come back to bite, if they were life examples, and you got the lamb part.

"He'd know Jeremiah or me," Rance said.

"Maybe Ollie would do it," Jeremiah suggested.

"He could know him too," Jesse said. He wouldn't put that old man at risk, and Ollie had once rode the owl hoot trail. He would have to do it. Bars weren't anywhere he liked to frequent. To get information, they were the likeliest.

And he'd do it as soon as he could. He had been reluctant to leave Bear and even more to stretch out his time away from him. He was beginning to hate that because the big head always looked at him so sadly, ears cocked, when he realized he'd been told to stay. He would not though see the dog hurt and couldn't protect him in town-- so he was safest out there. Hopefully, Charlie would keep an eye out for him. Or was that the other way around.

Nearing dark, he had found a cafe, eaten a tough steak, and boiled potato, before he headed for the Pedrales. Saloons were bad news for him on several levels. He couldn't afford them but even more wasn't one to drink a lot. He had enough trouble thinking straight when he was cold sober.

Saloons offered another problem that went deeper—those who went there. He was a big man and that immediately made him a target for reasons he would never understand. Maybe it was because he was slow. It had gone back to childhood. Whenever he was around other children, they ridiculed him and wondered why he wasn't in the one-room schoolhouse. It didn't take them long to decide they knew the reason, and the brutal names followed.

He had no choice this time and walked to the bar, where he ordered a whiskey. The barkeep seemed friendly enough, but when Jesse didn't respond, he went onto others.

Lighting a cigarette, Jesse turned and leaned on one elbow to survey the room. Nobody fit the description he'd been given. The place was lively with laughter and slurred voices. Women roamed around going from man to man with smiles that he knew meant only one thing.

"You lonely, big boy?" an older woman came up to him.

"No."

"Buy a gal a drink?"

"No."

She sneered at him then. "Maybe you prefer boys."

He looked at her with amazement but turned his back. That's what he had against women. Turn on you in a second-- even his mama, would get mad at his slowness.

"Not very nice to the lady," the slurred voice growled. The man grabbed Jesse's arm to swing him around. He was not as tall as Jesse, softer looking, but belligerent and looking for trouble.

"Sorry."

"You heered me, ya big ox."

"I did."

"Apologize to her."

The bartender came back to stand in front of them. "Jackson, get out of here and don't come back." Jesse saw the shotgun in the barkeep's hands and that he looked ready to use it.

The drunk glared at Jesse but stumbled out of the bar.

"Sorry for that," the barkeep said. "My name's Ridge. I seen you in here before, didn't I?"

"I've been here."

"You look like... Hey, you wouldn't be Vince's brother, would you?"

Jesse didn't think he looked anything like Vince but wished he did.

The barkeep chuckled. "It's the eyes, mister. Same eagle eyes."

"He is my brother. I am Jesse."

"Yeah, that would fit. I seen your pa around too. You all have a mark on ya."

That was for sure. "You wouldn't have seen someone new in here, blond, with tough looking friends?"

"Not tonight."

"Thanks."

Jesse had had his fill of the noise and stink of a saloon. He walked out the door heading for his horse, when his arm was grabbed. It was the drunk.

"You're going to get that beating now that your friend's not here to save you."

"Beating for what?"

"For being stupid. That's enough reason," the man said as he leveled a blow at Jesse, which he blocked by stepping back. It was then that he felt other arms around him, grabbing him around the waist, tightening to yank him off his feet. The arms were like iron. To break the grip, he slammed his boot backward into a shin and heard the satisfying oomph as the man dropped his grip. From then on Jesse felt fists slamming into him, his face, his belly, but he was free and his own reach was longer than any of theirs.

One blow after another and finally he was standing facing only the first drunk. The man now looked less certain with his friends lying on the ground.

"I didn't want this," Jesse said.

"What's going on here?" The loud voice was not drunken and sounded angry.

"He started it," the drunk slurred.

Jesse turned to face a man with a badge and gun in his hand. He let out a breath and straightened.

"I should put you all in a cage and sort it out in the morning," the sheriff said.

"Not me," Jesse said as he tightened his jaw.

The sheriff turned his gaze then onto him. "I know you?"

Ridge came from the doorway of the Pedrales. "This is Vince's brother. He didn't start it. Let him go."

The sheriff studied the ones on the ground now starting to rise and then Jesse. "I can see that. All right, but stay out of trouble. He looked back at the five men now standing and looking worse for wear. "That means all of you."

Jesse looked for his hat that had been lost in the fray and dusted it off. He looked back at Ridge who was watching. "Thanks," he said.

"Just told the truth. Sorry for what happened." Ridge then looked back at the drunk. "You stay out of my bar for a week, or you'll see what you got here was just a taste."

Jesse managed, despite a sore jaw, a smile. Ridge looked like the kind who could deliver what that look promised. He made a semi salute with his hand and then went looking for his horse. He'd done enough for his pa for one night—maybe at all. He might come back and ask that sheriff. He might be the type who'd be fair. He smiled then. When had he ever known a lawman to be fair?

By the time he got back to his adobe, the moon was almost setting in the west. He was surprised to see the old man sitting on his bench, sound asleep, Bear at his feet. When he had Judas in the corral, he felt exhausted and ready for sleep himself. A candle had burned down but the sun was faintly beginning to light the east. "Old man, you better go to bed."

Charlie's eyes opened. "I been worried. Where ya been? Didn't know you'd be out all night. Me and Bear was a frettin'."

"I can see that." He smiled and sat at the other end of the bench. Worn out, he lit a cigarette anyway.

"You get yore answers?"

"Some." He told him the gist of what Rance and his father had said.

"Billy Evans, huh. That one is a snake," Charlie observed.

"He might not be coming. Could be two old men just rambling." He'd thought of that possibility as he'd ridden home.

"So Rance and Jeremiah turned legal," Charlie shook his head. "I didn't ask you about your old man, figured it was your business, but he did swing a wide loop in his day."

"So I hear." He watched as the cigarette smoke trailed into the air. The pale glow to the east was beginning to get a little color. His gaze was caught by movement as Bear growled. "Let them be," he murmured putting his hand on the tense dog. The coyotes were loping north, just beyond the line of mesquite and rabbitbrush. One full sized the others three pups.

He liked the smell of the desert first thing in the morning. The scents of the night seemed to fill the air for one last burst before the heat sucked out their energy.

"You ever ride the outlaw trail?" Charlie asked.

"No."

"Too honest."

Jesse took another long draw on his cigarette. "Too slow."

"I seen you with your horse. I don't buy the slow."

"In the head, Charlie." It was the first time he had called him by his name.

"I don't see you as slow, son. Just as thinking it out more than the ones who run off hot at the handle. That's smart."

"Yeah, well..." He blew out the smoke.

"I can teach you to read."

"Let it go."

"Can you write your name then?"

"Yes."

"But not read what you'd be signing."

"Is there a reason we're talking about this?"

"Reckon not." Charlie rose and headed for the lean-to.

"Charlie, you snore?"

"Not that I know of."

"Use the bunk in the cabin, not the double bed but the one on the other wall... if you want that is."

Charlie stopped and turned to look back at him. "Finally decided ya trusted me, did ya?"

"Maybe. I do know this. You take good care of my dog." He

continued to smoke as the old man went for his possibles and then took them into the adobe. Its wide, earthen walls kept it bearable even on the hottest days.

Jesse stroked Bear who had again nestled at his feet. Tired as he was, he wasn't sure he could sleep. Seeing his father had stirred up feelings, ones he preferred to bury. Sometimes he could—sometimes not.

Staring at the sunrise, colors beginning to light the entire sky beyond the Tortolitas, he thought then of the forbidden. He was not a man to lie to himself. That was bothering him most, what had led to that headache. It hadn't come from his father, not even the danger that might also ensnare him. No, it was the woman. He'd been thinking of her since he'd ridden her home.

The woman in the bar had reminded him, as if he could have otherwise forgotten. He'd pushed women from his head. They were not for him. Least of all, a beautiful woman like Lily Jacobs. He kept remembering her eyes, those big eyes that had looked up at him asking... What the hell had she been asking? He took another long draw on the cigarette hoping he could find calm. There was only one way to find calmness at least where it came to her—stay as far away as he could.

Except he kept remembering her curly hair. Was it soft? How would it feel if he touched it? Then those lips. They were full and seemed soft. He had never kissed a woman. Oh, he'd had a few pull his head wanting a kiss, but he'd seen it as their way to ridicule him, and he'd pushed away to their laughter. No woman wanted a stupid man—not even the whores.

He had one day to get control of his reckless thoughts, to get a handle on himself before he gave her that next riding lesson on Monday. He needed to chop a lot of firewood. That might help, or maybe he'd clear the dead mesquite.

He looked down toward the two horses in the corral. They were nuzzling each other, which wasn't always how two geldings took to each other, but these two had from the start. One was chosen stock, from the highest breeding. The other had been out of outlaw stock, lucky he hadn't ended up dog meat. Both though made good mounts now—with the right handling. Too bad it wasn't that way with humans.

CHAPTER 6

Sunday morning, Lily dressed and debated going to a church service. She had gone with Rose a few times to the church nearest her home. She wasn't particularly a believer or for that matter, not a believer but she had liked being with the people, hearing the words, the singing, and the energy of being part of an old ritual. She equivocated long enough that time ran out, and the decision became moot.

If Rose stopped by after the service, which she sometimes did, it would be a sign she could ask her some questions on her mind. In the meantime, she got out the cookbooks she had found in the kitchen and looked for the simplest possible dishes to prepare.

When Rose tapped on her kitchen door, Lily was quick to open it and pull her inside.

"Cookbooks?" Rose asked as she looked at the table. "I thought you were buying meals from the deli on Fourth."

"I decided that I should learn to cook. I make breakfast but where it comes to dinners, I haven't done anything. What if the deli closed?" Of course, that was true, but not all of her truth.

Rose smiled and sat at the table. "And that's the whole reason?" she asked taking the lemonade from Lily.

Lily sat across from her. "No, actually I want to fix a meal for someone."

Rose's smile broadened. "Your artist friend, the man I met here before?"

"Well, no... It's Jesse." She looked up and saw the surprise on her friend's face.

"Jesse... Taggert?"

"Yes."

Rose sat back in her chair. "I uh... why?"

"I want to repay him for the riding lessons if he won't take money —Well, even if he did, just..." She looked into the older woman's eyes. "Is there a reason I shouldn't?"

"No, just you caught me off guard is all. Is there more to this than repaying?"

"Would it be wrong if there was?"

"Oh my." Rose sipped her lemonade. She frowned as she considered. She didn't appear to approve. "You are aware that Jesse is... well, slow-witted?"

"Not so much he can't function."

"Of course, not but he does best with animals."

"Perhaps people haven't tried with him."

Rose studied her thoughtfully. "I don't want to see you hurt, girl."

"I don't either. You think Jesse would do that?"

"No... but expecting something from him, that he can't give might."

"I guess that is a risk."

"It is. He's a beautiful man. Probably as handsome as any I've seen but..."

"I guess you won't help me with the other thing then."

"Other thing?"

"Well, I had in mind fixing a dinner and thinking I could get him to stay with me long enough to eat it—if it was good, but I was hoping I could get some information on something else."

"Oh my," Rose repeated.

Lily swallowed and tried to find the right words. "I have never been with a man... if you know what I mean."

Rose sat back in her chair and let out a breath. "How far are you hoping to take it with Jesse?"

"Well, if I was taking it anywhere, I would need to know... how to-- you know."

"No, I don't."

"I do understand about biology if that was your concern."

"If not biology, then what?"

53

"How would I seduce a… uhm man?"

Rose began to laugh. "For a gal who hasn't been with a man, you really are thinking of taking this a long way."

"Well, maybe not but supposing I wanted to. If Holly was here, I'd be asking her, but she won't be back soon enough."

"You can't wait until she is?"

"I'm not a girl, Rose. I am twenty-three."

"Jesse is much older. He's never married and likely isn't interested in marrying."

"I suppose." She wished she had never brought the whole thing up. She was being foolish.

"I don't want to control your life, Lily, or make decisions for you, but have you thought this through?"

"What do you mean?"

"You might be hurting him is what I am thinking. Jesse has innocence about him. He's been hurt by others for how they see him as not a… whole man. If you were to… Well, you know, and then didn't want more. Where would that leave him? Knowing about things he can't have."

"Why couldn't he?"

"Oh my." Rose just looked at her. "I wish your sister was here. I don't know how to help you and fear you might be…"

"In a rather peculiar way, Rose, my mother married for money— not to get it but because her family had it and they wanted her to marry a suitable husband. They thought he could take care of her, but he only married her for her money and the power he felt he could have with it."

"Holly told me once that it wasn't a happy marriage."

"It was not. I think she wanted to die long before she finally could. She had lost her freedom and her choices. If she had ever had joy in life, she had lost it before I was born. It was a well-thought out match, very appropriate, or so it was said. That was one example in my life. Another was Holly. She married for love. She thought she had known him in other lifetimes, but whether she had or not, she knew what she wanted, and it was him. She seems very happy. You married for love, and I guess both times."

"You can't think you love Jesse in such a short time?"

"I am not saying that yet, but there is something there I've never known before. There have been other men, who expressed an interest. I never even wanted one to kiss me. Mr. Jamison asked me to dinner tomorrow night, and I turned him down because I wanted the freedom to be with Jesse if he would stay with me for even a while. Maybe it's not there with him, but he's the first one I ever thought— him, it's him."

Rose sat staring at her. Lily could see the wheels turning and had no idea what she was thinking. "He is a very handsome man. You aren't considering him someone to play with?" she asked finally.

"Oh my Lord, no."

"You understand his limitations?"

"You think besides being slow maybe he can't love someone?"

"It's possible. I don't know that though. I don't know him well. Maybe Ollie would have a better idea of... Goodness, I just never imagined." She stared at Lily again and then smiled. "But... I mean if you really did come to love him." She stopped then and shook her head. "Not this fast though. You barely know him. What you know now is all that physical beauty. That isn't enough, but it likely did draw you, you being an artist and all."

"It could just be that. But I think it's his eyes. They are like Vince's. There is something in them that speaks of knowing things, things I'll never know except through being with those eyes."

"My goodness." Rose shook her head. She smiled again and stood. "All right, let's start with a simple dinner that you can fix. What do you have on hand?"

An hour later, Rose had taught Lily the basics of grilling steaks on the outside stove and mashing potatoes. "A tender steak and lots of potatoes are the way to a man's heart," she said as they sat at the garden table with glasses of cold tea. "That and cold beer."

"What kind of beer?"

"You can't get any today and tomorrow he comes at what time?"

"I said morning. What would that mean?"

"First light," Rose said with a grin at Lily's expression of chagrin. "That's how these men roll. If you didn't know that, you are about to find out."

"How did you... well, interest Ollie in you or was it the other way around?"

"He knew it first for us and went about making it happen. I though... well, very quickly realized I wanted it too." She looked at the garden. "I do need to get back to him and Royce. Would you mind if I took some of the poppy heads with me to try and get them started up at our ranch?"

"Of course not." Lily went for the shears she kept on a bench. "Take all you want and a bouquet too. The artists yesterday loved your creation. There were some lovely paintings that came from their time."

"Will they be back?" Rose snipped off a few of the round heads that looked closest to dry.

"Perhaps."

"I thought maybe you'd find Mr. Jamison of interest. He's a fine looking man."

"I suppose so but... No, I don't want to see him again unless it's with others around."

"You don't trust him?"

"I'm not sure it was that. But something... well, he's not someone I want to see again."

"All right. I can respect that. Where it comes to Jesse, you might have to be the one to make him see, but please don't play with the boy-- if you aren't sure you can take it all the way."

"All the way?"

"I don't want to interfere, Lily, but I must say this. Don't try to make him fall in love with you unless you mean it yourself. Wait until you do—if you ever do. I think he'd be hurt more easily than those more used to playing games."

"I won't play games with him."

Rose smiled as she headed for the gate. "If Ollie comes back to town today, I'll send him with beer." She waved before she headed for the stable where her buggy was waiting.

Lily went back into her house thinking of all Rose had said. "Was love at first sight really possible? Was she putting too much emphasis on that thrill she had felt at first seeing him?

Still, she had seen handsome men before, many of them. It wasn't that. But what was it? She had no more idea about that then she had before she talked to Rose. Maybe more warnings though. Rose was right. What was best for Jesse had to come first.

The knock at the door was unexpected but even more so that it was Rose. Her buggy was out front. "I thought of something else," she said. "No, I can't come in." Lily stepped out to close the door and keep the heat from entering the house.

"All right."

"Don't do this because you feel sorry for Jesse as to his limitations. Sometimes a woman can do that."

"I won't, and it's not that. I don't feel sorry for him at all. To be honest, I don't believe he's that slow."

Rose stepped off the porch. "Well, it sounds as though you will be the one to find out." She gave a little laugh and hurried back to her buggy.

Inside again, Lily thought about what Rose had said. She had only known Jesse for a brief few hours and that wasn't long enough to be as certain of his nature as she felt. Somehow, in that brief time, he had become almost a mythical figure in her eyes. For all his lack of speaking fast or even very much at all, there was something in him, the way he stood, the way he handled the horses. Would he handle a woman the same way?

What she had told Rose was true—to a point. Jesse saw the world in a way she never had. That was part of his attraction. She wanted some of what he had. It would never be hers by nature. She knew herself. She had good qualities. She liked herself but she could only have that wildness through him and that would take being his woman.

She shivered as she realized where her thoughts had taken her. She'd never imagined wanting to be any man's woman. Maybe this was why. No man before had been Jesse.

Most likely, he'd not want a woman or if he did, he'd not want her. Maybe Rose was right, and she was rushing it, but she would not give this up without finding out if that first impression meant something— something that could turn her life in a new and yes, more exciting direction.

Jesse spent Sunday first chopping wood, then clearing the dead mesquite. By the time the sun was setting, he should finally be tired enough to sleep. At the adobe, Charlie had food ready. It was stew again, but he couldn't deny it felt good to sit down and eat something he hadn't cooked.

"You figured out yet what you'll do about Evans when he gets here?" Charlie asked sipping from the ever present whiskey bottle.

"No." When he had finished, Jesse shifted to straddle the bench, leaning one elbow on the table as he lit a cigarette.

"Want me to go to town and see if I can locate him?"

"Up to you."

Charlie considered that. "Don't like towns."

"Don't blame you."

"What are you doing tomorrow?"

"Giving a lady a riding lesson."

Charlie smiled his toothless grin.

"What's that mean?"

"Nothin'. Her name Lily?"

"Why do you ask?"

"Cuz you talk in your sleep."

Damn. He knew he was better off not having someone living in his home. Maybe he'd sleep outside. Hot enough anyway. He wasn't going to ask what he had said. Since he remembered his dream of the night before, it wasn't hard to imagine.

"Purty name. Is she purty?"

Jesse stared out at the night smoking and not answering.

"Would have to be with a name like that. She work at the Pedrales?"

Jesse smiled reluctantly. "She's not a dove, and she is only someone I know."

Charlie grinned more widely. "Like to know her a hell of a lot better though, right?"

"A man like me can't afford a woman."

"Truth in that, son. Real truth in that."

"Too stupid."

"Not that. Too smart."

"How do you figure?"

"Woman ties a man down. Never satisfied with nothin' he does. Smart man stays away from them."

"That what you've done?"

"Wal, there was one onct. When I was young and stupid. Not stupid like you, son. You're stupid like a fox. Nah, I was stupid about her. Thought she wanted me. She wanted to be married. So, I married her and nothin' was ever enough after that."

"You get a divorce then?"

"Just left. Maybe she got one. I didn't need no paper-- not to begin or end it. I just needed to be shut of her."

"Sometimes it works. My brother seems happy."

"Been married a long time?"

"No, just a year."

Charlie chortled with that cackle that had Jesse smiling and Bear looking up for what was going on. "See. You jest wait. He might be happy now, but he won't be."

"I don't plan to marry ever."

"Good fer you."

Jesse wasn't so sure about that, but it's what it had to be. He dropped his cigarette to the dirt and ground it out as he rose. "I'm heading for bed."

"I'll just set out here awhile longer," Charlie said.

At first light, Jesse was up. Charlie was still asleep as he saddled the two horses. He looked at Bear, who he had fed when he hadn't eaten himself. The sad face was the end of him. "All right come on. Not like Jethro minds you, but you stay close by me and Judas."

The dog loped happily alongside the horses and even resisted chasing rabbits as they rode to Tucson. As the sun rose high enough in the sky to light the desert, they entered the just waking town. He didn't expect she would be up, but he'd stop by there first. If she was, the ride would be a lot more pleasant than it was likely to be as the heat rose Most of the days were heading to one hundred, if not over.

To the south, he'd seen the first thunderheads that seemed likely to bring on the monsoon season. The heavy rains would cool the land but not good for riding on the desert, not with a tenderfoot. If it did storm, he would ride Jethro as he had had no chance to see how the horse would react to thunder and lightning. Judas handled loud noises with no fear. Maybe he'd been a military horse.

At her cottage, he tied the horses to the rail out front and walked up to her porch expecting to knock lightly and come back later. She had the door opened before he could put up his hand. "I'm ready," she said smiling.

"Where's your hat?"

"Oh... be right back."

In a moment, she returned with a straw hat on her head and closed her door. "Where will we ride?" she asked walking beside him down to the horses.

He pointed to the south. "The wind is rising. Storm clouds to the south. So not a long ride this morning."

She looked then at Bear. "Who is this?"

"My dog. He wanted to come. Do you mind?"

"May I pet him?"

He nodded and she put out her hand to let Bear sniff of it, then she patted his head. "Beautiful dog. What's his name?"

"Bear."

"What breed?"

He shrugged as he held her horse for her to mount. This time she did it by herself and settled into the saddle as he'd told her. He handed her the reins. "Don't know. He's a stray."

"He's got beautiful colors, gold, brown and even some black accents around his eyes. Whoever his parents were, he must've gotten the best of them."

He felt a little shocked at her reaction. He didn't think anyone would call Bear beautiful. He hadn't thought of him that way either. But now that he did think on it, he was pretty-- desert pretty.

"It's such a lovely morning, seems a little cooler," she said as they rode to the east.

"The wind is helping. If we get a real storm, it will cool it off for awhile," he offered. He wasn't sure what was safe as she looked so pretty on her horse, that cute little butt sat the saddle like it was made for her. And since Vince bought it for her, perhaps it had been.

"I've not been here through a storm, but we got them in Chicago too. They can be beautiful but deadly."

"Yes. Now let's try a trot. You ready for that?"

"Not really," she said with a smile, "but I will try it. How do I though get him to trot and not run?"

"Just a gentle nudge with your heel. What we want is slow trot. It can bounce you around if too fast. Lean a little forward and then backward as you get the feel of his gait. Try to relax your hips." He hesitated wishing he had a better word that less reminded him of her hips. Keep your... uh upper body upright and relax your legs." Damn another word he didn't want to use when hers looked all too perfect-- slender and well formed. He would have to get Ollie to teach her to ride. This was not a good idea. Today and that would be it.

"How about my hands?" she asked as she nudged Jethro, and he went into the relaxed trot he'd been taught.

"Just easy with the reins. Good."

They had gone almost ten miles before he heard the first boom of thunder. It had to be as much as forty miles away, but desert storms moved fast. Their ride would have to be cut short.

"We need to turn around now," he said slowing Judas and happy to see she also slowed her gelding.

"Why?"

He pointed again to the south. "It's going to be on us even now before we can get back. Turn your mount. Remember what I told you." The dark clouds moved over them, and the wind began whipping up. This wasn't going to work.

"Stop Jethro," he said. She wasn't ready to be riding as fast as they would need to do if they were going to beat the storm.

When she obeyed, he dismounted. "I need to put you on my horse," he said. "We need to get back to town pronto."

He picked her off her saddle and set her onto his. "Now you get to ride a running horse." She turned to look, but he had already leaped onto the back of Judas and taken the reins from her. He held onto Jethro's with his other hand and kicked Judas into a hard run, his arm around her to keep her in the saddle. "Good experience for you anyway," he said, wishing he wasn't also getting one. Her body leaned back against his and her soft breasts against his arm were sensations he didn't need or want.

He brought the horses to an abrupt halt in front of her home. Bear had kept with them and showed his enjoyment at the run by his smiling face. Jesse dropped from Judas and lifted her from the saddle as he heard the boom of thunder and flash of a lightning bolt much closer. The rain was just starting.

"I'll take Bear inside with me," she said as she headed for the house, "while you put the horses in the stable. It's only two blocks down. Hurry back." With that, she ran into the house. To his shock, his dog had followed her without a look back. He didn't like any part of this, but he didn't have a solution either as he heard another slam of thunder. He leaped back onto Judas and rode as fast as he could to get the two horses in the stable.

By the time, he had them unsaddled, rubbed down, and given oats, the storm was fully on them. He considered staying in the stable with the horses, but then she'd worry. He didn't know how he knew that, but he did.

He ran back but was still soaked to the skin when he got to her porch, and she pulled him inside.

"You are soaked," she said, stating the obvious.

"I'll wait it out in your kitchen," he said as he looked back at the downpour outside. He wanted to go, to escape, but with lightning now hitting all around them, it would be a stupid risk for man and beast.

"No need for that," she said with a smile. She handed him a quilt. "Take off your clothes, and I'll hang them up. You can use this until the storm lets up and they at least have drip dried."

He looked at her with shock. Take off his clothes?

"Just do it right here in the hall," she said. When he didn't take the quilt, she hung it over a hook by the door. "I'll go to the kitchen and fix some tea. Bring your clothes when you come back and I'll hang them to dry in the little room. It stays warmer in there than the rest of the house. They might only be damp by the time you need them again."

He watched her until she closed the door. Then he looked down at his muddy boots, his soaked clothing. Outside, the rain was coming down heavily. The lightning bolts were hitting near the cottage. He couldn't go out. He couldn't stay. He definitely couldn't strip off all his clothes and walk naked into her kitchen covered only by a quilt. That was not possible.

CHAPTER 7

L ily rushed into the kitchen feeling like such a fake. She knew what she wanted. She wasn't sure how she would get it, but she knew. She had never felt more certain of anything in her entire life. Whatever it was she felt for Jesse, maybe it wasn't love as Rose had questioned, but it went way beyond the physical. She wanted to be connected to him in some elemental way. She though didn't want to do anything he wouldn't also want. It wasn't going to be easy.

Five minutes passed. She wondered if he would do what she had asked, and then he came through the door, his boots and soaked clothing in one hand, the other clasping the quilt to him. He had wrapped it toga style so it covered one shoulder and left the other muscular arm uncovered.

She tried to still her breathing as she took his clothing. He followed with his boots and watched without saying a word while she hung his clothing on the line. She turned back then and reached for the boots. "They can set on this table. We will brush off the mud when they dry some." With that, she walked back into the kitchen and poured the now boiling water over the tea leaves. She hadn't looked back, but she knew he had come and was sitting at her table.

At first, Bear had been as restless as his master, but now he was lying by Jesse's bare feet. She tried to think if she had something that he'd like to eat, besides the steaks she had for later.

"That's quite a storm," she said as she came back to the table with the tea to let it steep. She sat across from him, licking her lips as they felt dry and then she looked into his eyes and saw the mix of confusion and something else. She smiled then. His eyes had softened with that expression she had seen before on other men for other women. Desire. Jesse could feel desire and maybe love for her if he was given time to get to know her.

"This tea comes from Sicillas," she said as she poured it. "She said from the West Indies. Have you ever been there?" She nearly kicked herself for asking such a stupid question.

"No." He sipped the tea. She jumped as thunder and then the flare of the lightning appeared to be right overhead, the blast almost at the same moment as the flash.

"Jesse, I had hoped we could get to know each other. I am not off to a very good start, am I?"

"There's not much to know about me," he said. "I know you paint."

She smiled. He was at least trying. "Would you like to see one of mine."

He nodded. She went into the small closet on the other side of the kitchen and returned with one of the dry ones. She had painted the garden when the flowers were first beginning to bloom, earlier in the spring. The colors were paler than they were now.

He studied it for a long while. "I like it," he said finally. "Spring, isn't it?"

"Yes, Rose created this wonderful garden. All I have to do is go out there, and the paintings are almost done for me."

"Did you see the desert when it bloomed?"

"Some. I was trying to get this set up as a home. Holly took some of the furniture. You did know this was her home before she married your brother."

He nodded.

"I will go out more next spring. You live on the desert, don't you?"

"Yes."

"Is it pretty where you are?"

"Peaceful."

"Maybe you could take me there on one of our horseback rides."

"Maybe." He didn't look as though he liked that idea.

"What does your home look like?" she asked determined to get him to talk to her.

"Adobe, one room. Nothing special."

"What is around it?"

His smile was contemplative. So he knew what she was trying to do. "Desert," he answered finally.

"You must like the desert."

"Yes."

"Is it lonely?"

"No."

"Seems like it would be so far from people, someone to talk to."

"Charlie lives there for now."

"Who is that?"

"Old timer who showed up."

"And you took him in?"

"For now."

He wasn't helping, not one bit. He was biding time. The expression in his eyes told her he was thinking more about how soon he could leave than about her. Whatever she had hoped she had seen in those eyes wasn't there. "I know you grew up in Utah. Is it pretty?"

"Some parts."

"Do you want to go back?"

"No." She knew what he did want. Suddenly, she was determined, more than about anything in her life that it would not happen. She was not going to let him walk out of her life. He would though if she didn't provide him a powerful reason for staying in it. The riding lessons weren't enough.

When the phone rang, she wanted to ignore it, but the storm appeared to have moved to a different part of the valley. Maybe it was Holly, with a problem. She picked up the receiver, watching Jesse as he sat uneasily at her table.

"Lily, thank God. I have looked for you everywhere." It was the voice she least wanted to hear.

"I didn't ask for that, Harold."

"Well, I am coming to Tucson to get you and take you home."

She felt panic surge through her. "That's impossible."

"It is not. I will be on the next train. You poor girl, to be in that godforsaken land at this time of the year."

"Harold, please leave me alone."

"I will stay until you realize where you belong."

His voice sounded angry and unwilling to listen to reason. The law would not take her side. His coming to Tucson wasn't illegal. She realized there was one way to stop him.

"I am going to be married, Harold."

She heard his gasp. "Impossible."

"No, it's not."

"When?"

"Never mind when."

"This is too sudden."

"Perhaps, but it is what it is. You would be wasting your time to come. Goodbye, Harold." She slammed down the receiver.

Jesse watched her as she came back to the table. The expression in his eyes had darkened. There was no softness. "You are going to be married?"

"I hope so," she said knowing there was no way to confront this but directly. It certainly was not how she imagined a proposal, her being the one offering it, and the recipient not enthusiastic. She smiled.

"Congratulations," he said and then looked away. "I should go."

"Not before we talk."

"About what?"

"Jesse, have you ever thought of getting married?"

"No."

"Why not?"

"No woman would have me."

"I am sure that's not true."

"It is true."

"Maybe you don't want a woman."

He shrugged.

"Jesse, that man who called, he was a problem to me in Chicago. He wanted a relationship with me that I refused. He was not taking no for an answer. I came here hoping to escape him, but he has found me."

"He's dangerous to you?" He frowned.

"He could be." She was unsure whether Harold was actually dangerous. She knew so little about him beyond his being involved with the stock market and some sort of commodities trading—whatever that was.

He had assisted her father before he grew so sick. When Holly had taken over running the businesses, Harold was told his services were no longer needed. He had argued against that as being unwise. One visit to Chicago, with Vince Taggert beside her sister, had ended the arguments. It was then that Harold had turned his aggressive attention toward Lily.

"I have to make him leave me alone," she said knowing she had one way to do that, and it pleased her on a number of levels. For the first time in her entire life, she was going to be the bold one.

"Your husband will do that," he said, his jaw set.

"He could if I had one."

"You said you soon would."

"Do you want to know the name of the man I want to marry?" She saw him hesitate. Finally, he nodded. "Do I know him?"

"Quite well actually."

"Who is it?"

"You."

"Me?" He nearly dropped his hold on the quilt. "What are you talking about?"

"Would you marry me, Jesse?"

The idea had been growing in her head since Rose had said she couldn't use him, and if she wanted him, it had to be for something more than sex. She liked Jesse a lot. Moreover, she trusted him, which was strange since she did barely know him. Maybe they could be married friends. Maybe Jesse wouldn't desire a woman as a woman. If he didn't, he wouldn't mind marrying her. There could be advantages for him in such a union.

"That's not possible," he said staring at her now as though trying to understand what her words had meant.

"Why isn't it? I wouldn't limit your freedom in anyway. It could just be in name only... if, well, if that's what you wanted."

She saw him trying to reason through what she was saying. "You don't want a husband like me."

"What's wrong with you?"

"I am dumb."

"That I know you are not. You just take time to think things through. How is that bad?"

"I can't read or write."

"Not even your name?"

"I can write my name."

"Jesse, I am not asking you to love me but just marry me." She knew that sounded a little stupid even to her.

"I need to think."

"You'd be protecting me from the man. I am afraid he'll come to Tucson despite what I said. We need to be married quickly, before he can get here. His name is Harold Brooks. He is used to getting his way. I tried to keep him from even knowing where I was, but he found out. He's rich. He has ways."

"Being married to me would protect you?"

"I believe so." She supposed there were other ways, but this was what she wanted. It would normally have taken longer. Maybe though with Jesse, this was the only way. "It could have benefits for you also, Jesse?"

He smiled then with an amused glint in his eyes. "Like?"

"Well, I am an artist. I could paint your portrait... for free." She smiled back at him biting her lip.

"Would that be an advantage or drawback?"

She laughed then. He had a sense of humor. She hadn't known that. "Of course, an advantage. I have never painted a nude man."

"Well, you aren't starting now," he said rising but keeping a good grip on the quilt.

She came to stand beside him as he looked out the window. The water ran in rivulets down the street. She imagined the gullies would be full. "You can spend the night in the downstairs bedroom," she said. "Safer for you and Bear to go home when the water goes down a little. I hear the washes can be dangerous to cross after a storm. Think about it and let me know in the morning before you leave."

"Our worlds don't mix," he said without giving away any of what he was thinking.

"They haven't. It doesn't mean they couldn't. Wouldn't you like a good friend who is a woman?"

"Don't know. Never had one."

"You haven't had long to think about it, but if you will marry me and you later decide you don't want to be married, we can have it annulled."

"My name isn't a proud one," he said as he walked away from the window and sat back at the table.

"I like the name Jesse." She smiled as she knew what he had meant.

"You know about the family name because of Holly."

"It didn't bother her. Why should it me?"

"It's gotten more complicated lately. My father's drawn some trouble to him."

"And that could hurt you?" The thought of that led to pain in her stomach. Nobody should hurt Jesse.

He nodded. "It might be dangerous to be related to me."

"I suppose we could keep it a secret for a while, that is except from Harold if he comes anyway."

"You think he will?"

"I'm not sure. He said he would. I told him not to, but he didn't seem to care what I wanted."

She went to her refrigerator. "Ollie brought me some beer. Would you like one while you figure this out."

He nodded. She opened the beer and handed it to him. "Is beer good?" she asked.

He smiled then. "You never had one?"

"No, I've had wine but not beer."

He handed it back to her. "Woman about to be married better know what beer tastes like."

She smiled and took a sip unable to resist making a face.

"Didn't like it?"

"Is it an acquired taste?"

He laughed then. She liked his laugh a lot. "Maybe," he said as he took his own drink.

"I know you smoke," she said then as she sat back at the table and took a sip of her now cold tea. "You can do it in the kitchen if you wish. This will be your home if you marry me."

"I won't take anything from you." His tone was somber.

"A husband has certain rights." She looked up at him from under her lashes.

"What is yours will stay yours."

"Even if I want you to have it?"

She saw him try to figure out what she meant by that. "Even then," he said finally.

"Will you stay tonight?" she asked.

"No."

"Then no wedding?"

"Didn't say that."

"Harold could get here in three days."

"How long does it take to get a license?"

"I think a day would do it. I will talk to Mr. Angus."

"Who is he?"

"My lawyer. He can work out a contract if you insist on that."

"I do. There are reasons for it."

"And they are?"

"If something happened to me, my pa might try to take something from you if we don't make what this is clear from the start."

"Jesse, if we marry will you ever stay here?"

"When this Brooks is in town." He smiled then. "Bear might scare him off too."

"He didn't me."

"No, he didn't you."

"When will you come back?"

"Wednesday. Have everything ready."

"Can we have Ollie and Rose come to the wedding?"

He considered that. "Better nobody knows, except this fella you want to get rid of. It'll be safer for you not to be a Taggert and easier to end it later." he headed for the small room to dress.

She didn't like either of those thoughts. The first because it meant Jesse saw danger to himself. The second because she didn't intend to end it. She was certain of that-- whether it stayed a marriage in name only. She wanted to be this man's wife. She smiled then feeling an inner joy that she hadn't expected.

"If the gullies are full, maybe Bear should stay with me," she suggested after he had come out wearing his damp clothing and buckling on his cartridge belt.

He looked at her as though she had lost her mind. "He's a desert dog," he said. "He swims fine."

"He might like staying here."

"Protecting you?"

"He would be that when you aren't around."

"He can do what he wants." She saw he didn't like the idea. Bear was important to him. He loved the dog.

"I shouldn't have suggested it," she said wishing she had not.

"It's fine if he prefers it in town." He walked to the door and didn't call to his dog. She followed and stood with the door open as she watched Bear run after Jesse. She understood that. It was what she wanted to do too.

She lay in bed that night, not having fixed herself the steak or potatoes. She only hoped they'd keep until he came back. She had made more progress than she imagined possible. She felt certain the time would come when Jesse would want to acknowledge her as his wife. For now, she would trust he had his reasons. She had dumped a big load onto him.

If she had truly believed Harold was physically dangerous, she'd not have asked Jesse to marry her. He was an annoyance, but she didn't believe he was more than that. Although, she admitted she didn't know him that well. The truth was, he had provided an excuse to do what she wanted to do. It might seem strange to marry a man she knew so little but there had been women who married men based on letters or arrangements by mail. This wasn't that strange. They both did know each other at least.

Smiling she remembered Jesse's face when she had said what she wanted. Shock and disbelief were primary, as his mouth had dropped open, then slammed shut. Was he displeased? He had indicated he didn't plan to marry. So she wasn't taking him from another woman. She thought someday he'd be glad of it, of marrying her. It just might take some time.

Riding into the yard around his adobe, Jesse had not left Jethro in the stable but also brought him back to his lean-to and corral. . The two horses got along. Stables weren't the kind of places he liked leaving animals. Maybe tomorrow he'd let the two graze around the house, tie them together and they'd not get far.

He had nothing he had to do but was thinking of a few projects that would be good for the property. It wouldn't hurt to put up some barriers in case unwelcome friends of his father showed up, and he needed something he could shoot from behind.

At the corral, he was glad to see Sarie looked content. He unsaddled the two horses and then walked up to the house where Charlie waited.

"Sure was a gully whomper," he said. "Thought maybe you'd stay in town tonight."

"Looks like no damage here."

"Nah, wind blew, and I wondered some about that lean-to, but you did a good job on it. It held up."

"Good." He sat at the table and lit one of his cigarettes as he considered his strange day. There was no way under heaven he had dreamed what Lily would ask. He still found himself struggling to believe it had happened at all. Maybe he was going more insane than some already thought he was.

"You are troubled, son. What is wrong?" Charlie said sitting across from him.

"I will be back in Tucson on Wednesday."

"Come across Billy Evans?"

He shook his head. "Other business."

"Not good business from the look on your face."

"Not sure."

"Want to talk about it?"

"No."

Charlie rose and offered a large bone to Bear who ran to a corner of the yard to chew on it.

"Where'd that come from?" Jesse asked.

"Rest is hanging in the shed. This time it ain't beef." He chuckled.

"The big buck?"

"Nope."

He was relieved to hear that. The mule deer who visited the spring was beautiful. He admired how he had grown to his age and managed to survive when so many didn't. The spring had a drawback for how it drew predators to prey.

"So what is it then?"

"Javelina. Big boar. I shot him beyond the corrals." The herd had come through off and on, sometimes with young, maybe fifteen at the highest. "Big boar like that can prove dangerous, to your dog too. Rip his chest open—or a man's leg. Good eating."

"Then good job."

"You're glad it wasn't the buck?"

"Yes."

"You got a soft spot for animals, son."

"So do you." He gestured with his cigarette toward the corral.

"Sarie is all I got."

"You take good care of her."

"I try. Worry though, getting old like I am. What if I die? What happens to her?"

"No age has a guarantee about that." He knew how fast life could end, how fast his yet might.

"You're a fatalist, son."

"Sometimes."

CHAPTER 8

I t seemed strange to Lily that she was dressing in a pale green, silk
dress, for her wedding but without anyone with her—not that
she'd had a lot of experience in weddings. She had not been in Tucson
when Holly had married Vince, but she'd told her about it, described
how they had married at Ollie and Rose's with flowers and friends.
She would have liked that. But that would not have happened with
Jesse. No, this was how it had to be if she wanted to be his wife—and
she did. The more she thought on it, the more she knew she would
feel luckier than any woman in the world, if she could stand at that
man's side.

She wrestled with her hair before she gave up and let it hang down
her back. She carried her straw hat downstairs and busied herself
making more lemonade. There was also a bottle of white wine in the
refrigerator. Nothing special for a wedding supper, but she had
bought some rolls from the bakery, sweet and dinner rolls. She had the
steak, and it still looked fine.

Tuesday, although surprised at her requests, James Angus had
quickly drawn up a simple contract. "Are you sure you want this?" he
had asked as he handed it to her to read. She had decided that she
could do what Jesse requested where it was important. The contract
declared that while married to Jesse, he would have equal access to all
her funds. If she died, anything in her name would be left to Holly. He
would inherit nothing, which had been his main concern. She was
unwilling to be married and have him not sharing in her wealth.

"Yes, it looks exactly as I wish."

"I have never met him but did meet his brother. He's a fortunate man to win such a beautiful bride."

"Thank you."

"You two can sign it tomorrow, and I will file it along with your license."

"Can you be a witness?" she had asked. Judge Phillips said I would need two. His secretary can be one."

"Of course. What time."

She wished Jesse had told her a time. He'd just said Wednesday. James had smiled and said just tap on his door, and they could sign the paper. Because he had no clients for the morning, he had said any time before noon would be fine. She just hoped Jesse meant morning.

When she saw him ride up, she felt relieved. He had brought back Jethro too. She walked out onto the porch and smiled at him. He was wearing a white shirt, dark pants, and the ever present cartridge belt, holster, and revolver.

"Groom is not supposed to see the bride before the service, but guess they don't mean when people get married by a judge," she said.

His expression was stern as he dismounted and walked to her. "You sure you want this?"

"I am. Where is Bear? I hoped you'd bring him back with you."

"Figured you might steal him if I did," he said with that teasing light that had surprised her before.

"I might."

"That's why I left him with Charlie."

"All right, but in the future, when you come, I hope you bring him. He can use the yard and the house."

"You like him."

"I do. He's not only beautiful, but he has a good heart."

"How do you know that?"

"I feel it."

"That reliable for you?" he asked again with that soft smile. It melted her heart.

"It has been so far." She looked then at Jethro. "I don't see how I can ride him with this dress."

"I hadn't thought of that. I'll take them to the stable and come back with a buggy."

"Wait," she said, "what if you take Jethro to the stable, but you ride me to our wedding sort of as you did the day of the storm, in front of you on the saddle, except sitting sideways. Kind of."

He stopped and looked back at her. "You want that?"

"I do." She knew her own smile had grown soft as she felt warmth flow through her.

"All right." He tied Judas and rode Jethro down. He was back in a few minutes, which had given her time to put on her hat and stick the pin through it to hold it in place. He had put on a tan jacket.

He looked at her then as she walked toward him. "You are beautiful."

"Thank you."

"Not like a woman who should be marrying the likes of me. Sorry I don't have fine clothes for a wedding."

"You look fine to me, Jesse. We need to stop first at Mr. Angus' office. He drew up the paper you wanted. You know it's not important to me."

"I know."

"We can sign it before the wedding. He will be one of our witnesses. You said you can't read."

"I can't."

"Don't you want to know now what it says?"

"I trust you. It's just to secure your money for you now and if something happened to me."

"Don't keep saying that. I don't want to even imagine that happening."

At his horse, he stopped. "Are sure you want this?" he asked again.

"Don't keep asking me that either," she said with a little laugh. "Maybe it's you having second thoughts."

"No, this is all right." With that, he picked her up and set her on the saddle, this time with both her legs on one side. In another second, he had leaped onto the back of Judas and nudged him into a slow walk. "Where do we go?"

"I'll show you when we get there. It's next to the courthouse. It's where Judge Phillips will marry us. He said anytime would be all right as today he isn't holding court."

"Not much experience with judges... or law."

"I guess considering your family, that's good."

He laughed.

At James Angus' office, the contract was quickly signed. If Angus was surprised at any of it, he hid it. "You can leave your gun here if you wish," he said looking pointedly at Jesse, who hesitated only a moment before nodding and unbuckling it.

Together they walked to the courthouse and Judge Phillips' office. His receptionist came with them to a small room that used for official functions. The judge smiled and quickly began saying the words Lily had heard but thought little about their import. Now they seemed very meaningful as she looked up into his eyes. She promised to have and to hold, from this day forth, in sickness and in health, to love, cherish and obey, until death do them part. The until death do them part seemed even more significant with Jesse's strange warning about someone endangering his family.

Finally the judge asked, "May I have the ring?" She had forgotten about that, but it didn't matter. Then Jesse reached into his pocket and handed a ring to the judge. He handed it back to Jesse, who took her hand and slid it on the appropriate finger.

"With this ring, I thee wed," he said in his deep voice repeating what the judge had said, "and all my worldly goods I thee endow. In sickness and in health, in poverty or in wealth, 'til death do us part."

"I now pronounce you man and wife," the judge said, "and you may kiss the bride."

Jesse turned and took her into his arms. He bent and lightly kissed her lips. The kiss was soft, tender and innocent and yet, it had her wanting to melt right into him. When he stepped back, she had to steady herself to manage a smile and accept the congratulations from the judge's receptionist and James Angus. The license was handed to them, and they both signed where he pointed.

It was over. She was his wife. If she had at one time imagined she could let him go, if he wanted to walk away, she knew now she never would, at least not willingly.

At Angus's office, Jesse buckled back on his cartridge belt. "Thank you," he said as he shook the man's hand. Then they were outside and the sun was shining. "I keep thinking we should have Bear with us to celebrate," she said as they walked back to his horse.

He lifted her up into the saddle.

"Jesse, hold up, boy," an older man said as he came walking to where Jesse now stood with his hand on the back of Judas.

"What do you want?" he asked turning to watch him.

The old man looked from him to her on his saddle. "I haven't seen you in a while." He looked up at Lily. "You look familiar to me. Do I know you?"

"I don't think so," she said. It wasn't hard to figure out that this was Jesse's father. Even with the silver hair, there was a strong resemblance. Those eagle eyes. She also understood he was the last person that Jesse wanted knowing they were married. She saw the muscle jump in Jesse's cheek. He was clenching his jaw.

"Sorry but I'm busy now."

His father chuckled. "I can see that." He looked again at Lily. "You look real familiar to me, ma'am."

"We haven't met," she said. She then looked down at Jesse and put the most disdainful look she could manage. "You did promise to get me home, did you not, my good man." She had heard that tone from many of the elites. When she looked down at him, where his father could not see, she winked.

He looked away from her and back at his father. "As you can see, I have a job."

"I didn't realize. Sorry." The older man backed off. "Glad to meet you, Miss..."

"Good day," she said, ignoring the hint for her name. Jesse didn't mount but led Judas as any hired man would.

"You think he believed us?" she asked when they turned a corner, and she could no longer see him.

"Probably not." He leaped onto the saddle and gigged Judas into a slow trot.

"He has no way to find out anything."

"He could ask around," he said, "but he probably won't."

"Will you stay tonight?" she asked when they reached her cottage.

"Best I don't."

"I disagree."

"That jasper can't be here until tomorrow at the soonest, right?"

"Jasper?"

"Man."

He slid off the horse and lifted her down. She liked his hands on her waist and didn't want him taking them away. Such big, strong hands. She remembered that kiss. She wanted more of those.

"Listen," he said as he took off his jacket and tied it on back of his horse, "I am going to have to go by Pa's house now. Otherwise, he will go looking for where I have been, maybe start spying on me. I don't want him to know about you."

"I look like Holly. He will figure it out."

"Except for your beautiful brown hair."

She smiled at that. "You think my hair is beautiful?"

"Yes." Nothing about Jesse was pretense. In simple words, he told the truth as whatever he knew it to be.

She felt then of the ring. "I didn't expect a ring."

He walked her to the door. "It was my mother's. When she lay dying, she asked me to take it for someday."

"I like it being your mother's."

"I told her I'd never marry," he said then as he opened her door.

"What did she say?" She didn't want him to go. She felt like crying at the thought she couldn't hold onto him.

"That I would someday. The right woman would come along, and I would."

"Am I the right woman?" she asked, hungry for words of love from him.

"You are the one I married." He stepped back then. "I will be back tomorrow with Bear. And take the risk you will steal him."

She smiled but wasn't willing to let him go just yet and she held onto his hand. "I didn't have a ring for you. Would you wear one if I bought one for you?"

"No and you better not wear this one."

"For now?"

"Yes, for now." With that, he turned and stalked off the porch, leaping onto his horse before he took off at a gallop.

Jesse rode straight for his father's home. He tied Judas to the rail, knocked on the door, but was not surprised at no answer. He wondered if Rance had headed north. He sat on the porch step and lit a cigarette.

With nothing else to do, he could not keep himself from remembering the wedding. He'd never imagined he would have one. That it might not be for long didn't matter. She was his wedded wife. His. A woman like her. He had never imagined what those words would mean to him. He had promised to have and to hold, for better or worse, to love and to cherish.

He had to work to get control of his emotions as he remembered too what it felt like to have her body pressed against his as he had ridden her down to the courthouse. God, he had been filled with desire, something he had long ago pushed from his life. He hadn't wanted to desire anything. A man like him could not have anything. Yet, here it was, thrown into his lap.

He thought again of the vows. He would do that, keep her safe, die for her. When he had agreed to the wedding, he hadn't expected it to be more than just something to help her. Then he had said the words, looked down at that beautiful face beside him, and it all changed. It didn't matter about paper. They might annul this marriage, but she would be his wife until the day he died.

Then he remembered the problem he faced with his father's past showing up and presenting a possible danger. He needed to find Billy Evans before Evans found out there was something more that could be a pressure on the Taggert family. Jesse didn't know how wealthy Lily was, but Vince had felt what Holly owned was a barrier to their marrying. It had to be a lot. Someone like Evans would use that anyway he could. He felt a little sick as he thought of all the ways that could be. Nothing would hurt Lily, not if he could help it. But could he?

It was almost an hour later when his father and Rance showed up. They weren't riding but walking. "Didn't expect you here," Jeremiah said.

"Didn't you?"

"What kind of job you got with that woman and what's her name?"

"None of that is your business."

"Something you ashamed of?"

"No. I came to find out about Billy. You see him yet?"

"If we had, we'd likely both be dead," Rance said.

"Come on in. Have a whiskey," Jeremiah said.

Jesse was in no mood for whiskey, but in the tidy parlor he took a glass and a small sip. "How do you plan to find out if he's coming?" he asked.

"No idea. You got one?" Rance asked.

"It's not my problem." That wasn't the truth, less now than ever, but he would give neither of these old reprobates anything they could use.

"You are a Taggert," Jeremiah said taking a gulp of the whiskey. "Believing I cheated him, he could go for whoever looks easiest."

"You think he looks easy?" Rance cackled, gesturing with his thumb toward Jesse.

"I didn't create this mess," Jesse said, "but you need to find where he is and as soon as he gets to town, you need to let me know." He saw the wheels turning in his father's head. Jesse was slow to reason things out, but this took no reasoning. It was all experience.

"Who was the lady?" Jeremiah asked again.

"You need to know why?"

"You were with her. She looks a lot like Holly. She a relation?"

Jesse rose placing his barely touched glass on the nearest table. "As soon as you know, get word to me about Billy. I'll be around."

With that, he stalked out the door and leaped onto Judas. He decided to leave Jethro in the stable and rode out of town as fast as his gelding could go. He had pushed himself emotionally and mentally as far as he could. He had to clear his head and only a fast ride and hard work had any hope of doing that. Soon he'd have to be back with her, and all the temptations in the world would be going with him.

When her jasper was dealt with, assuming he really showed up, then he'd stay as far from Lily as he could—at least until Billy Evans was gone—one way or the other. After that, if he was still alive... he couldn't think that far-- just far enough to get her what she wanted, whatever that was.

He hadn't thought it was possible, but it turned out it was. He could love a woman and love her enough to die for her if that was what it took.

Lily lay in her bed wondering where Jesse was. She worried about him and realized it was a new experience in her life, to have someone out there, who she could not protect. He could be killed while she lay safely in her bed.

Tears ran down her cheeks as she imagined him lying dead some-where or suffering, and no one would be there. She remembered again that soft kiss. She had never imagined a kiss could feel like that. She had been so involved in her painting and then caring for her father's needs that she hadn't thought much about how it might be with a man. She knew other girls wanted those things. She had not until the day she saw Jesse the first time. Now she could only dream of another of those kisses. Or what would it be like to have him hold her in his arms. His arms around her, when he rode her on his horse, had been only a taste. A taste that left her wanting more.

When she slept, she dreamed of him, and the dream left her wanting him even more when she woke. When would he come back?

He said he'd be here when it was possible for Harold to get to Tucson. It could be today.

She dressed quickly and hurried downstairs to start coffee and fix her breakfast. Would he come? She got her answer before she'd had her first sip as a large animal bounded onto her porch. Laughing, she ran to open the door allowing Bear to rush in.

She saw him sitting on his horse watching her. "You are coming in, aren't you?" she asked as she stepped out.

"When I take care of Judas." He didn't move. Just watched her.

She smiled. "Well, hurry back." For the first time she wished her property had room for a barn. Maybe this home was not going to work when there were two of them sharing it off and on. She would hate to lose the garden, but she could plant another. Or maybe get Rose to help her plant another. She needed a barn on her property.

It was less than ten minutes when she heard his boots on the porch and she pulled open the door. Bear was curled on the quilt she had laid down for him.

"Was that mine?" Jesse asked as he entered the kitchen.

"I have several. Yours is still available." She looked pointedly at his gun.

"All right," he smiled and unbuckled it, setting it onto the table by the front door. He squatted to remove his spurs too and laid them on the floor by it.

"You aren't staying long?" she asked looking at the spurs, which he hadn't worn before.

"I had a few head of cattle to move this morning," he said nodding as she held up the coffee pot.

"This early?"

"They roam around at night this time of the year. Eat down the grass and don't move on soon enough."

"Would you like breakfast or did you already have that?"

"I'd like it, and no, I haven't."

She smiled, filled with joy, as she began mixing up the ingredients for hotcakes-- one of her few skills where it came to cooking. In moments, she had the flame high enough, tested the frypan and started the first pancakes.

"Do you think we'll get another storm today?" she asked as she flipped the first one.

"Clouds are building up."

"I asked about when the train comes in today. Eleven. I don't know if he'll be on it. Maybe he'll believe I meant it when I said he should not come."

"Maybe."

"Have you heard from Vince... I mean on their trip?"

He looked at her as though trying to think through what she had said. "Why would I?" he asked finally.

"Sometimes family write letters. I guess he couldn't call you, could he?"

He shook his head and smiled as she put the first cakes on his plate.

When Bear looked up hopefully, she got into her cupboard. "I bought this for him. If it's all right for me to give it to him." She held up a rawhide bone.

"You are trying to steal him," he said but nodded.

"With him, I get his master, don't I?" She gave him a saucy smile as she handed the dog the chew, and he started right in on it.

"Seems you got him already," he said as he dug into the hotcakes.

"I could only wish."

He didn't say anything. She refilled his coffee cup. "Would you consider posing for me today? You know, while we wait to see if he's coming."

"You don't mean without clothes."

She smiled then. "Not yet." When he quickly looked up, she put on as innocent expression as she could manage.

"It was a good breakfast," he said when he had finished eating several stacks of cakes. Before she could respond, a knock at the door forced her to go to it. She didn't want company and was even more displeased that it was Patrick Jamison.

"I hadn't expected you," she said.

"I was hoping to paint here again. Is it too early?" he asked and then looked beyond her.

Jesse was standing in the door, leaning against the jamb and watching him. "You have company, I see," Patrick said.

"I am sorry, Patrick, but it's not a good time." Never would be a good time.

"You going to introduce me to your friend?" Patrick asked looking at Jesse.

"Jesse, this is Patrick. He is a painter traveling through Tucson."

Jesse said nothing just watched the man, quietly assessing. "Do I know you?" Patrick asked him not taking Lily's less than subtle hint to leave.

"Not likely," Jesse said not moving.

Patrick then looked back at Lily. "I am sorry to have interrupted you with your... uh friend."

"It's fine. Goodbye." As soon as he went through the door, she closed it firmly.

"He a friend?" Jesse asked when she turned back to him.

"No, just a painter, which is what I want to be."

"With his help?"

She shook her head. "No, I want nothing to do with him." Something was not good about Patrick, but she didn't know what. Only that she didn't want him in her home ever again.

"Good." Jesse said and smiled.

"Is it?"

"Yes."

CHAPTER 9

An hour later, she had Jesse sitting in the wooden lawn chair with Bear at his feet. Well, as often at his feet as she could manage. She had pulled the chair so that the garden would be behind him, and he'd be in the shade of the big cottonwood. He let her do what she wanted with him but said little about it.

"If you really mind, we don't have to do this," she said.

"I don't mind but..."

"But?"

"I am not comfortable without my Colt nearby."

"Stay right there." She ran into the house and grabbed the holster, gun and even the spurs. Outside, she handed him the gun, dropped the spurs to his left and then brought over a small wooden table to be on his right. "Don't wear the gun. Lay it there. I think it'd be good in the painting." He looked up at her but with that faint smile did as she asked.

She walked around him trying to decide on the right angle.

"What are you doing?" he asked finally.

"Just trying to see where the light is best. Of course, that changes." She smiled then. "Maybe I am just enjoying looking at you." She went for her easel.

"Why?"

She had to remember he often took things far more literally than she expected. "You are a very beautiful man, Jesse. Surely you know that."

"Women are beautiful."

"Some men are too."

He laughed then. "Sorry. Don't see it."

She giggled. "All right, just you wait until you see my painting of you." She brought over her canvas, deciding a smaller one would be best since she had no idea how long he'd be content to sit.

"Don't make me beautiful."

"All right." She carried over her lightweight paint table, and quickly began adding colors to her palette. "How about handsome?"

"Not that either."

She took a large brush and laid a wash using linseed oil onto the canvas, a warm green. She looked back at him then studying how his nose rose out of his face, and that small smile. How would she ever capture that? Bear came over to see what she was doing but retreated to Jesse when she ignored him.

"What do you do with your paintings?" Jesse asked clearly growing uneasy at sitting even for this length of time. She quickly used strokes of ecru to get the shapes of his body and legs, the chair, sketching it all into place as she was sure he'd not last much longer than his dog.

"Would you like some lemonade?" she asked as she looked from her canvas to him.

"If I can move to get it," he said.

She smiled. "In the refrigerator. The glasses are in the cupboard to the left. Would you bring me one too?" While he was gone, she began using blocks of color for what she remembered of face and hands. She wished he would let her open his shirt a little farther. More skin tone there would be good for the composition, balancing out the cool greens.

Then she thought about his chest. She had never seen it. When he'd had the quilt, all that had been uncovered had been one arm and shoulder. Would he have a lot of hair there? Some men did. Maybe he'd have none. When she realized her breath was coming faster, she concentrated on blocking in colors for the garden behind his figure.

The closing of the door told her he was back. Even though she had been laying the colors down thinly, she would let it dry a bit before she went further. She came to sit on the other chair across from him. She watched as he sipped the lemonade all too aware his gaze was on her.

"Anybody ever paint you?" he asked.

"No."

"They should."

"You think so?"

He nodded. "Wish I was a painter."

"Maybe you are. Have you ever tried?"

He laughed at that. "Not hardly."

"You said you don't read. Does that mean you didn't go to school?"

He sucked in a breath and looked away. "They couldn't teach me. Ma taught the others, but she couldn't me."

"Would you like to read?"

He looked back at her. "I try not to want what I can't have." The hard look in his eyes told her how he had done that. She understood then the barriers he had put in place. They were what she would have to break through. One step at a time. *Be patient, Lily.* She stood up and came to stand in front of him.

"Jesse," she said as she knelt between his legs. She knew he was shocked. Good. "I can't always say things that won't upset you. I understand you have many years seeing yourself one way. It's not how I see you."

"It isn't?" His breathing was coming faster. She knew hers was too as she rested her hands on his knees.

"No, I see you as someone who knows things I'd like to know. I hope you will teach me. I can teach you things too. I think it's how it works when two people are married."

He leaned forward and took her chin in his hand, his eyes has softened. He bent then and lightly kissed her lips. She felt she could melt into him as just the simple brush of his lips had stirred her in ways she had never imagined possible.

Before she could say what she was thinking, if words even might do the feelings justice, Bear growled and a voice interrupted. "Hello the house." She looked toward the gate and saw the man she had most hoped she'd never see again. He opened the gate and walked through it. She didn't get up but stayed kneeling in front of Jesse.

"Be quiet, Bear," Jesse said in a low voice.

"Harold," she said. "I thought I told you not to come."

Jesse lifted her as he rose to face Harold, who came to stand on the other side of the chairs. He was a good foot shorter than Jesse and much wider around the waist. He seemed not remotely intimidated, as he smiled broadly. "Is this your model?" he asked Lily, looking at the canvas on the easel.

"Among other things," she said.

"I came to assure myself you were all right, dear Lily." He looked up then at Jesse, his expression one of aristocratic disdain. "I have to believe one of the other things is he's your intended—this time?" It was said as though she likely had had others and would in the future.

"He is my husband. And since we were just married, I hope you will understand we want privacy."

"Aren't you going to introduce us?" Harold asked his gaze never leaving Jesse's face.

She didn't know what to do about that and looked up to see how Jesse wanted it handled. He had that small smile we had seen before. "Introduce us, baby," he said using the endearment for the first time. She understood staking territory. Well, she was all for that herself. She reached out and put her arm around his waist, drawing him to her. "Jesse, this is Harold Brooks, a business partner of my late father's. Harold, my husband, Jesse."

"Does he have a last name?" Harold asked.

"Sort of no point to it-- is there?" she asked feeling increasingly annoyed. She felt the tension in Jesse's body.

"He ashamed of it?" Harold looked at Jesse with a smirk.

"Taggert," Jesse said. "T-a-g-g-e-r-t to be sure you get it spelled right when you investigate it."

"You seem to have a bit of a firecracker temper," Harold said.

"Sometimes."

"Hit women do you, when you get mad?"

Jesse looked at him for a moment blankly. Lily could see that the out of place comment had thrown him. "Harold," she said her voice rising with her anger, "you do need to leave."

Harold was studying Jesse but then smiled and backed away. "Of course, now that I can see you are fine, dear."

"Goodbye," she said.

In moments, he was gone, but the energy he had left behind wasn't. "Will he be a problem?" she asked Jesse who sat back in the chair.

"Maybe." His gaze flicked to a cardinal as it landed in the cottonwood.

"What can we do about it?"

"Nothing right now."

Something about the way he said that was disturbing. "What might he do?"

Jesse shrugged and turned his gaze back onto her. His eyes were warm, the smile the soft one she had come to like. "For now, I am not interested in him."

She smiled also. "What are you interested in?"

He beckoned her to him. "Another kiss maybe." He pulled her onto his lap. She liked that. She'd never sat on a man's lap. But then, until Jesse, she'd never kissed a man either.

"Think you can do that again?" he asked as she put her arms around his neck. She bent forward until her lips barely touched his, savoring the feel of his lips against hers. He opened his mouth, with a hand on the back of her head, he turned the kiss into a harder one.

When he released her, she could only sit and watch his face. She loved his face. Very masculine but as beautiful as she had said. "So your model huh?" he said as he ran a finger lightly down her cheek.

"Among other things."

"What are those other things?"

"Well, you do own my dog."

He laughed at that. "I do huh? You know he just came and claimed me."

She looked down at Bear who was now sleeping in front of the other chair. "Just like I did maybe?"

"Is that what you did?" His eyes darkened again.

"I have been trying to."

She realized he was staring at her as though trying to reason through what she was saying. She understood. Too much. Too fast for both of them. She rose and headed for the outdoor stove. "I have steaks for supper," she said. "Does that sound good to you?"

He nodded. She had no idea what he was thinking. She wanted to know but equally understood that she had to give this time. They had time. They both needed it.

In the evening, after they'd eaten, they sat in the yard again. She had worked a bit on the painting but would have to let it dry to do more.

"It's good how you have desert flowers and others mixed together. Wild with the tame," he said.

Sometimes he said things that amazed her. "Rose created it. I only wish I could be so creative with plants."

"You tend it though."

"I do and will as long as I stay here. But..."

"But? You thinking of going back to Chicago?"

Again, he had surprised her with how he thought ahead. There were places he could work through what he thought faster than others. The curves were what threw him.

"No, never. I love the desert. I just was thinking we'd need a barn and there is no space for one here."

He was silent. She supposed she should not have said we. Except, it was how she was thinking. She could not watch everything she said. He had to get used to her way of sometimes speaking without thinking.

"For the horse," he said finally.

"Horses."

"I should go into town tonight," he said avoiding a response to her.

"All right." She had no right to ask why, but she wanted to.

He smiled at her. "The Pedrales. I want to get an idea what your friend is up to."

"You think a bar will tell you?"

"Maybe."

"You will be back though?"

"You got my dog. I have to be back," he said with a smile. "Lock the doors when you go inside."

"How will you get in?"

"I can sleep out here with Bear."

"He will be with me... inside."

He smiled at that as he rose and fastened back on his cartridge belt. "He's not been a housedog."

"Anybody can change."

He sucked in a breath but smiled. "I will be back but closer to midnight than sunset."

"Drunk?"

He laughed at that as he pulled her out of her chair. "I don't drink that much, baby."

She liked him calling her that. Maybe there was hope, but then he didn't kiss her. When Bear started to follow him, he said, "Stay. Guard the property." He looked back at her and winked before he turned and stalked off.

She looked at the bemused dog as she took off her wedding ring. She had been wearing a plain gold chain. She unfastened its clasp and looped it through the ring before fastening it again around her neck and letting the ring drop between her breasts. Someday he'd put it back on her finger. She could wait.

"What do you think, Bear?" she asked at the dog, who was

watching the gate but looked back at her when he heard his name. "Come here." Surprisingly, he did, and she petted his head as she considered her options. She could pout, or she could work on a new painting. She opted for the latter.

Tying Judas to the hitching rail, Jesse walked into the Pedrales looking for any faces that could fit Billy Evans. He saw his father and Rance at a back table. No Billy Evans. He went to the bar and ordered a whiskey. "Any strangers showing up here?" he asked as he took a sip.

"All the time. Anybody in particular?"

"Maybe."

"You are a talkative fella for someone asking for something." Ridge said.

Jesse smiled. "I don't know what I am looking for. Maybe somebody who hires out his gun."

"You mean like me?" his father came up behind him and put his hand on Jesse's shoulder.

"You doing that again?" he asked as he met his old man's gaze.

"Too old for it now. Come on over to where Rance and I are sitting."

He had no reason to refuse and took his glass with him. At the table, he moved a chair so he didn't have his back to the room, then lit a cigarette.

"What are you up to, Jesse?" Jeremiah asked.

"Looking for a hired gun."

"To hire or kill before he gets you?" Rance asked as he sipped his beer.

Jesse took a long draw on the cigarette. "The second."

"Who would want to kill you besides my son?" Rance asked and he'll be after us first.

"Someone who has reasons but couldn't do it himself."

"He from here?"

"No."

"A dude?"

"Yeah."

"There was a guy in here earlier. Pudgy, not very tall," Jeremiah said. "Fancy clothes. He was in a rotten mood for sure, but I didn't see who he talked to. He nursed a beer." He looked at Rance. "You see him talk to anybody?"

"I'm trying to remember. Not the kind of guy I usually pay attention to."

Maybe he was looking for trouble where there wasn't any. He had a feeling though. Brooks not only had no use for him, but he still wanted Lily. There was one way to accomplish his goals. The city man wasn't the type to brace anyone himself. From what Lily had told him, the man had money to get that kind of job done by someone who could.

Jesse recognized Del Sicilla when he came in and bought a beer before looking around. When he saw Jeremiah, he came over. "You two hang out here a lot these days." He then looked at Jesse with curiosity. "Do I know you?"

"We met a year ago... briefly."

"That's right. You talk to the other side like my wife."

Jesse didn't like being reminded of that but nodded.

"You get a vision that someone is going to pay to have you killed?" Jeremiah asked showing more concern than Jesse would have expected.

"No."

"Let's hear it. What did you do?" Jeremiah asked now showing irritation mixed into the concern.

"It's not your problem. You have your own, it seems."

"Which might also be yours," Rance said. He looked at Del with interest. "Your wife really talk to the other side?"

"You know the answer to that."

Jeremiah shook his head. "Wish I could say I don't, but yeah, I do and she does."

"I should talk to her then," Rance said. "Maybe she'd tell me where Billy is. I'd like to convince him to stop before he does something stupid."

"She doesn't always get anything," Del said. "I owe this family something though." He looked back at Jesse. "Vince likely saved her life and mine. She'd probably try if you asked."

"Better not," Jesse said.

"Why not?" Rance asked.

"There is a cost."

"Oh, like a curse."

"A price," Jesse said. He didn't like the topic and wished he had said nothing.

"What kind of price?" Rance was not letting it go.

"Never mind."

"How much your wife charge?" He turned back to Del.

"Nothing," Del said sipping his beer. "But the sprout here is right."

"I'm thirty-four," Jesse said. "Not much young left in me." He was tired of people calling him son and boy.

Del chuckled. "You are young to me."

"Explain the price," Rance repeated refusing to let the topic go.

"You really want to know the future?" Jesse asked.

"Sure."

"Even if you were going to die tomorrow?"

"Wal, not then."

"You can't control what you get or even the truth of it." Much as he hated talking about the other side, he felt compelled to warn Rance. It was not something to take lightly, and that happened most often to those who didn't believe and considered it a game.

"When I went to Mrs. Sicilla, my wife came from the other side-- and said she had been murdered," Jeremiah said sipping his beer. "I'd rather not have known that."

"But she also said that she felt bad for how she treated you," Del reminded him.

"Don't believe that. She never showed none of that while alive."

"So you believed she got murdered but not that she forgave you." Del laughed again.

"We believe what we want," Jesse said and then wished he had not. His father looked at him with interest.

"You are talking more, boy. What's going on? That woman hiring you also pulling you out?"

Jesse smoked and ignored the question.

"I will tell you one thing," Jeremiah said, "and it don't take talking to the other side. If you want that woman, you will live to regret it. Nothing you do will ever be enough. A woman like that, they want more than either you or me can ever give them."

"I don't need to hear this," Jesse growled. His day had gone from heaven to hell, and it wasn't over yet.

CHAPTER 10

"Hey, that guy just come in," Rance said. "I know him." He looked over at Jesse. "He does hire out his gun. I saw him in a shooting, little more than a year ago in Sonora, Texas. Later the talk was a rancher outside of town paid to get rid of a rival for his son's sweetheart. Ugly business."

Jesse studied the man as he bellied up to the bar. He wore his gun down low and tied to his thigh. That alone meant little in Tucson. Who he was asking for might. Jesse rose and walked to the bar.

"He come in tonight?" the man was asking Ridge.

Ridge looked at Jesse, who had leaned one elbow on the bar, but said nothing.

"I asked you a question," the stranger said.

"I don't respond to demands," Ridge said.

"Who you looking for?" Jesse asked. "Maybe I can help you."

"Jesse Taggert."

Jesse smiled. "This is your lucky day. I'm Taggert."

The stranger turned to look at him an expression of shock followed by his own grin. "It is indeed."

"Somebody pay you to come looking for me?"

"Why'd you ask that?"

Jesse shrugged. "Just a possibility. Like maybe Brooks."

"Not heard the name." Jesse could see the lie in his eyes.

"Well, what do you want now that you found me?"

"You killed my brother."

"Where?"

"Doesn't matter, does it?"

"What's your name, stranger?"

"None of your business."

"It is if you think I killed your brother. Might be I want to see if I did."

"You calling me a liar?"

"How much did he pay you? Dying better be worth it."

"You'll be the dead one."

Jesse laughed. "And I didn't even get paid."

"Take it outside," Ridge said putting his shotgun on the bar.

Jesse realized Jeremiah had come to the bar and was standing at his left. "Let this go, son."

"Old man, stay out of this," the stranger said.

"Can't do it. This is my son."

"It's not your business." He glared at Jesse. "But you are."

Jesse had killed two men. He hadn't had a choice on either. He knew this man was the brother of neither. He debated whether he could walk away this time. He didn't want a shot in the back or maybe the man would show up when he was with Lily— or even target her. He couldn't prove it was Brooks who set him up, but it seemed most likely this close and for no reason.

"Tell me who paid you, and we can call this quits," he said giving it one more try.

"I don't want to call it quits. Outside."

Jesse shrugged. He didn't look away from the gunman. "Pa, you stay out of this."

"Rance said he's fast with a gun," Jeremiah said. "He will kill you, boy."

"We'll see."

The man turned to go, and Jesse heard Jeremiah reach for his gun. "No." He slammed his hand down hard against his father's wrist, making the revolver fall from his fingers. "Let me handle this." He followed the man out into the street, lit now only by the streetlights. "How much you get for this?"

"What's it to you?"

"Curiosity."

"Want to know what you are worth?" He chuckled.

"Curious as to what you're willing to die for."

"I won't be the one dying."

Despite the lights on the corners, the night was dark around them. Others came out of the Pedrales. Maybe some went for the law, but it wouldn't arrive in time. Jesse didn't like knowing he was willing to kill a man. Sometimes there was not a choice. He also could be the one who died. It wasn't impossible. It just hadn't happened yet.

"What's your name?" he asked as they faced off on the street.

"Why? I ain't got a rep."

"Man should have his name on his grave."

The stranger looked disturbed but shook it off. "Bill Sykes."

"Well, Bill," Jesse said. "Think about this. Money doesn't last long, not as long as death."

"I have thought of it." With that, he reached for his gun. Jesse was firing as the man's was still coming up. Jesse's bullet hit him square in his chest. It threw him back a step. He tried to level his gun but then dropped it and sank to his knees before going flat out.

Gun loose now in his hand, Jesse walked to the man and knelt beside him, turning him over. He knew his shot had been deadly. "Sorry it came to this. It was Brooks, wasn't it?"

The man stared up at him, pain and shock in his eyes. Frowning he met Jesse's gaze. "Don't matter now. Yes. Three hundred dollars. That man wants you dead, son. Thought I could do it. Needed the..." He tried to smile as his eyes went blank. Jesse knew he was dead before he felt for the pulse.

He rose and leathered his Colt as his father came to stand beside him. There were other footsteps. He looked around unsure if Brooks would have hired more than one.

"I heard what he said," Ridge said he came off the boardwalk to stand behind Jesse. "That Brooks hired him." He looked at the sheriff as he ran up. "It was a fair fight. Sykes drew first. He was paid."

"By who?" the sheriff asked.

"Harold Brooks, but nobody will prove it with him dead," Jesse said.

The sheriff looked from the body to Jesse. "I can talk to him."

You can," Jesse said feeling as though a heavy weight had descended on him. He was getting one of his headaches. No surprise, but not a good time.

"I'll ask him about it in the morning. As you said, unless there's proof, the most I can is strongly suggest he leave town," the sheriff said.

"I know."

"You better head for bed, young fella. You don't look good."

Jesse managed a smile as the pain pounded his head, and the aura began to block some of his vision. "I will." He headed for his horse aware his father, Rance, and Del were there as he mounted. He had no words for them and rode off.

At the stable, he took the time to curry and give Judas oats and did the same for Jethro. The aura was gone, but his head was hurting so much he had to work to concentrate on even those simple tasks. Slowly he walked back to Lily's home. The house was dark except for a dim light in the kitchen. He went into the backyard intending to sleep in one of the lawn chairs, hoping his headache would be gone by morning.

The kitchen door opened. "You are not sleeping out there," she said with irritation.

"Better I do," he said. She was beside him, had his arm, and pulled him into the house, Bear on the other side.

In the light of the kitchen, she could see his face for the first time. "What's wrong?" she asked, her voice full of concern.

"Just a headache."

"Just? You look as though you are in terrible pain."

"Some."

She kept his hand and led him through the house to one of the bedrooms. "You can sleep in here." He remembered the room from when they had all stayed there when Holly owned the house. She pulled back the spread. He unbuckled his cartridge belt and laid the weapon on the side table before he sat on the bed, feeling relief at being off his feet.

"Sorry," he said as he bent to get off his boots, but she was there first. She pulled them both off and the socks. He lay back then with a sigh.

"Do you get headaches like this often?" she asked as she sat on the edge of the bed watching him in the dim light from the moon.

"No."

"Since childhood?"

"Yes."

She reached out to stroke his forehead. "I'll be right back," she said. When she returned it was with a glass of water, cloth, and a small bottle. "Have you tried aspirin for them?"

He shook his head. "What is it?" He had avoided laudanum, which some swore by. He knew how it could addict.

"They came out a couple of years ago. They can ease pain." She shook two into her hand and gave them to him.

"Don't need it."

"Don't worry. They aren't addictive."

He let out a breath. The pain was so bad that he would try anything to ease it, and he swallowed the pills, surprised when she lifted his head to help him drink the water. "I am not weak," he said with a faint smile despite the agony.

"What if I like touching you?"

"Do you?"

She smiled then as she took what he found to be a damp cloth and stroked it over his face before she laid it on his forehead. It was cool. "Sometimes this helps too."

"You get headaches?" he asked as he looked up, struck again by her beauty. He realized she was wearing a robe, which meant a nightgown under it. Thinking of that led to a surprising swelling in his loins. He would have thought this level of pain would block desire. Apparently not.

"No, but my father did when he was ill."

"You were right. The cloth helps." In the past, he'd done nothing to ease his pain. He'd just endured it.

"How long do they last?"

"A few hours."

"Can you sleep with it?"

"Sometimes."

"Do you want me to help you get out of your clothing?"

At that thought, the swelling grew, and he shook his head. "No, I'll just sleep in them if you don't mind."

"Whatever is best for you." She rose off the bed. He immediately felt the loss. "I will see you in the morning."

When she was gone, he lay, thinking of the day. He'd gone through so many emotions that it was hard to put any of it together. Time with her had become one of the sweetest things he'd ever known. His life hadn't been filled with much joy. Bear had brought him some. Vince and Cole a bit but of the questioning sort. Even Charlie with his love for his mule, his wanting to help in his strange way. With her though, well, with anyone, it couldn't last. In the morning, he'd tell her what he had done. She'd not want anything to do with him after that.

Starting coffee in the morning, Lily thought about the man sleeping in the bedroom down the hall. Her husband. She had learned something new about him. The headaches. She also knew now that he endured pain without a groan. He was nothing like her father who had responded to any discomfort by making sure all around him were miserable. She had seen Jesse's pain on his face, but he'd not uttered a word of complaint or a groan.

She only knew he was standing at the door when Bear got up and came to him for a pat.

"How do you feel?" she asked.

"The headache is gone. The aspirin did help. Where do you get them?"

"Sicillas has them."

"Guess I should get some."

"Do you feel like eating?"

He smiled then and sat at the table. "Depends. What?" He had that expression in his eyes that made her heart seem to fill her whole body.

"I can offer scrambled eggs and bacon... for now." She smiled back.

"I have to tell you something first." His tone had grown somber.

"Coffee's ready. Want some before you tell me whatever it is?"

"All right."

She poured them each a cup, set his in front of him, before she sat across the table, and waited.

"Last night I went to town to find out what your friend had in mind. I thought I'd find out at the bars. I did."

"And?" she asked when he hesitated.

"Just trying to find the right words." He sighed. "I believe that he paid a man to kill me."

"My Lord."

"It was what I expected."

"How could you expect such a thing?" She felt shocked.

"You don't come from the world I do. It is what some do when they want something and someone stands in their way."

She let out a groan. "You. You stand in Harold's way? To what?"

"To you."

"I never dreamed, never imagined he'd do something like that, that our marrying would endanger you."

"I am glad you don't think like that. It's a better way to live."

"Well, what can we do about it?"

"The sheriff will talk to Brooks this morning."

"The sheriff? How did he get involved?"

He looked away and then back to her, his gaze firm and unmoving. "I killed a man last night."

"Oh no." She felt the tears welling up. "How?"

"He came to the bar and was looking for me. He made it impossible not to fight him. He would have come after me somewhere else. Maybe somewhere you were. Better to face it there."

"You went there expecting this?"

"It was a possibility."

"A gunfight?" She had heard of such but never imagined. Tucson had guns going off, and she had known some involved killings. Chicago didn't have such things. Or did it, but just not where she had lived?

"Yes. It was a fair fight, and when it was over, the man admitted he had been paid before he died."

She tried to steady her voice. "And others heard?"

He nodded. "But it won't be proven. Not for a man like Brooks. He will say he didn't and that will be the end of it from the legal end."

"Will he do this again? Hire someone else?"

"I don't know. I'll talk to him."

"You have to talk to him?"

"Yes."

She rose then but instead of leaving the room and walking off as he had expected, she came around the table and put her arms around his neck. He shifted and took her onto his lap where she cuddled against him. "You could have been killed," she whispered, her tears wetting his shirt.

"I know."

"I want us to leave Tucson." She lifted her head and looked into his eyes.

"You think you can run from things like this?"

"Can't we?"

"No. Besides, this is your home. My home."

"Don't separate us that way, Jesse. Yes, this is our home, but we can make a new one where this sort of thing doesn't happen."

"Where would that be? Heaven?"

"I wasn't thinking quite that far." She gave a little laugh.

"Lily, I don't run."

"Never?" she asked and a smile overcame the tears.

"Well, maybe not never."

She laughed and stood up. "Scrambled eggs, bacon, toasted bread. Anything else?"

She saw it on his face that there was something else. There was for her too. It would just take time. They had time... She hoped.

After he had eaten, Jesse went into the bedroom and came out wearing his gun.

"Can I go with you?"

"It's better you don't. It appears he already is mad at losing you. Seeing you won't make what he sees as his loss any easier."

"You don't plan to shoot him?"

"It won't go that way. It's not how he fights."

"You know this how?"

"Animal nature. Humans have one too." He smiled then and reached down to tip her chin up to give her a light kiss.

"I wish you wouldn't run off all the time after you do that," she said with a pout.

"Are you ready for what would happen if I didn't?"

"Are you?" she shot back.

He laughed then. "Maybe. Maybe not."

"Let's find out tonight," she suggested.

"We'll see. You stay in today, baby, at least until I get back."

"Food supplies here are limited."

"Maybe I could take you out tonight."

She smiled at that idea. "You would do that?"

He considered that a moment. "Let's see how this goes."

"Jesse, this isn't going to be dangerous is it?"

"Lily, do you know how to shoot a gun?"

"No, I never have even held one."

"I think you should learn."

"You are scaring me."

"I don't mean to. It's just a good thing to know."

"All right. I guess you could teach me to shoot."

"Next horseback riding lesson. We'll find a place on the desert. I'll buy you a gun today."

"They terrify me."

He smiled at that. "So did horses."

"So, horses still do," she corrected.

"You will get past both." When Bear started to follow, he said, "You stay." He found it amusing how the dog had taken to Lily but not surprising. It certainly was a softer life in town. Bear had been looking for a home when he came across the adobe. Not unexpected he would find it better here than out there. Safer for sure.

At the stable, he was still working through why he had to leave her again. She was a constant challenge to him-- like nothing he'd known in a good way. He had only thought he found reasoning hard before she came along. Now, with Lily, he found it sometimes impossible. What did she want? What was she hoping for where it came to him? Trying to figure that out went beyond his capability.

He gave Jethro and Judas some attention before he saddled his horse and rode to the San Xavier hotel. If Brooks had checked out, he'd see if he was at the train depot. He intended to have words with him before he left Tucson. Words weren't easy for him, but if this was truly to end, he felt they were important.

At the hotel, Brooks was at the desk paying his bill. When he saw Jesse, he smiled, nodded, and came out onto the porch.

"The sheriff already talked to me about the tragic events of last night," he said. "I have business in Chicago. I gather you are not requesting charges against me based on what a liar said."

"He lied?"

Brooks looked up at him. "I want you to know that I was drunk last night. I'd never have even talked to a man like Sykes had I not been. I could hardly believe what he claimed when the sheriff talked to me."

"Just out of curiosity. How much did you offer him to die?" Jesse asked lighting a cigarette.

"Of course, I did no such thing."

"I know you did. Dying men often talk truth."

"They might though be delusional. I lost my head even to talk to such a man. He misunderstood my words." He smiled and with that smug smile, Jesse knew this wasn't over. He might be leaving, but he hadn't given up. The question was what did he really want, and what did that smirk mean? Maybe Vince would have known, but Jesse took a step back to consider it.

"I am sorry for the trouble you had last night and that any words I said had anything to do with it." Brooks shook his head. "I had to come here to be sure she was well. I see that she is. It appears you can protect her and keep her safe, that you are a worthy husband of her."

The words were the expected ones to indicate repentance. The eyes said none of that. Jesse could prove none of what he knew. He smiled then. "Have a good trip."

"Jesse, may I call you Jesse?"

He shrugged.

"Are you somewhat well, disabled?"

"In what way?"

The smug smile was back. "Something about the way you speak

makes me wonder... Well, silly, of course. You are not disabled at all. You are good at killing, aren't you?"

Though he'd had experience with the kind of emotional attack that he understood Brooks was doing—he had no defense. He nodded and turned to go, surprised when Brooks put his hand on his arm to stop him. "You are certainly a muscular devil. Apparently you have to work hard with those muscles to earn your living, don't you?"

"What do you want?"

"Just Lily is a very bright woman, artistic and beautiful. I hope you... er understand all that she is."

"I do."

"She will want a bright man. Muscles are only satisfying for so long."

Jesse sucked in a breath. "And for my own good, you would be warning me that she won't stay with me?"

"Of course. I admire you. You are a magnificent physical specimen. Beautiful really as a man. Like a majestic animal."

"Take your hand off my arm." He felt some satisfaction when Brooks dropped his hand.

"I only meant to warn you as a friend."

"You are not my friend."

"I could be on many levels if you were needing a friend."

"I am not."

"You might need one someday." Those eyes bothered Jesse. The man smiled, but the eyes were almost reptilian. He could well believe Lily had been repulsed by him. He also was. He shook his head to clear his thoughts. "Good luck on your trip north."

"Thank you. I thought you might hold a bit of a grudge against me since at one time Lily and I were together."

Jesse just looked at him.

"Oh, I guess she never told you that at one time she led me to believe she had feelings for me, might even eventually accept my hand in marriage. Young women and their games, you know." His smile was calculating.

"I'm done talking to you, Mr. Brooks," Jesse said again turning to leave.

"Well, just remember," Brooks said to his back, "if you need advice someday, perhaps in investments." There was a small chuckle. "Feel free to contact me... in Chicago."

"Goodbye."

"You might someday want to have a friend. I did some research on your family after finding out Lily had chosen you instead of me."

Jesse turned back. "You're telling me this why?"

"Just I know how it can be for some who come from such families. They end up with nowhere to turn when... things go bad for them."

"And it's why you paid someone to kill me."

Brooks smiled, and it felt unclean to Jesse. "I didn't pay anyone anything, of course."

"Yeah."

"I understood it was a fair fight from the sheriff."

"One that never had to happen."

"Didn't it?" The smirk was the last straw. If Jesse wasn't going to slam him in his face, he had to get away from him.

"I've learned my lesson," Brooks said. Something about the way he said it turned Jesse back to look at him again. "I should be careful about casual talk to those I don't know well," Brooks said. "Sykes simply took on my own unhappiness at Lily's choosing another. Someone I saw... last night, of course, as her inferior."

"Uh huh."

"Anyway, I will be gone, and you won't see me again."

"Goodbye." Jesse stepped off the boardwalk.

"Uh, just one thing." Jesse turned back, the cigarette dangling from his lips. "Take care of her, Mr. Taggert." Jesse shook his head. He didn't turn again when he heard Brooks departing shot. "Someone needs to take care of... her."

As Jesse walked off, he doubted very much this was over. Brooks would be on the train, but nothing about that conversation made him believe the man had given up. Jesse couldn't do much about that. Would Brooks hire another man to come after him? He'd denied offering Sykes money, but Jesse knew he had lied. If he sent another hired killer and then another, eventually one would get him. In the end, everybody dies. Men who live by the gun do it just a little sooner than the rest.

CHAPTER 11

A t the cafe Patrick and his brother had chosen for breakfast, with his first cup of coffee in front of him, he opened the paper to the obituaries and legal notices as was his wont and let out a yelp.

"What the hell is wrong?" Rupert asked laughing. "Find you died and didn't know it?" He took a sip of his coffee and smiled at the waitress, who went off with their order.

"This is what's wrong." He shoved the paper in his brother's face and pointed to the notice.

"That's peculiar, isn't it? Is the groom one of *the* Taggerts?"

"How would I know. What's that supposed to mean?"

"Just it's, you might say infamous as an outlaw family. Kansas based. Wonder how she met him."

"More than met him, it appears."

"Well, you didn't figure she would marry you."

"I still feel shocked. I saw him there. Jesse is his name. He never said his last name. He was like a jungle creature, so beneath her."

"Jungle creature?" Rupert laughed.

"Artistic license."

Rupert sipped his coffee. "With him around to protect her, looks like that other plan of ours goes out the window too."

"You were still thinking of kidnapping her for ransom?"

"It wasn't totally out of my mind."

"Had you talked to Billy about it?"

"I hadn't had time."

"Were you planning to use him or cut him out too as you said you would with your big boss, whoever the hell he was?"

"It was a backup plan is all."

"Where's your little friend?" Patrick asked trying to think through how this changed things

"If you mean Billy, best you not call him little."

"So where is he?"

"I have no idea."

"Maybe you need to find out."

"What the hell are you talking about?"

"A widow might be more responsive to me."

"Pat, you must be joking. If we have him killed, she'll turn to you when she isn't now? I think you are the one living in the clouds to think that."

He knew Rupert was right but argued anyway. "She will look for comfort from someone who is of her sort, someone who can appreciate her finer qualities. I thought Billy would be going after the Taggerts anyway."

"You want this guy dead more than money, it sounds like."

There was truth in that. The man he had seen her with that morning, without even knowing the outlaw family background, he wasn't worthy of her. Jesse. Not just Jesse but Jesse Taggert. What had she been thinking? "Let me think." He felt a chill. "He's the one who killed a man last night."

"Yeah. Which tell us one more thing."

"What?"

"The man she chose is good with a gun. I will tell you another. So is his family."

"As fast as you?" Patrick looked up with curiosity.

"You only find that out when you go up against someone. All right, I better find Billy. Maybe we can get him to brace him."

"You really believe that's the best approach?"

The waitress refilled their coffee cups. "Food will be up in a few minutes," she said as she disappeared again.

"I don't know. While we think about it, we get someone to keep an eye on the Jacobs-- or make that Taggert home," Rupert said with a grin. "We need to know what's happening there."

"Why?"

"Just thinking as we talk. Kidnapping might not be out of the question. His being fast with a gun could be countered by his being softened by a woman.'

"It wasn't last night."

"She wasn't with him last night."

"Kidnapping has warped your brain. It won't work. Not to get money anyway."

Rupert chuckled. "Maybe he's not hanging around there much. If we kidnap her, his muscle won't help him if he can't find her. Her sister has the money to pay a ransom. But there is something else now."

"What?"

"She married him. You said he's a fine looking male specimen, which means she's enamored of him for now anyway. Honeymoon phase and all. Maybe we grab him instead, and she pays."

"Wait, didn't you just say he was dangerous?"

"I wasn't thinking far enough ahead." Rupert grinned. "I don't want to brace him. And frankly, you and I couldn't pull it off anyway. Billy could."

"Billy will go for that?"

"I think so. Distract him from his own annoyance getting here and being asked to wait around with no orders for why. He's not happy."

"Well, find out where he is," Patrick said staring again at the newspaper. His brother left without another word.

Patrick realized he'd been talking crazy. Rupert's lawlessness must be brushing off on him. Putting aside his disappointment, over the possibility no longer existing that he could marry Lily and solve his money problems, the potential for this to go wrong had so many possible directions. He felt a headache coming on.

"Where'd your friend go?" the waitress asked as she returned with two plates.

"Urgent business. Just leave mine. Keep his warm in case he returns."

She frowned but did as requested.

Pouring Tabasco on his eggs, Patrick tried to think it through. None of what he'd been hearing was making sense. Lily becoming Mrs. Jesse Taggert was the last impossible element in what was clearly a fiasco. He had yet to meet this mysterious boss or even understand why any of this was happening. If they weren't very careful, the little outlaw would turn on them— even before he solved his own mystery. On the other hand, why did he care? Life was getting too complicated. He poured more Tabasco on the eggs.

❧

Lily stood at the stove stirring what she hoped would be a good stew. She had followed the directions in the cookbook but as to exactly what the results would be, she was iffy. What she knew for sure was she liked cooking for Jesse and only hoped he would actually be home to eat it.

It was only when she heard his boots on the porch that she knew. Since he had insisted she lock the doors when he wasn't there, she flew to open it with Bear at her heels. She threw herself in his surprised arms but was happy he laid a package on her hall table and clasped his arms around her.

"Would you like a beer?" she asked as she led him back into the kitchen.

"If we can sit outside where I can drink it. It's hot but not that bad yet."

"Another storm due?"

"Looks like it." He went back in the hall for his package and then outside. She reached into the refrigerator for a beer, gave the stew one last stir and followed him out. The breeze was starting to pick up.

He unbuckled his cartridge belt and set it on the table beside him then took the beer. "That one is yours," he said gesturing to the wrapped package. She knew by its shape what it was.

"You sure I need this?"

"If you don't, you don't need to use it. Unwrap it. It's not loaded." She undid the string and opened the paper to see a small revolver in a leather holster. "It's a .38," he said. "Not too much recoil. Not too heavy."

"It is pretty."

He smiled. "I don't think of them are pretty but maybe."

"I guess I can learn to shoot. Holly is good with a gun."

"I remember. She saved Vince's life because of that."

She hadn't thought of it that way. If it was to save Jesse's life, she could learn to shoot. She would learn to shoot. "How did it go with Harold?"

"He took the train heading back for Chicago."

"I still can't believe he did that."

"You don't?"

She realized she had to be more careful how she phrased things. "I mean I do because he did, but it just seems so strange to imagine anyone doing such a thing."

"When he wants something, he's the kind not to care what he has to do to get it."

Before she could respond, the bell at the gate rang as it was being opened. Bear rose to look aggressively toward it but relaxed when Jesse put his hand on his head.

"Aren't you two the ones," Rose said as she came in laughing with Ollie right behind her.

"Would you like some lemonade?" Lily asked. When they both nodded and took a lawn chair, she went into the house and came back with the cold drinks. "Maybe you'd prefer a beer too, Ollie," she said ready to go back.

"Nah, just fine with this."

"Now, the ones what?" Lily asked.

Rose shook her head and laughed again. "You know what."

"I do?"

"Heard about the shooting last night," Ollie said looking at Jesse. "Too bad."

"Yeah," Jesse said.

"I want to have a reception for you," Rose said reaching over to pat Lily's hand.

"I am not following you."

Rose laughed again. "Thought you pulled a fast one getting married on the sly."

"How did you know about that?" she asked looking worriedly at Jesse. Might Harold have told someone?

"The newspaper, sweetheart," Rose said. "Didn't you know they post the wedding announcements?"

"Oh." She looked again at Jesse, who had put on that cold face she had seen before.

"We hadn't thought of that." She wondered how many read that section of the newspaper.

"We want to have a celebration dinner for you, Rose said. "We will invite your friends and ours. Will Holly be back soon?"

"Not for a month." My goodness, she hadn't even thought of Holly. She had believed she would tell her when she returned. Might someone else tell her first? Or would the Chicago Jacobs name end up being well known enough that the papers would pick up this story.

"It's not quite how it looks," Jesse said.

She gave him a look. "It's not?" she asked.

"I mean it's not a regular wedding."

Ollie smiled, pulled Rose to her feet, and said, "We will let you two work this out. Give us a call when you do."

Clearly, Rose didn't want to go, but she followed him.

"Please don't say anything," Lily begged as she stood at the gate.

"Of course not, dear," Rose said and then turned and left.

Lily turned back to Jesse. Did he believe she had tricked him into marrying her? "I had no idea that they printed such in the paper," she said watching uneasily as he lit a cigarette.

"This is a problem. It could be unsafe, especially right now, for you to be married to a Taggert," he said smoking and not looking at her.

"I don't think you are worried about me," she said. A two-day marriage. Was that a record? A marriage that never became one.

"What else would I be worried about?" he asked now turning and looking at her.

"You don't want to be married to me." She fought back the tears. She had been so excited at fixing a dinner and now... nothing.

"Baby, it's not about what I want."

"If it's not, what is it about?"

"What's best for you."

She felt furious. "You aren't even asking what I want. You just want out. Of course, we can do that. You only did this to help me, and that reason went north."

He rose and walked over to the cottonwood tree smoking and not looking at her.

"Do you even want to eat dinner with me tonight?" she asked brushing away tears. "You are free to go when you want."

He turned then and she saw the pain on his face. Was he getting another headache? "Lily," he said, "I don't want to see you hurt."

"Even when you are the one doing it."

"Staying married to me could have you hurt in ways you don't understand. It's not just the family reputation, but there's more."

"So because of some possible fear, you want to walk away from me."

"I'm trying to think what is best."

She felt suddenly furious at him. "How dare you say such a thing," she snapped. "You don't care what's best for me. You haven't even asked me what I want. You still haven't asked me."

"What do you want?"

She came to stand in front of him. "I want you to want to be my husband." She stepped back then, reached for the ring on the chain, pulled it up, and held it up. "I want you to put this ring on my finger when you want to be married to me."

"What do I have to offer you?"

"Are you talking about money?"

"That and security."

"Jesse, I am so mad at you right now that I can't speak about this rationally. It's not your fault. I understand that. I pressured you into marrying me. You have every right to walk away now. Just please don't you dare tell me it's for my best."

"I need to think."

"All right, think. I need to stop thinking." She ran into the house and slammed the door.

The knowledge that their wedding was now public information forced Jesse to consider things he hadn't wanted to... not yet. Was Brooks still a danger to her? In some ways, now that he'd met the man, he could see how he might be more of a danger than she imagined. Where would she be safest?

He didn't want to walk away from her. The thought that something could happen to her was unbearable. How could he best keep her safe? She was his, and yet she never could be. He sat back in the chair and smoked as he considered possible choices.

He realized that Bear had come to put his head under his hand. "Don't much like it when we argue, huh?" he said, understanding that feeling well from his childhood.

He did not know what Lily wanted. She had been right about that. He found it impossible to imagine her wanting to stay married to him. To protect herself from a man she feared, that he understood. But to want to be with him for any other reasons, to want to be his wife? Could she want that? He was stupid, uneducated, and part of an outlaw clan that would always have enemies and consequences.

She opened the door. "The phone call is for you," she said in a cold voice.

Who would call him here? That wasn't good. He stubbed out his cigarette, grabbed his revolver, and went into the house.

Holding the receiver to his ear, he said, "Hello."

"Glad I found you. Jesse, Billy Evans is in town," his father said.

"How did you know to call me here?"

"The paper."

Hell. "I didn't know you read one."

"Rance was looking through it and... Never mind how. I know. Evans got into town. He's got five rowdies with him. Rance saw his son at the Pedrales, but he thought he got out of there before he was seen. You need to get out of town for a while."

"Damn."

"I'll try to get hold of Vince and warn him not to come back. Not sure when he was due here again."

"I think another month."

"Good. I wouldn't have called you here except..."

He understood. If his father knew about Lily than so could Billy. "All right, thank you," he said, feeling sick as he put the receiver back on its hanger.

"What is it?" she asked still looking angry but now equally concerned.

"Remember I told you my past could catch up with me. It has, and now I don't know what to do about it."

"Obviously, your father also reads the Citizen." She dished up a bowl of stew and put it on the table. "You might as well eat."

She put some into another bowl for herself and then a third for Bear, which she set on the floor for the appreciative mutt.

As he ate, he struggled again to think it through. If she got on the train, she would be out of town before Billy learned of her. Surely, newspapers didn't also put addresses in them... or did they? He was unsure what all information had been on the form he had signed. He studied her as he thought about the problem.

"The man that I am worried about is a killer," he said finally with no way to edge into the problem or soften it. "He believes my father and his father cheated him, stole from him. Revenge appears to be what he's after."

"Did they cheat him?"

"They say no."

"Then couldn't they explain that?"

"Before or after he shoots them dead?"

She shuddered. "Would he also try to hurt you too?"

"I don't know. It's possible. I have the name. Now, you do too."

"I am sorry that I am complicating your life." Her tone sounded annoyed.

"It's not your fault."

"It certainly is." She pressed her lips tightly together. "So what do you plan to do about it? Head for the bar again?"

He smiled. "I am not anxious to see Evans, so no."

"Then your problem is? I see you feel you have one."

"I can't protect you here. It's too open. Too easy for someone to come in without us seeing them. The best idea is you get on the train tomorrow morning, go to San Francisco and stay with Vince and Holly."

"What about them? Would they also be endangered if someone is going after revenge on your father?"

"Billy isn't likely to go to California. They do though need to stay away for a while." Not that he thought Vince would do that if he knew about Evans.

"Has your father warned them?"

"I don't know."

"Call him back and ask."

"He doesn't have a phone. That was from a neighbor's. I can ride over there, but then that would mean leaving you alone."

"You can't worry about me all the time."

He walked outside trying to clear his head as he buckled on his cartridge belt.

"I am not getting on a train anywhere," she said as she followed him. "Besides, maybe they'd find that out too. People do buy tickets, get seen."

She was right. Hell.

She sat on the chair. "Would he know about your place?" she asked.

"I don't have a place."

"The adobe."

"For what?"

"Me to go if you feel I shouldn't stay here."

He opened his mouth and slammed it shut. "It's not much of a home."

'You live there."

"With Charlie now."

"I guess we could work around that."

"You have no idea how primitive it is. Scorpions, tarantulas, rattlesnakes. You aren't used to anything like living with the desert."

"Were you used to this when you came here?"

He clenched his jaw. "I wasn't planning to come here."

"I am not getting on any train. I can stay by myself if you don't want me out there with you."

"You know that's not it."

"So we go to your place where you can teach me how to shoot. Holly left their tents and camping gear in the spare bedroom downstairs. If you got us a pack horse, I could even take my paints, couldn't I?"

He felt like a wind was carrying him away. He tried to think whether she was right. He could do a better job protecting her out there. It'd be harder for Evans to find him too. It wasn't as if his place was on a map or that he had an address. Maybe it would work. Except..."

"Lily, you will hate it out there. This is the hot season, and the adobe doesn't stay as cool as your house. No electricity. No fans. Then there are the storms. Looks like this one passed us by, but there will be more and in a small adobe, they can be scary."

"If it doesn't work, I'll get on a train or whatever you want. Let's try it though." He looked at her and saw the smile, even excitement in her eyes. She clearly wanted to do this. The fact that he knew she'd hate it wasn't going to stop her. He didn't have a better idea—yet.

"Let me think." He tried to remember how much food he had there. Potatoes, carrots, salt pork, flour, salt, sugar, lard, whiskey, beer. No refrigerator though to keep anything cold.

It was almost dark. He could probably get the rest of what they would need. Not like Evans was likely to look for him yet. For now, he'd be concentrating on finding Jeremiah and Rance. It would take time to get to him.

"I have an account at Sicillas," she said. "I could go there and..."

"Whoa." He put up a hand. "You will stay here or I'll head for that bar and find Evans right now."

"Don't do that."

He nodded. "All right. I'll be back in an hour with our horses, a packhorse, and supplies. Be ready." With that, he was gone.

In the house, she packed her painting supplies, including a roll of canvas. She ran back outside for the gun he had bought her and laid it on the table. In a sack, she packed medicinal supplies that she had found useful including aspirin, hydrogen peroxide, carbolic, iodine, and material for bandages. She bagged up all of the food she had in the house, which wasn't much, but at least would give them tea and coffee.

She dug through the supplies Holly had left in the small room and found a tent. Maybe it wouldn't prove useful but wouldn't hurt to bring it if he did find a packhorse. Then she went upstairs, changed into her pants, boots and shirt. She stuffed a bag with a pair of sandals, undergarments, a nightgown, extra socks, a shirt, and one dress, not that she expected to need it. She carried the bag and her quilts downstairs.

The sunset was long gone before he returned and began carrying out the sacks, securing them on the packhorse. Jethro was tied to the front gate. She wondered then how soon it would be before she saw her cottage again. "I should let Rose know I'll be gone. She comes by and will worry if I'm not here."

He considered that as he was tying on the last of the gear. "All right, but don't say where. Better they don't know."

As she walked into the house, she thought he was being a little melodramatic, but then he understood the risks they faced far better than she did. She hoped the Olivers hadn't gone to bed. Rose answered on the second ring.

"I just wanted to let you know Jesse and I are talking a little vacation."

"A honeymoon?" Rose asked quickly.

"Sort of."

"How long will you be gone?"

"Awhile but not sure. I didn't want you to worry."

"Thank you, dear. I am sorry I upset him today. I wasn't thinking."

"It's all right. Take care."

When she came out, Jesse was smoking his cigarette and watching her. Bear waited at his side. "You sure about this?" he asked. "It's not too late for you to stay in the hotel tonight and take the train tomorrow wherever it goes."

"I am sure." She walked to Jethro and mounted him. "I am ready."

"God, I doubt it," he said but stepped into his own saddle and gigging Judas in the side, took them off at a slow trot. She quickly remembered his instructions. Jethro had a good gait, and she found riding him increasingly comfortable. The only strange part was riding without sunlight. Even the moon has yet to rise. She knew to stay with Jesse. Bear stayed ahead of them only looking back now and then to assure himself they were still there.

She wished Jesse had been in a better mood about the whole adventure. Then she remembered the fear he had to be feeling. His father was at risk and so was he. Well, maybe so was she. At this point though, she could only think she was with him. She would be out on the desert he knew so well, where she was ignorant, but eager to learn. She should have been afraid, but she felt only a heady sort of excitement.

Lily's life had been one of restrictions. Painting had been her only outlet to escape the rules and limitations of the wealth her family had and her father's need for control. She was now following a man who had no desire to control her at all. She was following him into a wilderness that rather than frightening her left her excited, filled with a strange exhilaration.

When she came close enough to his horse, she decided to confront his irritation. "Did you want to tell your father where you will be?"

"No."

"He might worry."

"What he doesn't know, he can't tell anybody."

"Would he do that?"

"Hurt someone enough and they'll do anything to get it to stop."

"Torture?" She couldn't hide her shock. "My God, you think someone would do that to him?"

"No. I think he'll be out and gone too."

"Forever?"

"Just until this clears out."

"Billy Evans won't wait around forever, will he?"

"Unlikely."

"Are you mad at me?"

"Why would I be?"

"Well, I did push you to marry me and now you are stuck with me."

He turned and looked at her. She could barely make out his features in the darkness. "Lily, I am not stuck with you."

CHAPTER 12

With late night, Tucson's bar district was bustling with laughter and activity. Patrick hated it all. He should have been in his room, in bed. Instead, he needed to be with Rupert when he finally had the opportunity to learn more about Billy Evans. Patrick had met the man before dinner with no chance to ask questions. He had hated every pretentious inch of which the little outlaw had precious few. He saw the kind of hair-trigger temper that he always avoided being near. Worse was the mean look in those cold blue eyes.

Evans, with a smirk, had agreed to meet for a longer talk, but it had to be at eleven in the El Toro. As much as Patrick hated Evans, even more he hated the seedy bar. All the patrons looked ready to shoot anyone who looked at them cross-eyed. He was the only man there not wearing a gun.

All Patrick wanted was to get on a train and head east hoping to forget this whole fiasco. Unfortunately, he did not have enough money to get him so far as Benson.

"Quit moping," Rupert said as he sipped what had to be his fourth beer of the evening. "Hey, here he is."

Billy, handsome, slickly dressed, and shorter than any man in the place, arrived with a flourish and a garishly made-up whore on his arm. He glanced around the room, whispered something to the whore who giggled before she headed up the stairs. He sat at their table and looked straight at Patrick. "Get me a beer," he ordered with a look that didn't brook no for an answer.

Patrick considered refusing, but he had enough money for that and saying no to the little Napoleon seemed a poor idea. He returned to find Billy had his chair. He placed the beer in front of him and sat across from him, now forced to have his own back to the room. He knew another thing now about Billy Evans—he liked to maneuver people, to get control. He hoped Rupert understood what this man was.

"Where are my pa and Taggert?" Billy asked in a surly tone.

"Did you know there is another Taggert in town?" Rupert asked.

"I just got here. Why would I?"

"It adds a dimension and adds options, could change the plan," Rupert said his voice only a little slurred from what he'd been drinking.

"In what way?" Billy asked not showing much interest in the answer.

"Just it's a new entry into the equation," Rupert said.

"Don't use big words with me," Billy snarled. "It makes me mad and you don't want me mad."

"Lily Jacobs married Jeremiah's son."

"And this matters why?"

"She used to live alone and ... well, her family's rich."

Billy cut off a chaw of tobacco and began chewing it. "Which son she marry?"

"Jesse."

"Hmmm. Seems like I met him once years ago. Ain't he the slow-witted one?"

"Maybe slow-witted," Rupert said, "but fast with a gun. He killed Bill Sykes last night."

"Don't know that name."

"He used to fancy himself fast with a hogleg."

Billy sneered. "Lot of men did—the dead ones mostly. I don't see how this changes the plan. What I'd like to know is why ain't the boss here?"

"He'll be here when need be."

"Well, you tell him I need more money. I ain't hanging around here, doing nothing. Me and the boys need gambling and whoring money."

"I can get you the money, but it is going to require laying low."

"Why don't we just grab her and kill the new husband? That oughta bring the old man out of his hole."

"I went by her house. Dark. I checked at the depot. She didn't take the train. Not the stage either. Most likely besides marrying her, Taggert got her out of town with no way right now to know where."

Billy looked suspiciously at Patrick. "Your brother didn't rat us out, did he?"

"I beg your pardon," Patrick said feeling offended and more than a little lightheaded from his own whiskey. "I would not do that."

"Beg my pardon, huh? All right." Billy grinned and sipped his beer. "While we wait around for orders, we find out where they went, and I get some fun with the girl and a Taggert." He smirked.

"You can't hurt her. That order was firm."

"How about him?"

"No problem on that." Rupert chuckled.

"She won't be gone long," Patrick said wishing instantly he'd not said it.

"How do you know that?" Billy put those cold eyes back on him.

"It won't take her long to realize Taggert was a mistake. Then she'll return. She has a home she loves, a garden she tends. She won't stay gone a week if that."

Billy chuckled. "You may not be the total loss I figured. When she returns, what then?"

"If it's her, we kidnap her and get money from her sister to get her back," Rupert said.

"Whoa, the boss is going to okay that?"

"Would he have to know?"

Billy smirked. "All right, I can buy into that. He was the one not here when he said he'd be."

"And if Taggert is the one who shows up, you'll find out where his father is. You like the ways you have of finding information, I know about that."

"He shows up without her and he'll tell us where she is too," Billy said with a wider smile.

Patrick felt swallowed by guilt. He wondered who his brother even was. He wanted no part of kidnapping and torture, but he was in it. He couldn't get out of it now without enough money to get him away from this godforsaken desert.

"We've just been waiting around anyway until we know the boss's plan," Rupert added. "Why not make something extra for ourselves. So long as we don't hurt the girl, we can do what we please."

"As long as it brings in money," Billy said as he looked from them toward the stairs. He had clearly lost interest in the conversation.

"That's the idea," Rupert said. "One way or the other we make money."

Billy rose. "All right, I'll get some of the boys to keep an eye on her home. You wait here and take them to it. We'll work it in shifts." He turned that cruel gaze onto Patrick. "Including fancy pants here."

Patrick managed a smile that he didn't feel as the little dictator walked away from the table, clearly in a better mood. Watching the gunman climb the stairs, Patrick hated himself but he saw no way out. He could only go forward. He felt sorry for Lily Jacobs, but on the other hand, she'd had the bad taste to marry that outlaw. Whatever she got, she deserved. He wouldn't mind seeing the half-wit taken down a notch or two or three. Then he felt a surge of fear. What kind of man was he becoming?

~

Jesse did not take the direct route to the adobe, as he wanted to avoid any possibility of being seen. Billy Evans would be looking for his father and Jeremiah first, but just in case, Jesse didn't want any reports going back. He was uncommon enough looking, with his height and then having a beautiful woman with him, which even wearing her pants, curly hair tucked up into a hat pulled low, Lily clearly was. No, best not to take chances.

When they finally took the last trail that led to his adobe, he looked over to see how she was doing. "This is it," he said as Bear ran contentedly ahead to look for whatever bones or treasures he'd left behind.

Even with a nearly full moon, she wouldn't be able to see much, but he could imagine she'd be disappointed. She doubtless expected more of a home despite her saying she would be all right.

Before she could say anything, if she intended to, Charlie came out from the shed. "You're back finally... and what the hell is this?" The old man cackled then when he got close enough to see who was with him. "No wonder you took a while."

Jesse dismounted and helped Lily from her horse. "I imagine you're sore."

"Some," she agreed looking toward the adobe which showed up only dimly as the moon began to set. He led her to the outdoor table.

It occurred to him that the casual attitude he and then Charlie had toward nature's call would have to have more of plan now that a woman was here. He needed her to have a safe place, open enough to avoid being bushwhacked by snakes and yet private. Then he had to find a way to tell her where without embarrassing himself in the telling.

"Jesse," she said as she stretched. "Could I use the left side of the house for... well er a private need?"

He smiled. He shouldn't have worried. He walked to the outdoor shelves where he'd leaned a shovel against the wall and handed it to her. "Take this," he said, "and watch for any movement."

"No shooting a snake?" she teased.

"No shooting your own foot 'til you get some lessons. Shovels better for a snake anyway or you can give out a scream and I'll come... if..." And then he got embarrassed to go further with the thought as he imagined her state of dress if that was needed.

She laughed and took the shovel, heading or the appropriate open but private enough space.

"I'll be back," he said," "after I get our horses in the corral. Then I'll unload the packhorse." He secured the mare's lead rope to the post by the house before he took the reins of the other two and headed back to the corral. The mare followed his process with interest. "You'll get your turn," he said.

At the corral, Charlie had his bedroll in a corner in front of the shed. "You sleeping down here?" he asked the old man, who watched as he unsaddled the two geldings and gave each a small portion of oats.

"Yep, for now. There's been a cougar nosing around. Wasn't going to leave Sarie without protection." He pointed to his rifle stacked against the railing. "Good having Bear back. He'll let us know if the cat comes back." He pointed his thumb toward the adobe. "Who's the woman?"

"Lily. She'll be with us awhile."

"What's up, son?"

"Does it matter?"

He went into the adobe and brought out a lantern, which he lit. To the east, he could see the first dim light of dawn. This was another day where his life had changed so abruptly from light to light that he was having a hard time keeping a grasp on what was real.

He unloaded her gear first and put it on the table to let her sort through. Then he carried the food they'd both brought to the outdoor cupboard. It was secure enough to protect it from the rodents and convenient to the brick and adobe oven. In the winter, there was a small cook stove inside, but this time of the year to cook in there would make it impossible to sleep or endure during the day.

He took the packhorse down to the corral. She immediately went for the water trough, which was filled by a narrow pipe from the spring. Sarie greeted her with interest while the geldings ignored her. He hadn't heard a name for the plain brown mare, but he called her Esther, while he fed her a portion of oats and protected her from the boys while she ate them.

When he got back to the table, Charlie had gone up to sit across from Lily. "You a painter, ma'am?" The old-timer was staring at her tubes of paint and rolls of canvas. Jesse was surprised she had brought them. He hadn't imagined she would stay long enough to use them. Two days at the most, and she'd be asking to go home.

"Call me Lily," she said, "and yes, I paint. I thought I'd find lots of good subjects out this way." She looked then at Jesse. "He is one, but now that I see you." She looked back at the old man. "You'd be a good subject too."

Charlie cackled again. "Me? An ugly cuss like me?"

"You seem very much like a desert man. And if that's your mule, I could paint her with you."

Charlie smiled with a warmth that Jesse had never seen. "Lily, I'd like that a lot, a plumb lot."

Jesse saw then the medicinal supplies she was pulling out of a sack. "You expecting trouble?" he asked.

She smiled up at him. "One never knows, does one?"

He sat at the other end of the bench and pulled out a cigarette to light. "You need to lie down," he said. "You must be tired."

"I am, but with the light just coming on like it is, how it highlights those distant mountains and then accents the corral, horses, your shed down there, oh and look how it hits the saguaros. I would not miss this moment for anything."

He looked then at where she was staring. It was pretty enough. He had always liked this moment in the morning but hadn't expected she would.

As the light grew, he went to the oven and lit a fire to start some coffee. At least they had plenty of that. He was past exhaustion and now operating on adrenaline. So far so good and no headache, which often came when he got to this point.

He brought tin cups and the coffee pot to the table. "No milk for coffee," he said as he poured the cups. Bear again settled near Lily and chewed on a bone he had dug up.

"I take it black," she said her eyes still pinned on the sunrise slowly starting to wake the desert. Now the night animals would disappear and out would come the day ones. Much as he liked the desert, Jesse liked it even more in the summer when so many hated it. The season of monsoons had a rhythm that called to him, seemed to energize him when it sucked the energy from others.

It was only when the colors had faded and a blue sky had taken over that she turned back to look at the adobe. "Your home is beautiful. And that rock cliff behind it. Perfect setting."

He had never thought of the adobe as anything but a shelter and not a very solid one at that. Now he tried to look at it through her eyes. The only thing he could think of to say was, "It's not my home. I live here while I work at the XY."

"Too bad. It'd be a wonderful place to live." He saw then that her eyes looked tired. Coffee wasn't going to do enough.

"You should lie down until it's too hot to sleep anyway," he said as he blew out the lantern and then rose and walked toward the adobe. He didn't know if she would follow, but she did. Bear watched them but remained outside with his bone.

When they got inside, he wondered how she would see it. At one end, there was a well-used fireplace and a small cupboard was on the wall next to the bed. He had paid little attention to it but saw it had a carved wooden horse on the top of it. The bed was rope, slung between wooden supports and a stuffed mattress with a simple quilt on top of it. A small chest was at its foot. There were also two rocking chairs, which he'd been too big to use even if he'd been so inclined.

"You told me it was nothing," she said as she turned in a circle looking at each wall.

"Fair warning."

She smiled then. "It's not nothing. It's a wonderful room. It's warm and inviting. Yes, simple but I love it. A family lived here once, and it's been a loved home." He saw then for the first time the small crib and a child's chair alongside it. He looked back at her face and saw the glow. He swallowed trying to readjust his thinking from his expectations to this reality.

"You were raised in a mansion," he said finally. "Holly told me that once."

"Did she also tell you it was a cold home full of rules and disapproval, a home without love?"

He nodded.

"This room has known more love than that mansion ever had." She sat then on the bed. "It's soft. Lie with me, Jesse. You have to be tired too."

"I should..."

She interrupted him. "Whatever you should do, it can wait, can't it? Share this bed with me." She began pulling off her boots but left on the pants and shirt as she lay back and looked up at him with a wistful smile. God, he had no idea what kind of woman she was. He almost felt afraid to find out, but he guessed he was going to—want to or not.

"I'll be back," he said. "I need to tell Charlie to watch out and that I need some sleep."

Her smile widened. Outside he saw Charlie had gone down to the corral. "How often is the big cat here?" he asked as he leaned against the post beside him.

"Too often."

"You see it?"

"The tracks. Just once, I saw him at a distance. Big un. Gone afore I could get my rifle. He wants my Sarie. He damned well ain't gonna get her.

"You keep watch then while I sleep... and also for any strangers."

"Rance?"

He shook his head. "His son. I'll tell you more when I wake up. I need rest if I want to make sense."

"You going to sleep with her?"

"Charlie, she's my wife."

Charlie did a double take. "You serious?"

"I am."

"Wal, I gotta say, that surprises me. She looks like a lady."

"She is."

"You're an unlikely couple."

"I know. Keep the information to yourself. I can't explain more now. My head isn't thinking straight, but it won't last with her."

Charlie snorted. "Time will tell, son. Time will tell."

Jesse walked back to the adobe. It seemed its whole energy had changed. He had never thought of it as someone's home. It had been where he slept. He had barely looked around at what was there. He hadn't thought of himself as unseeing, but he guessed he had been where it came to the adobe—and maybe a lot of other things. He supposed it had been protective. Do what you have to do and don't try to think about anything else.

He had never slept with a woman. Walking through the door and seeing her lying on the bed, tender emotions surged through him. He stood for a moment just watching her. She opened her eyes and looked up at him. "Come to bed, Jesse," she said beckoning with her hand.

He knew he shouldn't, but he unbuckled his cartridge belt and set his gun on the small table before sitting on the edge of the bed and pulling off his boots. He was tired. No way they'd do more than sleep, but the thought was coming strongly to him that he wanted to do more.

When he lay down, she turned over and curled against his side. "I like your home," she whispered against his neck. "But you know something else?"

"Not likely."

"I like you even more." When he looked down at her, her eyes had closed, and she soon was breathing softly. He lay awake thinking of what she had said. He liked her too. More than liked her. That scared him.

When Lily woke, she had to orient herself to where she was. What she didn't have to orient herself to was waking next to Jesse. That felt so natural and right. Her hand was on his chest, curled just under his shirt. She was tempted to delve deeper but feared it would wake him. It was hot in the room, but she didn't mind that. She loved the overhead beams where they crossed the room with a feeling of strength. Outside she could hear the wind picking up.

"It's going to storm," he said; so he had been awake. She wondered for how long.

"Are the horses safe where they are?"

"No big trees to fall on them or be likely strikes. They can get under the shelter."

"How long ago did you come here?"

"A little over a year."

"Was this all here then?" She could resist no longer, she ran her fingers under his shirt. She loved the feel of his skin, muscles as they flexed and her discovery that he had crisp chest hair. There didn't appear to be too much but just enough. She wanted to see it.

"The adobe was. I built the corral and shelter. There had been one, but it had fallen down."

"And it belongs to a big ranch?"

"Big ones swallow little ones."

"Who owns the ranch?"

"Jason Tibbets. He's a banker, lives in Tucson, has a foreman at the headquarters to ramrod the place. I work it two days a week unless there is branding or something more."

"Do you have to go there soon?"

"To check in. But not until I feel confident about your safety here."

He had shifted and now was lying on his side. She reached up and unbuttoned a button. "You must be hot," she said as she moved to unfasten another.

"You too."

She felt his hand move to her shirt and he undid her top button and then another, spreading the material with his strong fingers. She knew he would be seeing the swell of her breasts. She looked up to see if he liked that, but his eyes were closed as his fingers moved to undo another button. If he kept going, he'd come to the ring. Was he ready to put it on her finger? She sighed and undid another of his. This time she looked at what she was revealing.

"You two ever goin' to wake up?" she heard Charlie's voice outside the door.

Jesse smiled and rolled to his side of the bed. "Always shake your boots out before you put them on," he told her.

"Scorpions?"

"Black widows too."

"Tarantulas?" she asked as she did as he suggested.

"They are here, but they aren't poisonous like the smallest scorpions. Ignore the big black spiders or tell me and I'll move them outside."

He stood up but didn't fasten his shirt. She liked that as it revealed a lot more of his flesh than she'd seen other than that time with the quilt and that hadn't been his chest. She had to suck in a breath to stop thinking how much she wanted to see more of it.

With Charlie outside, she had to fasten her shirt, but she wished she could leave it open. It was hot. The shirt open would be cooler, but more she hoped Jesse would like watching her as much as she did him. She had never been so aware of the beauty of a man. There was something about Jesse that drew her gaze again and again. Of course, she appreciated him as an artist did an interesting subject, but it was so much more. She had to force herself to drop her gaze to the floor as they walked outside.

"See what's comin'?" Charlie asked as he pointed to the south.

The sky was nearly black. There was a thick streak of a lightning bolt and then another. She counted to thirty before the thunder followed.

"Will it come here?" she asked wondering what they had to do to prepare for a storm.

"Most likely," Jesse said. He went to the oven and began to stir up a fire. "We need to eat now before the rains." He reached into the cupboard and pulled out a big frypan that he set on the grill. Then a few potatoes. "Any of that javelina left?" he asked Charlie.

"I dried some strips but a hindquarter is still hanging. I'll cut off some steaks." He headed for the lean-to then turned around. "You like javelina, ma'am?"

"I've seen them come through town but never eaten any. What does it taste like?"

"Pork with a wild taste to it. We should smoke what's left of it." Jesse said.

"Where do you do that?" she asked looking around.

"Backside of this oven has a chimney. Just have to keep the fire going slow, and it'll take care of itself." When Charlie returned with a chunk of the meat, he threw one of the pieces to Bear, who snapped it up and ran to the corner of the adobe to eat.

Within an hour, they had consumed everything. The meat did taste like pork, although she was hungry enough that she'd have eaten it whatever it had tasted like. The wind picked up, and the first rain-drops began hitting the dust sending up puffs. The desert had a wonderful fragrance. It was as though the raindrops had released the scents of everything the dust had experienced over the dry days.

Jesse and Charlie brought the remaining hindquarter and began slicing it thinly to put on skewers. Bear's sad expression earned him a few more slices.

"May I help?" she asked watching them and thinking she must have something she could contribute.

"Feed the fire," Jesse suggested.

As the rain increased, she put in sticks until the first lightning bolt struck too close for her comfort. She ran for the ramada that provided a sort of porch and sat on the bench, her feet tucked under her, wishing Jesse and Charlie would come with her. Bear settled at her side to watch the storm from shelter.

Lightning could strike them. Another bolt hit a nearby ridge, and the thunder was deafening. As the wind blew the rain nearly side-ways, she was relieved to find it was coming from the direction that the house mostly protected her. From being too hot, soon she'd be cold.

Jesse and Charlie made a picturesque pair as they worked with the meat trying to get it all into the smoker part of the oven. Charlie as an old man, with white hair and a long beard, was skinny but looked as tough as the desert. Jesse was handsome and youthful with grace even working with the knife as he bent and shifted to get the meat where it would be preserved. With his shirt plastered to his torso, she could see all the muscles outlined, and her imagination was taking her places she likely should not be going.

"Shouldn't you come out of the rain?" she asked as it now was coming in torrents. Another lightning bolt hit the other side of the ridge.

Jesse nodded. "It's done." The two of them came to join her on the bench— one on each side of her. Charlie brought a bottle up from beside the bench. "You want a swig?" he asked her.

She shook her head. Jesse was lighting a cigarette and also refused the whiskey. They sat then watching the storm move up the valley as the full force of it came upon them now with more bolts striking but most on the ridges. Only one hit somewhere south of them on what had to be the valley's floor.

"It's majestic," she said. She'd only seen the other one when she and Jesse had ridden to escape its brunt. Then she'd been inside and never felt the fury as she did now. It seemed to be filling her with a strange sort of energy, as though making her one with all the wildness around her. She wanted to belong to it, be one with it at the same time it frightened her with its power. It was a part of how she felt about Jesse.

The mule and horses had gone into the shelter of the lean-to—only their heads looking out at the rain. Slowly, the worst of it moved past. Jesse went out and fed more sticks into the oven. The smoke was fragrant with a blend of the scent of mesquite and the slowly drying meat.

"This is so beautiful out here," she said. "In Tucson it's removed from the desert. I've been out a few times, mostly to visit Ollie and Rose but I never imagined how wonderful it'd be to be here, able to live with those giant saguaros. And what are those trees?"

"Mostly mesquite, paloverde, and the one over there is an ironwood," Jesse said, "willow and cottonwood by the spring."

"Spring? Then that's where you get your water?"

"I have some for the horses from a pipe down there. For the adobe, it's by the bucket." He added with a teasing smile, "No pump."

"Is that where you bathe?"

"Bathe?" Charlie said with a cackle. "Don't need no stinkin' baths." He laughed again.

"Well, I like them. In fact, the Tucson house has a bathtub. It's a luxury, I admit but..."

"I'd have used the storm," Jesse said, except you being here."

She sighed with pleasure as she imagined what he would look like standing naked under the downpour. Well, she couldn't imagine that but sure would like to see it. She felt a warmth moving through her body at the very thought of it. She looked over at him. "You shouldn't have let me stop you. I could have joined you."

He gave her a look.

"Well?"

"I told Charlie we're married... for now."

"You mean forever," she corrected. "It's what we promised."

"Yeah, well forever often isn't that long."

Charlie shook his head and took another swallow of whiskey. "You hold onto a good thing when it comes yore way, son."

"Sure." Jesse lit another cigarette.

"I know storms can lead to flooding. Is this near where that could happen?"

"It will fill arroyos between here and town," Jesse said. "We're above it."

"How about you explain how this purty little thing come to be here. You kidnap her?" Charlie asked with another chortle.

"I'm afraid it was the other way around, Charlie," Lily said with a smile.

He laughed again. "Now tell me why ya brung her here, or she brung you."

Jesse explained what he had been told regarding Billy Evans. When he finished, he took a long draw on his cigarette. Charlie was silent as he thought about it. "I heard of him. A mean, sadistic bastard." He looked at Lily. "Sorry, for how this worked out for ya, ma'am."

"Lily."

He smiled again and took a swig of the whiskey. "He there now?"

"That's what Pa told me."

"Smart move to come out here but why bring her?"

"Our wedding was in the paper. We thought we could keep it

secret but found out otherwise. I couldn't risk her being there by herself, couldn't protect her in that house, too many ways in. She wouldn't take the train to California." Jesse took a long draw on the cigarette.

"Stubborn one, huh?" Charlie said with another laugh. "All right, so what if he shows up here? How many men he got with him?"

"Five is what Rance said. And maybe you would be safer if you left."

Charlie shook his head. "Ain't doin' that. But we better make some plans."

"I've been thinking on that." Jesse blew out the smoke. "How do you plan for a sadistic bastard?" He gave her an apologetic look.

"I'm not that soft," Jesse," she said with a frown. She wasn't experienced. She knew that. She also knew, having dealt with her father and cared for him as he died, she was tougher than Jesse believed. He'd find out.

CHAPTER 13

L ily was disappointed that when it grew dark, Jesse said he'd be sleeping down at the lean-to. "What if it storms again?" She could see more clouds coming from the south.

"Whatever comes, it's safe there, but those clouds don't look like they'll do much."

"All right."

"Do you mind if Charlie sleeps on the bunk at the opposite end of the adobe? He's been sleeping on the ground in the lean-to to protect his mule. I think he needs a more solid night's sleep."

"No, it's fine. Er... does he snore?"

Jesse laughed. "A little."

"Hopefully I'll be so tired that I'll get to sleep first. Why do you need to sleep at the lean-to? The cougar?"

He nodded. "I will probably sleep in the corral with the animals to be on the safe side."

"Safe? Wouldn't that mean you could get attacked by the cougar?" That didn't sound good.

He smiled. "I meant for the animals. I have a rifle and a revolver. They are levelers."

She sighed. "All right. What about Bear?"

"I'd prefer him to sleep with you. If he hears the cougar, he'll growl, and I won't get a shot at it."

She didn't like any part of it, but she took Bear. From the way he responded, she felt that the two of them felt equally in exile. Not long after she had gotten into bed, Charlie came in. "You sure you don't mind?" he asked. "I can sleep out there."

"I came here to be part of Jesse's life, not change it. You are welcome in your bed. I hope I am welcome here."

"You are a special lady. Thank you."

"I am not remotely special."

"Oh, yes, you are. You just don't know how special yet." Charlie was asleep almost instantly. For Lily it took longer. She had things she wanted, that she ached for, but she had no idea how to get them. The one certainty was she had to be patient. Pushing Jesse would not get her what she hoped to have. Maybe with time, he'd want her as much as she was sure she wanted him. She pulled the ring out where she could hold onto it and with that, she fell asleep.

The crack of a rifle came when the birds were starting to wake and light was barely gleaming in the east. She lay wondering if she imagined it.

"He got it," Charlie said with a chuckle as Bear ran to the door and waited.

"How do you know?"

"One shot. And he ain't the kind to shoot if he didn't have a good one." He sat on his bunk pulling on boots and then was out the door.

Lily knocked her boots on the bedstead and then pulled them on. When she was at the door, she saw Bear below the corrals sniffing and growling. Jesse was up at the outside kitchen and beginning to stoke up a fire.

"It a big one?" Charlie asked.

"Biggest I've seen. Shame I had to kill it," Jesse said moving to the cupboard to fill the coffee pot.

"Why did you?" she asked as she watched him work in the dim morning light. His hands were steady, didn't seem shaky, the way she would've expected having just killed a dangerous predator.

"He was nosing around. Eventually he'd try for the horses, mule or one of us. He was a good one hundred and sixty pounds, big even for a tom. But he's not young. Likely not so fast anymore."

"How can you tell that?" she asked.

"Some broken teeth, fur worn, loose under the jaw."

"I will get ya the pelt of ya want."

"I don't," Jesse said, "but even worn, you might be able to sell it. City folks like such."

"Good idea." Charlie looked up at Lily. "You want it?"

She shook her head. "Will there be more around then?" she asked Jesse as she looked around with a little nervousness. Predators. He had said they'd have predators. She hadn't fully considered what that meant.

"When they realize this territory is open. He likely kept others away. When they come, we'll see their sign, but they won't likely hang around the adobe. Usually they avoid humans," Jesse said.

The coffee had started to boil, and Jesse cut off slabs of salt pork to put into a fry pan. She needed to find things she could do to earn her keep. She would start with cleaning. It didn't look like the adobe had ever been swept or dusted. Probably on the desert with blowing dust, it was a losing task. Still, it should be done now and again.

She turned then to watch the sunrise as the sky turned crimson, changing with the clouds moving through. She had seen many sunrises in her life, but nothing like these out here with the sun coloring the distant mountains. "You want this?" Jesse asked handing her a cup of coffee.

"Oh yes. I need to learn to do things to help here." She sipped the strong brew. "I don't want to just sit while you serve me."

He smiled. "I will have to be gone some today. Maybe you can do a painting, make the adobe prettier."

"You have to go the ranch headquarters?"

"Just to let them know I'll be busy for a few days. As I go, I will look around to be sure the cougar didn't kill any calves. I shouldn't be gone all day. Charlie will watch over the place." He smiled as the big dog nosed his hand. "And Bear."

"All right." She would miss him.

"Tomorrow, I'll show you the desert," he said as he turned back to the fry pan and turned the salt pork.

"I'd love that. I have never really been out on it, just ridden through to Rose and Ollie's."

"Then tomorrow, I'll show you what it has to offer."

"Not many love the desert, not like me and Jesse," Charlie said as he came back up. "Or Bear here."

"It can be dangerous I am told."

"For the careless. Yes," Jesse agreed.

An hour later, he had fastened on chaps, strapped on spurs, and was riding north. She missed him the moment he was out of sight, but she was excited at cleaning the home and then painting. She started with an old cloth and dusting. That was followed by washing the outside cupboards.

"Woman gets the cleans, jest stay out of the way," Charlie told Bear as he came back from nailing the hide to the shed wall.

"What did you do with the flesh?" she asked. "We can't eat it, can we?"

"Could if we was starvin' but otherwise, not. I threw rocks and dirt over it. Likely it'll be uncovered tonight. Some ain't so picky about what they eat."

"Like the buzzards? I've seen them circling."

He chuckled as he put more sticks in the fire to keep the smoking process going. "They'd circle you iffn' ya lay down long enough."

"What's this?" she asked holding up a metal object.

"Meat tenderizer. Pound it enough and even I can chew it."

She continued sorting through items, putting baskets one place and the wooden bowls another. When she had more or less organized the outdoor kitchen, she headed for the adobe where she swept out piles of sand and dust.

When she finished, she went to the spring for a bucket of water. "How can I bathe at the spring when we drink the water from there?" She felt sweaty enough to need a bath desperately.

"You do it at the outflow and get yourself a bucket of clean water first to pour over ya and rinse off the soap."

"I forgot to bring soap. I didn't notice. Does Jesse have any there?"

"Yep. Don't know why a man would want to wash off the body's natural protection but..." Charlie shrugged.

"Will it be safe? I mean no more cougar?"

"Why don't ya wait 'til Jesse gets back. He could keep an eye out for ya." He cackled. "Not that I'd mind."

She smiled and decided she'd do just that. She could live with hot and sweaty for a few hours. She got out her paints and the roll of canvas.

"Want I should tack that on a frame for ya?" Charlie asked watching her process.

"I'd love that. Could you cut me one a foot and a half by two feet or as close as you can get?"

"Shore can."

Fifteen minutes later, she had propped the canvas against the table's bench and was laying on a thin wash of colors. It wouldn't be as good as stretched with a layer of gesso, but it would let her paint. She decided to start with the adobe.

"Want I should make up some more for ya?"

"That would be wonderful. One a little bigger. I'll use that one for you and Sarie."

He smiled broadly and got to work while she filled another brush with the right color for the aged adobe walls. As happened when she was painting, she lost track of time and was surprised when she heard the approaching horse, Bear's excited bark, and realized Jesse was back. She bit her lip as she put the lid on her chrome yellow. Now maybe the bath... or something a little more. She smiled as she put away her paints and the palette. She might work on it again later when sunset colors might enrich the adobe—rather like the aging of the structure.

Jesse walked up from the corral looking as hot and sweaty as she felt. When Charlie offered him a whiskey, he shook his head. He dippered out water from the barrel and drank it in one long swallow. Taking off his hat, he wiped the sweat from his forehead.

"How about a bath?" she suggested.

He looked up then with a faint smile. "You or me?"

"Both of us."

His smile became ironic. "You think that's a good idea."

"Very much. Charlie said I shouldn't use the spring without a lookout... I could be yours, and you could be mine."

"I'll hold down the fort here," Charlie said reaching for his whiskey bottle. "And keep Bear so he don't roil up the water... or nothin'." He grinned.

She could see Jesse debating, but finally he nodded. He went into the adobe, poked his head right back out. "What happened in here?"

"Do you mind?" she asked hoping he didn't.

"No, just surprised." He disappeared again and came out with a shirt and some worn towels that she had seen in the bottom of the corner cupboard. He picked up his rifle and a bucket. "Ready?"

She ran in for the quilt. He only looked at it but said nothing as he headed down the path to the spring, which was shaded by cottonwoods and desert willows. Walking ahead of her, she saw him scanning the side of the path probably for rattlesnakes. She felt a nervous energy that had nothing to do with the possibility of snakes.

At the spring, she spread the quilt on the grass. She looked up then at him. He had lit a cigarette and was not looking at her but instead at the small pool. It was reflecting the leaves above and the sky. It looked clear and maybe two feet deep at the center. "The bar of soap is on the string on the willow branch," he said, his lips tightly set.

"Charlie said to use the soap where the water flows out and the bucket to rinse off afterward where it won't hurt the water for drinking later."

"Charlie is right." His voice sounded tense. She took the bucket from his fingers being sure to brush them as she did. She dipped it into the water and carried it to where she would wash, then came back for the soap brushing past him as she did. He stood like an oak—stiff, clearly determined. Well, now so was she. She wasn't sure how to go about it, but she knew it was time this marriage was consummated. Jesse would never accept it as permanent if it wasn't. She wanted him and in ways she barely understood. This spring was the right place to change the dynamics of their relationship. She had the courage to do it. She hoped.

Jesse was tired, had had an unpleasant talk with the ramrod, Rasmussen. The arrogant bastard wanted him working more days than he had been and coming into the headquarters more frequently or even living there. He'd be forced to quit if those requests became demands. He was not going to live in a bunkhouse with six other hands.

"Tibbets is thinking of selling off part of the ranch," Rasmussen had added with a smirk. He had known how Jesse liked living in the adobe. It had probably been his idea to put an end to that. Rasmussen liked dominating, and Jesse wasn't about to let him do that to him.

He looked above the spring to the rocks, anywhere but at the woman where he could hear the sound of clothing rustling and knew what she was doing. He felt himself swelling with desire, something that wasn't far from the surface even when she wasn't taking off her clothes.

Would she take them all off or wash with her underwear on? He wasn't about to look to see, but it took all the determination he had to resist. He could only imagine how beautiful she would be without any clothing. No, he forced his mind away. Think about anything. Think about Billy Evans or...

Then he heard the sound of the soap bar and water running over her skin. He took a long drag on the cigarette again trying to think of something that would cool him off. "The water is delightful," she said with a purring sound to her voice. Pleasurable, yes, it was. He sucked in a breath as he rigidly kept himself staring at the rocks. Rocks. Solid. Dependable.

Then he heard as she took the bucket and was splashing water on herself to get off the soap suds. He wondered where her hands were and imagined possibilities. He'd seen naked women. Asa's whores had tried to lure him into becoming a customer or offered to let him have their wares free. He had never felt tempted. In fact, it had been repulsive especially since some would go so far as to touch him to arouse him. His brother had laughed, but Jesse had gotten as far from them as he could.

He didn't feel repulsed as he imagined Lily naked or nearly so. He heard her walking away from the overflow. Finally, she would get dressed. She didn't stop until she stood in front of him. He couldn't resist looking down. She was naked, water running in rivulets down her golden skin. He stood frozen but then realized she wasn't just standing as she reached for his cartridge belt buckle and unfastened it. Taking the gun and belt, she put it on the quilt and was quickly back to begin on his shirt.

"What are you doing?" he asked hoarsely as she slide the shirt off his shoulders.

"You need to wash," she said as she reached for his pants. She would feel the bulge there if he let her do that.

"I can do it myself," he said breathing harder.

"You could," she said stepping now to where her breasts pushed against his chest. "But I want to do it."

"Lily." There were reasons they shouldn't do this. She might get pregnant. She wouldn't want to stay married. He didn't voice them though as her nimble fingers again reached for the buttons on his pants and began unfastening them.

"We are married," she reminded him as she pushed those pants down, and he was revealed fully aroused.

"You sure you want this?" he asked as he could resist no longer and pulled her into his arms.

"More than you will ever know."

"I need to wash first," he said as he dropped his cigarette to the dirt and ground it out with his boot. He then sat on the quilt and pushed off his boots and pants. He rose and walked to the overflow.

She followed. "Let me." He stood as she sudsed the soap and used it on his body, first his shoulders and arms, then his chest, moving down but not quite touching his erection. She moved then to his back and sudsed it, including down over his buttocks.

Jesse had never let a woman touch him intimately, but suddenly he wanted that very much, unsure if she would. Maybe Lily was more experienced than he had assumed as she moved to wash his legs and then come back to kneel in front of him and work her way up from his feet to his hard erection. He had had erections before, a few he had taken care of himself, but never felt anything like the surging desire at her soft touch.

She moved away long enough to fill the bucket and begin rinsing off the soap. He then reached for her and turned her so that her back was against his torso, where she would feel his arousal as he began to stroke her breasts, teasing her nipples into hard little nubbins. He moved his hands down her belly to where he most wanted to touch her. She had hair there but not a lot and he pushed her legs apart as he teased her in the places he'd only imagined touching a woman.

When he turned her back to him, he bent and kissed her. This time he thrust her lips apart with his tongue. He wanted to enter her, to feel the warmth of her mouth. He was surprised when she responded quickly by using her tongue in his mouth. He bent and lifted her into his arms, carrying her back to the quilt where he laid her down and then himself beside her. He played with her body, learning what she liked by the writhing movements and little sounds. Although inexperienced, he was not naive about how sex was done. When he knew he was close to climaxing himself, he pushed between her legs and found the place he most wanted and pushed inside. When he came to the barrier, he nearly stopped, but she was having none of it and lifted her hips, putting her ankles up behind his buttocks and forcing him past it.

The next moments were lost to him as he thrust into her trying to find the places she wanted as he tried to stop himself from immediately climaxing. It was only when he heard her cry out, that he let himself go, and collapsed beside her.

She had her arms around him and was kissing his chest when he came to himself. "God," he whispered as he reached out a hand and pulled her tighter to him.

"It was everything I'd imagined," she whispered against his sweaty chest.

"Me too." He smiled as she pulled back.

"You never did it either?"

"No."

She cuddled back down against him. "You are pretty good at it for a first time then."

"I didn't want to do it with you."

She let out a breath and sat up then walked back to the overflow and washed again.

"It's not because I didn't want you," he said as he followed her and washed himself.

"Then why?"

"It can't work for us. You know that. I can't give you what you need."

"And that is?" She walked back to the quilt and used the towel to dry before beginning to dress.

"You know I'm not smart."

"I am really tired of hearing that, Jesse. You may not be about some things, but you are very smart about others."

"I will never earn the kind of money to give you the life you deserve."

She let out a hiss. "You really do move from wonderful to annoying amazingly fast." She pulled on her boots and stalked off.

Jesse stood, naked and feeling vulnerable in ways, that he'd never known. He was trying to do what was right. Obviously, he was failing. She just did not understand what it was like for him. How hard it was to work out what others did so easily. Maybe her being angry was for the best.

CHAPTER 14

L ily worked to get past her feelings of hurt. In part, she understood how he felt. What he didn't have a way to know is that in critical ways, she'd grown up as deprived as he had. He didn't seem able to understand how that could be.

She was tired of being the aggressor, the one who had to approach him and somehow convince him to want to be with her. From now on, if he wanted her, he'd have to come to her. She would though, give him every reason to do just that.

Because Jesse didn't look as though he was mentally challenged, she found it easy to overlook his disability. He was so competent physically that it was easy to forget he had problems with change, with reasoning out something he hadn't had time to think through. She also understood that his disability had led him to feel inferior— even if others didn't see him that way. She could not afford to forget any of that.

One thing she had learned in being a caregiver for her father— patience. She hadn't exercised it very well with Jesse. She kept telling herself she would, but her desire for him had led to failure. It would be difficult, but she would try harder to be a friend and not ask for more. Maybe then, he'd want to give her more someday. She wasn't give up but just back off a bit.

Then she thought about what she had felt at the spring. She had known before she went down there that she wanted to entice him finally to make her his wife. She had made one decision though and that was to put the wedding ring and chain in her shirt pocket before she undressed. She would not use the ceremony they had gone through to hold him. She needed him to want her.

"The spring feel good?" Charlie asked with a teasing glint in his eyes.

"Yes, the water is perfect." She got her paints back out. Instead of working on the adobe one, she took the larger canvas Charlie had gotten onto a kind of frame, and did a thin wash of pale gray with a hint of green. Time to paint Charlie and Sarie. The challenge would help her get past her upset. She could not afford to keep thinking about Jesse and what he wanted. He could change his mind though. She had time.

She could see the mule down at the corral and didn't need her closer yet. Charlie was sitting on the bench outside the house, and she glanced over now and then to get the shapes right.

By the time Jesse walked up from the spring, she had herself well in hand, was laying in the basic shapes for her new painting. She even managed to smile when Jesse stood at the end of the table with a small glass of whiskey from his cupboard.

"I had a talk with Rasmussen," he said as he lit a cigarette. Lily and Charlie both looked at him. "It's possible this place won't be mine much longer."

"He firing you?" Charlie asked.

Jesse took a long draw on the cigarette. "It's more changing what the place will be. Tibbets is evidently selling off some of it. Maybe this piece."

"That's terrible," Lily said. "He should sell it to you."

Jesse laughed. "Like I could afford it even if he did want to do that."

"Of course, you could."

"What are you talking about?"

"It can't be all that expensive." She realized she had never told Jesse about the marriage contract they had both signed. He might not be pleased if she told him now that he had access to all her money. He might be angry with her for not doing exactly as he had asked. He clearly was in no mood to test that.

"Whatever it would be, it'd be more than I could afford."

"I ain't got the money neither. I counted on it stayin' empty to use it now and again."

"You thinking of heading on?" Jesse asked as he straddled the bench.

"Might have to."

Lily forced herself to patience, to doing what she had just set herself to do and had nearly abandoned. "Not right away though," she said finally.

"No, not right away. Rasmussen might've just been talking anyway," Jesse said in a contemplative tone.

"Why would he do that?"

"He likes to run things."

"You mean people?" she asked

He nodded and sipped the whiskey. "He wants me staying there at the headquarters. I'll quit first."

"I'm sorry you could lose your job, but sounds like you are right about not doing that," Lily said. She wondered where she would find this Tibbets. Unfortunately, she could do nothing about that until they returned to Tucson. The truth was she didn't want to return, but she did like the idea of adding onto the adobe, of them owning it. Possibly, with time, Jesse would come around to thinking it was a good idea-- whenever she could tell him that they could easily afford this land and the adobe. It being for sale was better than as it had been—unless someone else bought it first. She would think positive. But wait, what if Jesse didn't like the idea of always living here.

"How much do you really like this place?" she asked squeezing out a little paint onto her palette, not watching his face and trying just to concentrate on his words and the tone with which they were said.

"No point in liking what I can't have," he said. His tone left her no doubt that he meant more than the home.

"Should I fix supper tonight?" she asked with no idea how she would do that.

"Why don't I heat up some beans?" Charlie suggested. "Ain't had beans for a while, and it's plumb hot for cooking."

"Sounds fine with me," Lily said. Jesse just nodded. They sat and watched the sunset together. Lily put her wet canvas aside before they ate. Maybe tomorrow she would have another chance at it.

After the sun went down, Charlie rose. "I am sleeping in the lean-to. Young married folks need some privacy." With that, he headed down for it without giving Jesse a chance to argue, which Lily figured he might have.

"Would you pour me a little of that whiskey?" she asked as she moved to sit on the bench in front of the adobe.

He stood, refilled his glass, handed her one, and sat on the bench with her. The night birds had begun making their cooing sounds as some tried to settle into trees and others flitted around for one last bite to eat.

"It is so peaceful here," she said. "I have never been anywhere that felt so peaceful."

"Yet out there one animal is killing another. Did you hear that sound?"

"The squeal?"

"Rabbit and that cry of pain means he's likely dying."

"That's sad."

"It is what it has to be. Some eat another or die."

"I guess in that sense, it's good, just rabbits are so cute." She glanced over to see his smile. She took a sip of the hard liquor, managing not to grimace.

"And so are bobcats," he said.

"That's true. You really didn't want to kill the cougar did you?"

"No. I don't like killing, but sometimes..." He didn't need to finish the sentence.

"I've seen so little of life. You told me you'd show me the desert around here. Are you still willing to do that?"

"You want to?" Now he turned to look at her.

"Of course. I'd like to understand better what is here."

"All right. Tomorrow."

The stars were slowly coming out. "The sky is so dark out here and the stars so bright," she said taking another sip of the hard liquor.

"In the heat of the summer, night is the time to do anything. Hear that sound in the rabbitbrush?"

She listened. "A little rustling?"

"It's a rat. Bear, you leave it be." The big dog subsided by Jesse's feet.

"How can you tell?"

"It moves and then stops. Small rodent and most likely rat. Too big for a mouse."

"What does it want to eat?"

"Our scraps if we leave any out. Oats that Jethro, Judas, Sarie, or Esther didn't eat."

"Esther?"

"The pack horse."

"Esther was in the Bible, wasn't she?"

"Yes, a beautiful woman."

"As I remember the horse, she's not beautiful."

"So she needed a beautiful name." She smiled as she heard then a screech overhead. "Red-tailed hawk," he said before she could ask.

"Why does he make that sound? It is like a scream almost."

"I've heard it's to establish his territory. Stay away. This is mine. It's sure not for hunting as it alerts anything below he's there."

She heard then the whoosh of wings that seemed to plummet earthward. It had come from the far left of them.

"Maybe his mate. Their babies though should be out of the nest by now; so might be teaching them to hunt."

"I love this world, Jesse. It's so real, so vital, so alive."

"It is that."

She yawned.

"Go onto bed," he said.

"You will sleep with me tonight, won't you?"

"If you want."

"I want." This time when they went into the adobe, Bear came with them and settled at the foot of the bed. Instead of sleeping in her clothing, Lily stripped to her pantalets and chemise. She knew Jesse was also taking off clothing. She wondered how much. Then she reminded herself that she'd not try to tempt him to do what he didn't want.

When she felt his fingers on her breast, she lost her concern and turned toward him. For as long as he wanted her, she was going to be his. Later, she'd worry about what came after. For now, all she could think was how much she wanted him making love to her.

It was only after they'd both climaxed and were lying in each other's arms, hot and sweaty, that he took hold of the chain and her ring. "You still wear that around your neck."

"For now." He didn't say anything, but his fingers stroked down her arm. She wondered what he thought but soon forgot as again he made love to her and took her to the other world.

With morning, Jesse got up and dressed before Lily woke. He should not have made love to her again, but now that he'd had her, being near her would be impossible to stop doing it. That meant sooner or later, she would get pregnant. He couldn't let that happen.

Outside in the morning air, he tried to clear his head as he and Bear took care of their morning needs and then built up the fire to start coffee. Nothing that was happening made sense, least of all that a beautiful woman like Lily Jacobs would be lying in his bed. Why was she wearing his ring on a chain around her neck?

"How soon you figger to get kicked out of here?" Charlie asked interrupting his attempt to reason through what Lily wanted.

"I don't know. Will take some time likely."

"That ramrod sounds like a mean son of a bitch." Charlie watched the coffee as it boiled. "I like living here."

"He is, and I do too, but it's not my property."

"Wisht I could buy it."

"Well wishes don't do a person much good, do they Charlie, or have you learned otherwise?"

"Things can change, son."

"Not in my experience."'

"Maybe you need to broaden your experience," Lily said from the door as she reached down to pet Bear who had come to greet her.

He gave her a look but grabbed a cup and filled it with coffee.

"I miss eggs," she said as she sat down.

"Maybe I could get them next trip to town," he said.

"When will that be safe?" she asked.

"I don't know. I'll have to go in one of these days and find out."

"I don't like the sounds of that."

"We can't stay out here forever. If this is only about Evans, he'll give up and head out."

"What do you mean if?" When he just looked at her without answering, she said, "And if he doesn't leave?"

"It comes down to the same thing. I will eventually have to go in."

"But not today."

He smiled then. "No, not today."

Listening to the two men talk, she ate fried bread with her coffee but said no to the salt pork or fried potatoes. She still was amazed at the feel of a desert morning. She had thought her garden at the Rose Cottage was desert but understood now that she'd had no clue.

"Where's your gun, baby?" he asked as he poured himself another cup of coffee.

"In the bag."

"Get it and take it with us."

"You expect trouble?"

He chuckled. "I always expect it but no. This is for you to learn to shoot it."

"All right." She went back into the adobe and found the revolver, brought it out. "It's not loaded."

"It will be. Pick up your hat too. I want to show you something."

"How about Bear?" she asked as she stuffed the hat on her head. Jesse now had the cartridge belt around his waist and his own hat on.

"He should stay here and take care of Charlie." He picked up two canteens. "We will be back in about three or four hours," he told Charlie. "I am going to show her the cliff."

Charlie smiled his approval. "Me and Bear'll be here and keep an eye on things."

"I know, and if something shows up that shouldn't, fire two shots fast. I'll come running."

He led her off to the southwest. The desert had enough washes that they could mostly stay to the sandy arroyos and avoid the worst of the cactus barbs. He pointed to one and said, "It's the kind that will jump out and get you. Even a breeze can land spines in your knee."

"Ugh."

"Definitely and then it's not easy getting out. They kind- of burro into to you.."

"How do you get it out?"

He pointed to a Bowie knife on his belt. "Pry it out."

"I'll stay back from them."

She loved walking with him as they passed cuts in the mountain, but he clearly had a destination. He stopped once and pointed. She saw the coyote just before it disappeared around the bend in the hill.

"Do we have to worry about it?"

He laughed and pointed ahead where she saw a snake wriggling across the way they would be going. "Not him either. Look at the head. It's not triangular and no rattles."

"Okay, so triangular head and rattles, I worry."

"Just don't step on them. Most rattlers aren't interested in you. They mind their own business."

They walked toward the bluff she saw ahead and through what could only be called a forest of saguaro, which rose high into the sky, many with multiple arms also reaching up.

"It is so beautiful here and so many types of cactus."

"A garden."

"Is this part of the land you watch over for the ranch?"

"Not so much. The cattle stay mostly to the north of here." He pointed again to what looked like a stone wall. "Someone lived here but thousand years or more ago."

"The ones Holly studies?"

"She hasn't been to this one yet. See the stone with mud walls. It was once homes. She said these people are called Hohokam."

"Can we go into them?"

"If you want."

They entered through what looked to have been at one time doorways. Even so many years later, the floor was mostly open with only a bit of grass. It wasn't hard to see it had been a room.

"They had a nice view."

He smiled. "Over under that rock outcropping is a small spring, not as big as the one by the adobe but probably do enough for a small family. Some grew crops but planted mostly around the rainy season."

"And then they left?"

"Or became the O'odham today."

"Holly is supposed to figure that out." She smiled.

"She or those like her."

She was surprised he knew so much about the site. Then she remembered Holly saying he had wanted to stay when she had the excavation in central Arizona. Jesse might consider himself slow. Maybe it appeared that way even to others, but he could go deeper than many ever would when he took the time to think something through. She wondered if he knew that about himself.

"What are the hills called?"

"Malpais." He pointed to a tall peak rising south of them. "That's Silverbell Peak. Tallest one around here."

Coming out of the dwelling, he edged them around the cactus to get closer to a nearby cliff. She saw it was made up of a mix of rocks, some dark and almost black. Only as they grew nearer did she see the markings. "Petroglyphs?" she asked but had no doubt.

He pointed to the one that looked like a human shape. There was a snake alongside it and below that a kind of spiral. "Telling their story."

"I guess we all want to do that," she said thinking how much she'd like to paint this place.

He handed her one of the canteens, and she drank from it as she studied the markings left by these long ago artists.

"See that one," he pointed to an animal with another on its back. "That is either predator attacking prey or mating." He smiled when she looked at him.

"What is that one?" She pointed to one that was upright like a man but had what appeared to be horns.

"Maybe a sacred dance. Have you seen the Yaqui deer dancers yet?"

"No."

"They wear headdresses that look like deer and their dances are symbolic of predator, prey and the ultimate sacrifice."

"Which is?"

"One animal giving up its life so another can live."

She looked over at him how he was studying the drawings, the expression on his face one of contemplation.

"Do you come here often?" she asked.

"When I need to think, and it's not coming." He nodded. "It's quiet. At least for now. The mining is mostly south and west of here."

"These hills have valuable minerals in them?"

He shrugged "Gold, silver and copper mostly."

"I know it's going to be unbearably hot soon and probably hotter out here with these rocks, but can we find someplace for us to talk?" she asked.

"About what?"

"The things we haven't."

She saw him considering that. "All right." He led the way back and this time to the west, away from the hills. At first, she thought maybe he was going back to the adobe but realized his goal was another hill, one that seemed to rise out of the ground with a perfect round shape. When they got to it, he skirted it. On the side that she had not seen were trees similar to those by the adobe's spring.

"If you know where to look, small waterholes are all through the part of the desert," he said as he led her to the small pool.

"Is it volcanic?"

"Maybe."

The pool was surrounded by willow and a big cottonwood. "Is this on the land of the adobe?"

"Hard to say with no fences, but this is a special place. More than most will know."

"But you know. Just as you know animals better than most."

He shrugged as he looked behind and around the rocks for snakes. "Let's sit here. It's always cooler than the air around it."

"I would like to know about your childhood," she said to hopefully get this started.

"Why?"

"Because I then want to tell you about mine. Don't you think we should know some of those things about someone we marry?"

He smiled at that. "We kind of did this backwards, don't you think?"

"You mean marry first, then have sex and then learn who we are?" She laughed.

"Yes. All right, I knew I wasn't like others when I was little. Mama would try to teach me things, and I just couldn't understand what she was asking. And where it came to reading. Forget it. They kept me out of the little school when it opened. Papa said they might lock me away if they knew."

"Lock you away for what?"

"Being a half-wit."

"I don't like that term."

"There are worse."

"I wonder if you were slower then, and it's changed as you got older, but you never thought about it."

"Why would it change?"

"We all learn as we grow. You were a small child when your parents told you that you were different, right?"

He nodded but didn't answer.

"They feared for you and maybe that added to you not going around others."

"Maybe. They said the places they put people like me are bad."

"They would be, but you aren't like the ones put there, Jesse."

"How do you know?"

"I read books, and there have been some newspaper stories about the need to change how people treat those who are mentally different. They have done bad things, even..." She stopped not sure she wanted to go on.

"What?" He wasn't going to let it go.

"Well, they have made it so the women or men cannot have children because of fear their children won't be right. They call it eugenics."

"I've never wanted to have a child..." He stopped, his lips tightened and she saw the muscle jump in his jaw. "What if it went through what I did? I wouldn't want to put that on anyone else."

"Because those years of being a child were frustrating?"

He nodded. "Lonely, and knowing I was disappointing Mama. I tried. I tried but nothing came the way it did for the others. And then Pa saying I'd be locked away where I'd never be free again."

"There are many reasons someone can have the kind of difficulties that you did, Jesse. They aren't all something you'd carry on."

"That's what Abigail said."

"Sam's wife, right?"

He nodded. "She said it can come from a hard birth, but how would I be sure?"

"And it's why you didn't marry."

He smiled at that. "Never found a woman I wanted until..." He stopped then and looked away.

"All right, you told me about you. Now, would you like to know about me?"

He looked back and nodded.

"I had an older sister. You know her. She was the one my father doted on. Mama retreated from everything. She seemed like she just didn't care about any of us. Father turned me into his servant. Holly was the one he wanted to go school, but he got me a private tutor, refused my desire to go away to an art school. With Holly often off for one thing or another, I grew up very much by myself except for our servants and Papa."

"Not happy?"

"I found a different way to be happy. Painting. Papa didn't respect that either, but it kept me quiet, I suppose. He just didn't want me leaving. He needed me to run the household after Mama died. Well, even before. I think now Mama was drugging herself with laudanum, but at the time I didn't know."

"I have seen that," he said sympathy in his voice. "It's why I wouldn't use it for my headaches."

"We both grew up lonely," she said.

"It seems so."

"Your mama though, she loved you didn't she?"

"I think so."

"I doubt mine did. I think she was far from being able to love anybody and maybe it was the opium or something else, disappointment. She didn't get to follow her dreams."

"What do you mean?"

"Her family had the money. But, they pushed her to marry Papa. They thought he'd make them more money. It didn't work out that way, and I don't think either of them were happy. They didn't marry for love as he married her probably to get wealth."

"I know that money isn't always an answer." He drew out a cigarette and lit it.

"It's a cold answer."

"But it gives you luxuries and security. You have never lived without that to know what it's like."

"You have."

He nodded as he smoked. "I earned what I could from the time I was old enough to go to others and ask for jobs. My first was watching a flock of sheep at night from the wolves, bears, coyotes, and cougar."

"How old were you?"

"Seven."

"My Lord, you went out at night to protect sheep from those predators and you were a child."

"I knew how to shoot."

"Weren't you scared?"

He gave a little laugh. "At first, but you learn to get past it."

"And now nothing scares you?"

He looked at her then. "I didn't say that." She tried but couldn't read the expression in his eyes.

CHAPTER 15

W hen they finally headed back to the adobe, they had talked most of the day, and it was all they had done. Lily had come to understand that they had more in common than she had ever imagined. She was unsure whether Jesse saw it the same way. If he didn't, at least now he'd heard her stories, understood how her life had been-- as much as she understood it herself anyway.

She had loved hearing the stories of his life—especially his times in nature. If she hadn't been wildly in love with him before, she was now. He was all the things she admired in a man or any person. Where once he had talked little, with the afternoon, he had loosened up and shared his feelings even about his father. He told her about his last meeting with him. Jesse could be stern. She had seen that side of him also, but it seemed to her that he had no buried resentments. Things just were what they were. She hoped she could learn to do so well.

At the adobe, Charlie was stirring a pot on the stove. She was a little tired of stew but it was the easiest thing to fix.

"Javelina?" she asked as she sat on the bench by the adobe.

Charlie shook his head. "Got me a rabbit in one of my snares. Nice big jackrabbit, but they're tough. So I been simmering him two hours or so."

"Bear looks happy," Jesse said pouring himself a shot of whiskey.

"He got him a rabbit too," Charlie chuckled. "Selfish mutt wouldn't share his though."

"Careful about calling him a mutt," Jesse said sipping the whiskey. "He thinks he's a purebred."

"Thinkin' it don't make it so," Charlie said with another cackle.

"What we think often is what we become," Lily said dipping out water to drink.

"Sounds more like a fairy tale to me," Jesse disputed.

"No, it's positive thinking." She lifted her head and smiled at him. "We can often have what we think we want by how we think... or not when it's the other way around."

"Thought you didn't go to college," Jesse protested.

"I didn't, but I had a very good tutor and read a lot."

"Good. I guess."

"You could learn," Charlie said.

"Uh huh." He stood up and walked to the edge of the clearing.

"Walking off when you don't like hearing something is not a good way to learn," Lily said.

"I'm still listening."

"Can't prove it," she said teasingly.

He turned back. "Can I now?" His gaze met hers, pulling her right into him.

"Don't do that either," she said.

"Why not?

"Because." She walked up to him and pulled his head down, thrusting his lips apart with her tongue as she gave him a kiss that he met with his own passion as he lifted her into his arms.

"That ain't no way to train him not to do that," Charlie said laughing as he stirred the stew again. "Them what wants to eat, it's ready."

After they had eaten, they sat at the table, watching the sun as it started to set. Although Jesse had watched the sun set and rise many times, he learned it was different when shared.

"Gonna be a good one," Charlie said. "Right clouds for it."

"Charlie," Lily said, "where did you grow up?"

He looked at her with shock. "Why'd ya ask that?"

Jesse smiled. "Won't do you any good to run from it, Charlie. Might as well answer her. She won't give up until you do."

"I was born in Indiana, 1833. Little place ya never heard of."

"Did you go to school there?" she asked.

"No school. Our ma taught us to read and write. Good woman, she was. Done her best, but there was twelve of us. A lot of mouths to feed."

"And your father?"

Charlie looked at her and grinned that toothless smile of his. "Why ya askin' that?"

"Just curious. I mean you live out on the desert and no family with you. I just wondered how you came to do that."

"I like roamin' around with no woman to ask questions." He gave her a look, but she just smiled back. "No woman would have had me anyways."

"Did you ever try?"

He chuckled. "Once. Didn't take. A little mining, little trapping, sellin' hides. It's a good life. I can go where I want. Mostly just find deserted houses and live in 'em for awhile. It's what I figgered when I got here, and there was Jesse."

"You'd stayed here before?"

"Five, maybe six years ago. Pretty here, but I got restless and moved on."

"This time you might stay though."

"Might've 'til Jesse said it's gonna be sold, and he'll have to leave."

"You never know. That could change. If it did and Jesse owned it, would you like staying here?"

"Why ya askin'?"

"I just am curious. Sorry if I am prying."

"Nah, just nobody ever cared what I think or where I come from."

"Surely someone had."

"Nah."

She smiled then. "Maybe you didn't give them a chance." She looked then at Jesse. "Is that possible?"

"I get yore point," Charlie said and shook his head. "Maybe I didn't. There's a lot like me that way."

This time they both looked at Jesse. He stood up and moved to lean against the adobe and watch the sunset from there, as he lit yet another cigarette.

When it was dark, and almost cool enough to sleep, Charlie headed off for the lean-to to spend the night down by his Sarie. Lily rose from the table and came to where Jesse was sitting at the bench. "Are you sleeping with me tonight or still mad at me?"

"I wasn't mad at you."

"Then sleep with me."

"We keep on this way, and you'll be having a baby."

"Maybe I wouldn't mind that. We are married."

"Maybe I would."

"You want your freedom." Her voice sounded hurt.

"It's not that. I don't know if a child of mine would… I'd never want to bring a child into this world to have to face what I did and do." He also didn't want to have one raised when the marriage was over, and he was pushed out never to know his own child.

"Even if that was true, it wouldn't be the same, Jesse. He'd have different parents than you. People understand more now how to deal with differences. Besides, for all we know, it already happened."

"Is that likely?" He felt a cold chill.

"It's not the time it'd be most likely, but anything could happen. Those systems aren't written in stone. Come to bed. We don't have to do anything."

He didn't argue but followed her into the room, stripping off his clothing and lying down, aware she was also naked and beside him, not quite touching. There were things he could wear to protect her from pregnancy. Vince had mentioned it once for why he and Holly hadn't immediately had a baby. He did not have such a device, but he knew where he could get one. It would require going to town. He'd just have to resist touching her until he did.

"Jesse," she whispered against his ear as she turned toward him. "It's a good time for this. For another few days anyway."

He felt her hand slide down his belly not quite, to where he most wanted her touching him.

"You sure?" he asked trying to steady his breathing as her hand touched him and then went below to his thigh spreading his legs apart.

"Almost."

It was too late to stop what was going to happen. Where it came to her, his resistance was gone. He wanted her too badly. He would though have to get something. In a few days, he'd have to go to town anyway for supplies. He needed to know if Billy Evans was still there and a danger. When he went, he'd make sure he bought what would keep her safe from baby making for as long as she wanted him. He stroked down her hip and pulled her to him. Even with the heat, he wanted her pressed against him, wanted to taste her lips. Any chance of resisting that would require sleeping miles from her. Until then...

In the morning, after they'd eaten, Jesse brought out the gun and holster that he had bought for her. Not too big-- but enough to kill a man if the need was there. He hoped it never would be for her.

"You sure you want to be handing her a gun?" Charlie asked sipping his third cup of coffee.

"She needs to know how to use one. Safer than not."

"Is it loaded?" she asked as she held it gingerly.

He nodded.

"I don't like touching guns."

"It's the trigger you shouldn't touch, unless you are ready to fire."

He took her down below the corrals and set up a broken pot as a target about thirty feet farther toward the ridge of an arroyo. "Hold it with both hands to start." He came to stand behind her and adjust her hands correctly. "Straight out with your arms and get the sight leveled on your target. When it looks like it's there, pull the trigger. Keep your hand firm when you do so it doesn't jump up. You might need to fire again."

She fired and missed. "Do it again," he said, "but this time don't cringe as you pull the trigger."

"I was expecting it to push back against my hand more."

"That's why you are using both hands for now. Fire again."

For half an hour, she shot; then he had her use a rifle. She was better with it and broke the pot into pieces but hadn't hit anything exactly where she had hoped.

"Close enough though for what you'd need," he said to her protestations.

"Now," she said, "I want to see you shoot."

"All right. What?"

"How about that branch above the pot shards?" He had the gun out and had fired faster than she had imagined possible. When she looked at the branch, it was gone. "How long did it take you to learn to do that?"

"Need is a great teacher," he said as he reloaded his revolver, sliding it into his holster, and then reloading her gun, before handing it back to her.

The next morning, Jesse was saddling Judas when Lily came down to the corral. "Where are you going?" she asked as he dropped the stirrup into place.

"The XY. I have to be there today."

"I will miss you."

He stopped and walked to the railing. "Practice with the .38."

"All right. When will you be back?"

"Before dark."

"Be careful."

He bent and kissed her lips before leading Judas from the corral and closing the gate. "I will," he said as he mounted. "You be good."

She smiled at him. "I am always good."

"Except when you aren't?" he asked and gigged Judas in the side to head north.

When she could see him no more, she turned back to the adobe. Charlie was watching her. "I think you need to pose for me today," she suggested.

He poured himself some coffee. "How you figger that to work?"

"Well, bring Sarie up here and let's experiment. I put in the background and shapes but not sure until I start using the real colors."

An hour later, she had gotten the canvas more or less as she wanted it. She used intense colors to capture the essence of Charlie. As she worked, she said, "I bet you had your pick of ladies when you were younger, didn't you?"

He grinned and gestured with the rifle she had had him use as a prop that seemed to her to capture some of his kernel as a desert man. "I stayed away from *ladies*," he said with a cackle.

"Ah, so women?" She squeezed some crimson onto the palette and dabbed it alongside his canvas beard to add some energy.

"You betcha. Ladies, they don't have that much a man needs. A woman now, she's the one you can ride the river with."

"I've heard that expression and generally understand what it must mean," she said as she took a smaller brush and used a little purple alongside Sarie's smooth gray coat. "But actually I don't know. What is a woman, who you can ride the river with?"

"She's there when the going gets tough. Riding a river is a damned hard thing to do, as you never know what it'll be like from year to year. A woman who can stand by her man in a time like that, she's a real woman."

Lily had never heard him speak that much at a time. She glanced over and saw the intensity in his eyes. "Jesse is that man, isn't he?" she said.

"He is. A body could count on him and know he'd die to do right by 'em."

"You really like him?"

Charlie grinned. "I only met him when I came to this place. But it don't take knowing a man long to know what he's like. Jesse is a man I'd ride any river with and know he'd get me across or die trying."

She worked with her brush as she considered that, resisting dabbing away a few tears. "Does anyone ride the river with him though?" she asked finally.

"I don't know, but I shore hope so. He deserves it." She knew what he meant but didn't comment. She wondered if she had that kind of grit. It had never been tested.

She worked with the colors and shapes, glancing now and again at Sarie who had stood patiently for a bit but was losing interest. "You can put her back in the corral if you wish," she said as she added the last teal blue to the sky. She had never painted an animal and only hoped she was doing the spirited Sarie justice. Maybe she'd try Bear next.

On his way home from the XY, Jesse thought through what Rasmussen had said. After the branding and castrating were finished with the last herd, he had saddled Judas and then told the foreman he would quit if the condition of working there required living at the headquarters. The ramrod had only smirked, before nodding and walking off.

There had been something in the foreman's eyes making him wonder what kind of man he was. Where had Rasmussen come from before he became ramrod after Lester Adams was killed in that freak accident? How often did Rasmussen go to town, and when he did, who were his friends?

Might he know about Lily and their marriage? Or even more did he know Billy Evans? As long as Evans didn't know where Jesse was, the adobe was safe. It was unlikely that they would imagine a lady like Lily would consent to stay there. It would not be high on their list of places to look—unless he was their target.

He didn't trust Rasmussen but what was bothering him was his inability to know if Evans was still a concern. Maybe he'd left town and gone onto something else. He needed to go to Tucson and find out. They did need supplies.

When he rode into the adobe's enclosure, Lily waved from the outside kitchen, and he could smell tempting fragrances. He hadn't had a home for more years than he could count. It felt both strange and frightening at how comfortable his had become for him. He reminded himself yet again that he couldn't afford to become used to it. It wouldn't last.

Charlie came down to watch him unsaddle Judas. "How'd it go?" he asked. "He say more about how soon we have to leave?"

"No." He threw the saddle over the railing.

"How long you figger we got?"

"I don't know."

"She painted me and Sarie today. That gal is plumb talented," Charlie said as he followed Jesse up to the house.

"How was your day?" she asked standing at the oven and giving him a smile.

"Fine. What are you cooking?"

"It's an experiment as a way to avoid more stew." She grinned mischievously as she flipped what looked like patties with the spatula. "Charlie has been teaching me. Although the fritters are just potato, salt, and rabbit, it would be better if we can get onions, eggs and maybe cheese."

"I will go tomorrow."

She spun to look at him. "That cannot be safe yet, can it?"

"We need to know." He managed a smile. "I better wash up. Be right back."

After they'd eaten and he had complimented both cooks, declaring that the fritters had been good, they sat and watched the sun set. Jesse smoked and sipped on whiskey. Lily was drinking tea, which she had told him she had made earlier with the sun and allowed to cool. Bear contentedly sat watching them and then the brush whenever there was a movement.

"Wanta see the painting?" Charlie asked when he obviously could resist asking no longer.

"Sure if it's okay with the lady."

Lily gave him a look. "The woman," she corrected.

He smiled. "The painter."

She rose and went to where she had stacked canvases around the side of the adobe. She brought the one of Charlie and Sarie back and set it against the table.

He truly was shocked. She had captured more than simple images of Charlie and Sarie. She had somehow painted their love for each other, the beauty in the aged mule and man.

He shook his head. "Amazing. It's beautiful."

Charlie cackled and did a little dance. "Told ya so. I gotta save up money to buy it. That's what I got to do."

Lily laughed. "You must be teasing. That painting is yours. I did it for you."

The old man sat down abruptly, his face showed a mix of sadness and pleasure if such a thing was possible. "Mine?"

"Of course. I thought I told you."

"Nobody give me anything half so wonderful."

She smiled. "It couldn't belong to anyone but you. I hope though you will hang it somewhere we can all enjoy it at least for as long as we are together."

He gave off a little breath, shaking his head. "I shore will."

"This was one of the best sunsets," Jesse said after Charlie left to head down to the lean-to and sleep.

"Do you really have to go to town tomorrow?" she asked her voice reflecting her concern.

"We need more supplies and to know if there is a problem still there. I will be careful."

"May I come?"

"Not this time. Let me just see what's going on."

"I just wanted some things from my home."

He considered that. Would Evans have someone keeping an eye on her home? All along, the unknown factor would be whether Evans would find out about the wedding. He didn't seem the type to read legal announcements. How big a story would their wedding have been? The problem was he couldn't be certain of any of it. If Evans didn't yet know, her house would be safe.

"What did you want?" he asked trying to decide what the risks would be.

"A blue skirt. It's hanging in an upstairs cupboard. And also just be sure the flowers are all right. I should have asked Rose to be sure they were watered, but maybe she'd know to do it."

It wouldn't take long to do that. "All right."

"I want to go."

He laughed. "Stubborn little thing, aren't you?"

"About some things."

"So am I. It's not a good idea for you to go this time. Make a list though of the food supplies we need. I can give it to Sicillas, and we'll be set another two weeks if that is required."

"When will you leave?"

"Not early. I want to get there about dusk. Be less chance of being seen."

"Then you do think he's still there?"

"It seems unlikely as why would he hang around? But I don't know. I need to know."

"I have a bad feeling about this. Why don't you wait another few days?"

"Several reasons," he said tilting her head up where she met his gaze. "We are one of them."

"Oh."

"I don't want you pregnant."

"Ever?"

"We'll worry about the ever part later," he said with what he hoped was a light tone. He didn't feel light about it. He wasn't sure how he felt other a total unwillingness to bring a child into the world to go through what he had—the confusion, the difficulty in understanding what others found so easy. He felt certain that he couldn't bring that onto a child.

"Maybe you will pose for me tomorrow with Bear," she suggested, stroking his bristly jaw.

"Maybe."

"Will you take him with you to town?"

"No."

"Then you do think it'll be dangerous."

"I don't think one way or the other. I just know it has to be faced."

"Not tomorrow though." She turned his head so he was looking into her eyes. "Maybe the day after."

He shook his head but smiled. "We can't wait on that one item, and baby, if I am near you, I will be making love to you. I can't say no to it."

"I don't want you to say no."

"Which is why it has to be tomorrow. We've already been pushing our luck."

She gave him an exasperated sigh and rose, pulling his hand for him to stand. "I won't rape you," she said. "Come to bed."

He laughed then. "Maybe I'm worried I'll rape you."

"Not possible," she said as she began unbuttoning his shirt as soon as they got through the door.

CHAPTER 16

J esse dismounted, tied Judas to the rail, and looked to the Rose
Cottage. No lights. He had hoped that coming after the sun had
set would reduce the risk in what he was doing. It would be the
same at Sicillas. Keep a low profile, get what was needed, look around
but not be where he could be seen.

At the door, he used the key she'd given him and slid quietly
inside. He heard nothing. Not so much as a squeak of a floorboard.
She had said the skirt would be upstairs in a long cupboard. He took
the steps two at a time, eager to get out of the house.

Coming downstairs with the blue skirt, he went through the door
to the kitchen to check on the garden. He heard a step at the back door
and drew his gun. The door opened to a stranger's face. What wasn't
strange was the shotgun pointed at Jesse's belly.

"What is this?" he asked delaying for time as he and the stranger
each had a gun, where the end of firing was apt to be fatal for them
both. Before he could reason through his next step, he heard a sound
behind him. There had been two. A hard blow came down at the base
of his skull sending him to the floor and blackness.

When he came to his senses, the darkness had been replaced by
electric lights. Unsuccessfully, he tried to move from what was an
uncomfortable, stressed position. He wasn't going anywhere. He had
been tied backward to a chair, his legs straddling it, his wrists crossed
behind it and secured together with rope, which appeared to go under
his knees. He twisted his wrists against the rope. Whoever had done

the tying knew what they were doing. He was helpless and going nowhere.

"Not so big now, are you?" a voice asked as someone yanked his hair and forced his head up to look into cold blue eyes.

His head hurt so much that thinking wasn't easy. The man though had blond hair, a mustache. "Evans?"

"Glad to see you waking up, Taggert. We figured you'd be back or she would. I'm glad it was you."

"What do you want?" The pain from the answering blow was blinding. If he had thought thinking through things had been difficult before, now it was all but impossible.

"Several things. Let's start with the easy one-- where is the lady who lives here?"

"Don't know." The slap sent his head sideways. He fought his way back to consciousness unsure why he wanted it.

"Where's your old man?"

"Not at his home?"

Evans grabbed his hair and forced him again to look into gloating eyes. 'You think either of them would suffer to protect you?" Evans released his hair, and Jesse fell forward on the chair. Hands at his shirt pulled it from his pants and over his shoulders. The air on his back let him know what was coming next.

"I like this kind of thing, Taggert," Evans said whispering in his ear. "I suspect you won't so much. You can be sure that whatever you know, I will. You can save yourself some pain anytime you want."

A moment later, he felt the sharp sting of a strap on his back and then another. The width of the hits, the way it was striking meant it was a riding crop. Each blow was painful, but the one following more so. Of all the things he'd endured in his life, Jesse had never been whipped. He groaned as the pain became impossible to ignore before he blacked out again.

When he came out of the haze that seemed to be enveloping him, Jesse realized he'd been blindfolded. What the hell was that about?

"Ask about her?" a new voice said. Then he realized it wasn't new. He'd heard it before. It took a moment to realize it was Patrick Jamison. What the hell was he doing here. If he wanted to remain unknown, was there any chance they planned to let Jesse go at some point? He didn't believe that. Maybe the blindfold was just a way to frighten him.

"Where is Lily Jacobs, son?" His hair was yanked to force his head up. "Want a little whiskey," another voice asked. It was gruff but seemed unnatural. Maybe that the one who didn't want to be recognized.

"No."

"You got her hid away somewhere? Wherever she is, you know, don't you? I hope you understand this one thing, son-- from now on, it's not what you want, you arrogant bastard, but what we want." His nose was squeezed shut, and he was forced to open his mouth and swallow or choke. Hard liquor burned as it went down his throat. He hoped it was just whiskey.

"That should loosen you up a little. Come on and tell us what we want to know and you can go."

Jesse managed a laugh. He wasn't naive enough to think he'd ever get out of this. The blow caught him on the jaw again causing him to lose consciousness. Waking, his head throbbing, he found himself in the same uncomfortable constraints. The whiskey hadn't helped his headache, but it had made him desperately thirsty. He considered asking for water but begging would get him nothing from whoever these people were. Billy Evans. Jamison and the other voice—one he should know.

He realized that his shirt had been ripped from him when a rough hand touched his bare arm. "You are going to tell us eventually, son. Might as well save yourself some pain."

"Where is Miss Jacobs?" Jamison's voice asked. "We won't hurt her. We just want to keep her safe. Where did she go? Is she hiding with friends in town? Where? You tell us and your suffering is over."

Jesse said nothing. The only way his suffering would be over would be when he was dead.

"What about your pa?" Evans asked. "Where's that bastard and my pa?"

That reassured him that his pa had gone into hiding. Jeremiah might have not been much of a father, but he didn't want him dead or tortured by those like these sick bastards.

A hand ran down his biceps. "Ever wondered how cattle feel when they get branded?" It was the rough voice, followed by agonizing pain from a blazing hot object applied to his bare arm. It was lifted and laid down again. The pain forced a cry from his lips.

"Don't want a neighbor hearing him," another voice said. He came to stand at Jesse's other side and quickly bound a gag over his mouth.

"Damn," Evans said from the other side of the table. "I'd like hearing him scream. They all scream eventually."

Jamison made a sound of disgust. He bent over Jesse. "You can put up your hand when you want this to stop," he said. "None of us like seeing something like this done to a fellow human being, but you do see it's how it has to be."

The last time he'd seen this man, Jesse had been standing in a doorway watching him be rejected by Lily. Now the man held all the cards. He must be enjoying the reversal even if he didn't like the smell of burning flesh.

He had no idea how long the questioning went on as it alternated between blows and the whip. He lost consciousness and regained it always wishing he hadn't.

"He's not going to talk," a soft voice, in almost a whisper, said. He had not heard that voice before.

"Suppose not." That was Evans.

"It will take more than can be done here in town." A hand touched his neck. It was soft as it ran along his neck to his shoulder. "A lot more for this one." There was a soft laugh.

"What if we find his father? That might give him inducements to tell us what we want?" Jamison again.

"And how do we do that? The wily old fox is not at his house, neither is my father. Damn them both to hell." Evans.

"Would he know where she went?" the rough voice asked.

"He might make Jesse here more receptive to telling us what we want. Some can endure any torture but not to those they love."

The soft hand took his chin and lifted it up. He could hear the man's breathing. Who had a soft hand in country like this? "All right." It was the soft unknown voice. Or should it be known?

Someone moved around to be in front of him. "Big man like you and brought low by a little man like me," Evans said with a giggle. "Brain versus brawn. How's that feel, stupid?" He slammed his fist into Jesse's jaw causing his head to explode again in pain.

"That's enough." The soft voice had moved to near the counters. Was he the boss? "I'll talk to you and him later." A door opened and closed.

Jesse lay forward against the chair as though unconscious. He wasn't far from it.

"Go get a drink, Billy. I've had enough of this," the rough voice said. "He's right. It's not getting us what we want."

"I like it. Is that enough reason?" Evans said.

"No. We've gone as far as we can for now. We need to take him somewhere more secure."

"Where's more secure than here?" Jamison asked.

"Quieter at least for us." The chuckle was low. "I know of a place we won't be interrupted."

"I like that. Screams are better than the stupid gag," Evans said as he slapped Jesse again.

"It's pretty near light out. Someone might see us move him."

"We'll set it up and do it tonight after dark. He's fine here for now."

"Then somebody has to keep watch?" Jamison-- It didn't sound like he liked any part of it, but he wasn't going to help Jesse. Without the use of his voice, he couldn't try to talk the artist into letting him go —even if the man had the power or courage to do it.

"We kill him afterward?" A new voice asked.

"Just see how long he lasts is all," Evans said. The accompanying giggle was more nerve wracking than the beating. That man enjoyed watching someone tortured and listening to screams. Whatever it took, he'd not let them know where Lily was. The pain he was feeling was nothing to what he would feel if they hurt her.

"He sure ain't worth no ransom. Nobody would pay for a dummy." Rough voice again. He tried to think where he'd heard it.

"His family might," Jamison said.

Two voices laughed.

"He's out cold, and he ain't going nowhere when he wakes up. Let's get that drink," That voice was new and sounded like Jamison but different.

'You can but two have to stay."

"I don't want to be stuck here," a voice protested. He's hogtied better than a steer, boss."

"I'll bring whiskey back when I relieve you. For now, two of you stay. And don't take anything for granted. Someone might yet show up." He heard a door open and close. The room grew quiet, but he heard movement-- two had remained. It didn't matter. Rough voice was right. He was going nowhere.

Jesse had known times of helplessness in his life, where he'd felt impotent, but nothing matched this moment. Lily would come. He had told her not to, but she would. She was that kind of woman. He had no way to warn her or protect her when she did. He suppressed the groan only because it might lead to more torture, but no knowledge caused him more pain or fear. He'd rather die than have her come.

Lily had not slept at all as she lay awake waiting to hear Jesse's horse. When first light came, she knew it wasn't going to happen. Something had gone wrong. Wearing her britches, boots, with her gun belted to her waist, she walked out onto the porch. Bear followed and both stared to the south.

"I will go in and find him," Charlie said. He had been sitting on the bench holding his rifle.

"We will both go in."

"He'd shoot me if I let you."

"You can't stop me, and if he's been killed, I'll let you do it." She didn't believe he was dead though. She felt him, and he was alive. She just had to find him. Charlie helped her saddle Jethro and then saddled Sarie.

"What about the packhorse?" she asked.

"She'll be safe here with no cougar roaming around. That hide I got drying will convince any new one from moving in for a while anyways."

"Do we take Bear?" she asked as she felt nervously of the holstered gun.

"I'd like to see you stop him."

She nodded. Maybe Bear would help them find Jesse. She knew where they had to start—her home. But after that, she wasn't sure where they could go. He would have gone to Sicillas next. They would know if he'd been shot. No, she wouldn't let herself think that way. He was in trouble, but he wasn't dead.

A few miles from town, the sun higher in the sky, she could resist the question no longer. "What do you think happened?" she asked Charlie mostly to stop herself from thinking.

"Don't know."

"You think he's still alive?"

"He will be iff'n they wanted him to be and he's got something they want."

"You are scaring me, Charlie."

"You asked."

"How would they get whatever that was?"

He gave her a look.

"All right. I understand. They'd hurt him." He nodded. "So where are we going to find him?"

"Where is your home? It was his first stop, right?"

"Yes. It's in a bunch of other homes though. Not that far from the plaza. Could something like that happen in a place so close to others?"

"If they was waiting for you or him there, they might just still have him there."

"Me?"

"Hasn't it yet dawned on ya that you could be the target of this as much as his pa?"

"Why would you say that?"

"You're rich, ain't ya?"

"I guess figuratively."

"Either way you look at it. This whole thing smells. Why'd Evans come to Tucson or hang around? It ain't over his pa, you can be on that."

"Do we know he is here?"

"He'd be the most likely reason Jesse didn't come back last night."

She yelled for Bear to stay with them. He was racing ahead, and she didn't want to lose track of him. The fear she had originally felt was being overtaken by a nervous excitement, a strange feeling of pride. She could do this. Wherever her husband was, they would find him and would get him back—whatever it took. For the first time, she knew she could shoot someone if that's what it took.

Entering Tucson, the heat hadn't yet built up, and people were moving around taking care of early business. When she and Charlie got to her home, he motioned her to keep riding and called Bear to him.

"Why? That's Judas. He has to be inside." But was he alive?

"Lily, they left that horse there for a reason. They want you or his pa to go barging in to save him."

"Well, we have to save him."

"We do, but not how they expect." He led the way down the street and then up the block to come back the alley behind the cottage. Two houses past, he stopped Sarie and dismounted. She and Bear followed suit. "Let's think this through. Where they going to be holding him?"

"I am not experienced in kidnapping," she said unnecessarily as she reached down to give Bear a reassuring pat.

"Well, it ain't like I am either. Here's how I figger it. If they are messing with him, it's the kitchen. Where is it in your home?"

To keep herself from thinking what any of that meant, in the dust, she drew him a diagram of the rooms.

"Can you get into the kitchen from the back?"

"Through the garden?"

He nodded.

"There is a gate that leads to this alley. It isn't used much; so might have to be forced."

He gave her an assessing look. "Can you do it?"

"If it gets Jesse back."

"Here's the way we go at this. We leave Sarie and Jethro tied to this post. I'll go around front and knock on the door then bang on it, saying come on out, Taggert, I know you're there. Seen your horse. You owe me money. I'll make enough noise they won't have a choice."

"Won't they attack you?"

"Not likely on a front porch with folks around. No, they'll want to shut me up. They might ask me inside and figger to kill me. Or maybe try to threaten me to get me to leave. Either way, you and Bear are going around back with some time to get into that kitchen. If he's there," he handed her his Bowie knife, "use this and cut him free."

"He'll be tied up?" She was having a hard time following this and feeling as though her own reasoning power had disappeared. She would have to follow Charlie's orders on what to do. The thought of Jesse being hurt made her incapable of thinking rationally.

"Can you do it?" Charlie asked looking at her sternly.

"I can and will. Why not Sarie with you though?"

"Don't want her getting hurt if bullets start flying. A lot of these jaspers ain't all that good of shots."

"Charlie, I don't want you hurt." She reached out and grabbed him into a hug, which he returned.

"Lily, not neither of us can guarantee this is safe. Mornin' though is a good time. More'n likely they got hangovers or are sleeping it off. We can't leave him there, can we?"

"No."

"So?"

"I'll do it. If someone comes while I am there, will I have to shoot him?" She managed a smile.

"Let's hope nobody does." He smiled too with that toothless grin that had come to make him so dear to her.

"You take care of yourself."

"Likewise." With that, he took off at a lope to get around the house as she headed for the back gate. She had only been through it once, but there was no lock. One hard shove had it open. Once inside, she crept around to the back door, going low past the window. Bear followed her as quietly as she was going as though he understood this was a hunt.

If the door was locked, she would have to go through the window in the small room. She hoped it wasn't. She waited until she heard Charlie step onto the porch and begin banging on the door. He was talking quietly at first, but his voice rose. She heard a man's voice from the kitchen and then the door open to the hall. Quickly she tried the doorknob. With relief, it turned. She looked back at Bear. "Guard the door." The dog stood obediently. Pushing the door open, she saw Jesse without his shirt and slumped forward on her kitchen chair.

It took all the courage she had to go forward to feel of his pulse and determine he was tied in this torturous position but still alive. "Jesse," she whispered as she removed first a blindfold and then a gag. He didn't respond but despite his obvious injuries, including blood on the back of his head, his pulse was strong. She took the Bowie knife from her belt and sawed through the ropes that held his wrists. When they dropped, she realized the rope also tied his knees together. She cut through it. Charlie was still yelling and another man responding. She felt desperate to hurry. As the rope dropped, Jesse groaned.

When the kitchen door opened, she moved back from Jesse, shoved the Bowie knife in her belt and pointed her gun at the tall man who entered.

"Patrick?" she yelped in shock.

"Lily?"

"What are you doing here?" She didn't lower the gun.

He came forward, and she backed up until she could go no farther. She still heard Charlie and another voice out front. "Don't make me kill you," she said, "but I will if I must."

"My dear, I came here to help your friend, of course."

To Lily's relief, Jesse struggled to his feet. "He's lying," he managed in a hoarse voice. She didn't dare look at him to see how badly he was hurt, but he wavered as he stood.

"He's delirious, of course," Patrick said.

"Sit on that chair," she ordered him. "Can you hold the gun?" she asked Jesse. He took it from her.

Using some of the rope that had only recently tied Jesse, Lily tied Patrick's hands behind his back and looped the end through the chair securing it. "I'd kill you for what you did to him, but I don't want noise." She heard the kitchen door opening and a rough looking stranger came through. Jesse had the gun pointed at him. Behind the man came Charlie holding a gun on him.

"Where's my gun?" Jesse asked. His voice was little more than a croak, but the gun barrel didn't waver.

"In the hall," Charlie said looking over Jesse to assess his condition and then at the bound man. "Not enough rope for another one," Charlie said. With one of his cackles, he hit the second one a hard crack over his head. After the man fell and lay without movement, Charlie went for Jesse's gun and handed it to him. "Ya don't look so good. Can ya ride?"

Jesse nodded with a grimace. "Where is Judas?"

"Tied to the rail out front."

Jesse strapped on his gun. For the first time, she saw the marks on his back and burns on his arm. She clenched her jaw as she looked around and saw his hat. His shirt was in rags. She handed him the hat before she ran out back, ordered Bear to follow, and hoped nobody would show up before they could get away from the home she had once regarded as a refuge. In moments, she had mounted Jethro and was leading Sarie around to where she met Jesse and Charlie. When she started to head north, Jesse said, "No."

"Where then?"

"We need those supplies."

"The doctor?"

He shook his head with a grimace. "No."

"We need to get somewhere safe. There were more, weren't there?"

"Yes." He gigged Judas in the side and headed them to the back road and then toward town. It seemed all wrong but despite his injuries, he seemed to know what he was doing. By the time they got to the back of Sicillas, she understood his reasoning. Looking over at him, she worried. Was he barely holding onto consciousness?

Gritting his teeth, he dismounted and knocked at the back door. Charlie hung back with their animals, but she came to stand beside Jesse, unsure if he was going to keel over. He didn't need another head injury.

The door opened and Connie Sicilla looked out, then said, "Come in."

"Is Del here?" Jesse asked not moving.

Connie nodded and disappeared. In a moment, it was Del, who was at the door. "What the hell happened?" he asked.

"A lot. We need supplies. Helping us could be dangerous."

Del looked beyond him to where Charlie still sat on Sarie. He nodded and came out. "You two go on in. I have a barn in the back. Your horses and the mule will be safe there."

Jesse didn't move. "I have a dog too."

Del then looked at Bear and grinned. "He's welcome too. Is he house broke?"

Jesse managed his first smile. She didn't think it came easily given how bruised and cut his face looked. "He's safer than the rest of us."

Del nodded, and went to Charlie. "Follow me." He took the reins of the two horses.

When Charlie looked uneasily back at Jesse, he told him, "She'll be safe there. These people can be trusted."

Charlie finally nodded and followed Del while Jesse went into the house with Bear at his heels and Lily at his side.

CHAPTER 17

Jesse lowered himself carefully to the kitchen chair and then looked back at Lily. He had endured something he never imagined and thought he'd die for his careless stupidity, and then he'd heard her voice and roused himself. Now he didn't know what was safe. Except they needed supplies. He had to hold himself together long enough for that and to get her somewhere safe. Except where was that? It should be a long way from him and Tucson. He doubted she'd go.

"What happened to you?" Connie said as she entered the kitchen from their store.

"It takes more explaining than I have energy," Jesse said. "We need food. I had a list, but lost it when they ripped up my shirt. I guess I need a shirt." He looked at Lily who sat next to him at the table. "And a skirt." He looked apologetically at Lily. "I had it, baby. Not sure where it ended up after someone hit me over the head." Then he remembered his thirst. "Could I have a glass of water?"

Connie brought that to him. As he drank, she looked over his body for the injuries. "You were hit over the head."

He nodded as Del and Charlie entered.

"Those can be serious. Do you see double?"

"No."

"Well, I have some herbs that will ease your pain and help to be sure it doesn't infect."

"How about cigarettes?" Jesse asked finishing his glass of water. "I could sure use a smoke."

Del grinned and reached into his own pocket, handing him one, taking one himself. He looked over at Charlie. "You smoke, old-timer?"

"Used to. Lost the habit when I couldn't afford it no more. You sure Sarie's safe in that barn?"

"No one but us goes in there," Connie said. She looked then at Del. "You need to go out front and tend the store. I would close it; but if we do, someone might wonder—especially if anyone is looking for them."

He nodded and headed out smoking.

"Now then," Connie said, "let's look at you."

"Not pretty," he said.

Connie smiled. "You are pretty enough. You can afford a few scars." When he snorted, she laughed. "What did this?"

"You mean who. It was Billy Evans, some of his men. Patrick Jamison was with them."

"The artist?" She didn't sound as shocked, as he would have expected. He guessed that being a seer made shocks harder to come by.

He nodded and looked at Lily. "I know you considered him a friend."

"Not that so much but never imagined he'd be party to something like this."

"They blindfolded me then to keep me from identifying the rest— not that they likely figured I'd get away." He winced as Connie probed the back of his head.

"This is a big lump and it's bled some but has stopped. I have iodine, aspirin and some unguents that may help with that nasty burn and... your back... They are mostly welts but a few open wounds. Besides beating you, they whipped you? What kind of sadists were they?"

"The bad kind." He drew long on the cigarette. It had been one of the most humiliating and painful things he'd endured. "I got taken like a fool... which I was and am, I guess."

Connie probed the lump. "Let me get my medications and quit beating up on yourself. Someone else already did a good job." She looked at Lily. "You look pale, sweetheart. Do you want to lie down?"

"No, I'll help you if I can."

"Just sit there and don't faint.' She smiled then and looked over at Charlie. "I think I've seen you before but don't honestly recall your name."

"Charlie Provo is my friend," Jesse said grimacing as Connie lightly touched the area around where he'd been branded. "Charlie, Connie is a mystic."

Connie smiled and looked back at the burns. "Are you aware this is an X?"

He hadn't known anything but how much it hurt when it had been done. Looking down he realized that she was right. Did it have some kind of sick meaning? Bastards. He would feel a lot better when they were out of Tucson. "Lily, see if you can remember what was on the list and write a new one for Sicillas."

Connie looked back at Lily and Charlie, who both were looking pale. "While Lily writes the list," she handed her paper and pencil, "could you make the tea, Charlie, and I'll tend these wounds. It's always harder to watch someone you love being treated than to endure it yourself."

As they did as Connie requested, Jesse concentrated on being stoic with the stinging antiseptics and lotions that Connie used on the wounds. It seemed he had wounds of one sort or another on every inch of open skin. Just lucky the bastards hadn't stripped him and gone for more damage. That likely was in their plans after they moved him out of town.

When Connie had finished, she said, "I think we have a shirt big enough to fit you. I'll be right back."

Lily came to sit beside him again. "I was so scared," she said, as she lightly brushed her fingers over his hand.

"I don't know how you did it, but the two of you pulled my fat out of the fire."

"It was Charlie's plan." Lily smiled at the old man as he sat across from them. "I wasn't sure, but it worked."

"Shore did. Didn't I tell ya it would? Guess we should've killed those jaspers though. Just have to fight them again now."

"Better we got out of there," Jesse said smoking the last of the cigarette. "There were other voices, none I recognized. Jamison is likely to leave town now. Patrick must've been Rupert's brother."

"Who's Rupert?"

"He's the one who told Evans the lies to get him here." But why? What did he have to gain by doing that? Jesse wished his head didn't hurt so much. It made even his limited reasoning powers difficult.

"We should go to the sheriff," Lily said. "People can't go around hurting others like you were."

He considered that. He had never gone to the sheriff for

anything. He wasn't sure it'd help with this. By the time the legal system got around to deciding anything, Evans would have time to kill him and anyone near him. Why though? That was what was bothering him.

"What are you thinking?" Lily asked lightly stroking her fingers over the abrasions from the ropes.

"Trying to understand why. Evans wanted to find his father and mine. They though kept asking where you were."

"Me?"

"They expected me to know." He looked up at her with a faint smile. "I played dumb... not hard to do."

She reached out to caress his cheek. "I suppose they also found out we were married."

"You are married?" Connie asked from the door. She came in and handed him a gray shirt. "This should fit you."

Jesse nodded and pulled it on over his head leaving the buttons at the top open.

"I feel better about you not knowing," Lily said. "I was beginning to think everybody read the legal notices."

"Hardly have time to read the front page. I admit I am surprised."

"Didn't show up in tea leaves?" Lily teased.

"I only read those when someone asks," Connie responded with a laugh. "Does Holly know?"

"Nobody was supposed to," Lily said.

"Evans isn't the type to read those notices," Jesse said. "Maybe Jamison." Or was it that other voice, the one he still couldn't place.

"I still find Patrick, being mixed up in this, hard to believe," Lily said. "Much as I didn't like him, I never imagined him to be a sadist or a crook."

"There must be a reason," Connie said. "People do things for reasons that at least make sense to them."

"None of it has to me," Jesse said. "I don't ever find reasoning that easy, but this time it's impossible."

"Maybe there is something more behind it-- or someone," Connie suggested. "When you know that person, then it might come together like a puzzle."

Jesse had thought of that. Maybe his father wasn't going as straight as he had imagined. He had seemed though to like the idea of him marrying Lily. If he hoped to make money out of that, he would use guile, not muscle. Trying to reason it through made his head hurt more than it had.

"You look pale. You should lie down," Connie said. "You can all spend tonight."

Jesse shook his head and then wished he hadn't. "Not a good idea for your sake or ours. We need those supplies and then get out of here right after dark."

"At least lie down," Connie insisted pointing to an open door where beyond he saw a bed. "You and Lily can use our bedroom for today."

Not immediately following Jesse, Lily handed Connie the list. "I think this is what we need. You wouldn't have eggs would you?"

Connie smiled. "Fresh ones, and I know how to package them for travel too." She looked down the list and smiled. "Yes, we can handle all of this."

Jesse was lying on his stomach on the bed, when Lily entered. She watched him a moment before he opened his eyes and looked at her. "Come here," he said.

She smiled and lay beside him. "I'd like to touch you," she said, "but is there anyplace that doesn't hurt?" Outside, she could hear a storm starting up.

"Not many. Looks like we're in for a blow."

"Will it be past before we go?"

"If not, we won't until it is. Not like I am riding with you in a lightning storm." She heard the first crack of thunder.

"I was scared," she said as she cuddled against his side. She loved the feel of his skin under her fingers.

"I am sorry you got put through it."

"It wasn't your fault."

"I should have been more careful. I nearly got killed for it and could have gotten you killed too."

"You really think they wanted me?"

He nodded. "Seems that way. Maybe for ransom. You are a rich family. Otherwise, I don't know."

"I just want to get back to the adobe and home."

"It can't be home for long if Rasmussen is right about Tibbets selling it."

"We could build another."

"I guess."

"Jesse, I want us to be together. Do you believe that?"

176

"I believe it's what you want now."

She would have screamed if they'd been out at the adobe. She sucked it in instead. She couldn't slap him either as he was already too injured. "You are so stubborn, Mr. Taggert. Do you know that?"

He smiled then and brushed her cheek with his fingertip. "And that's not good?"

"It could be about some things but not about this. Don't you dare keep disrespecting me."

"I'm not doing that."

"Yes, you are. You don't think I know what I want and that I won't stick to something. Look, I know you have been through a horrible experience, a night of it. I will try to be understanding. You need to sleep, and I should add another item to the list for Connie. I'll ask her not Del though."

He smiled then and closed his eyes.

Lily walked out to the kitchen where Connie was starting supper. "Where's Charlie?"

"He worried about Sarie getting scared in a strange barn with the storm. He preferred to take a nap out there with her than in here."

"He does love his mule. Did Bear go with him?"

"No, he is roaming around out front with Del. Nobody will recognize him."

Lily nodded. "I had two things I wanted to talk to you about."

Connie turned from the stove. "Let's sit at the table while we drink some of that tea." With cups in front of them, Connie smiled. "So, tell me."

"First we need condoms. Do you carry such things?"

"We do. How many?"

"They are reusable?"

"For a few times but best not take the risk beyond that if you aren't ready for babies just yet."

"He's not."

"You would be?"

"I don't have the same fears?"

"He doesn't feel he can be a father?"

"He's afraid his disability will carry through to a child."

"Ahhh." Connie let out a low whistle. "That would be understandable. You know, Jesse doesn't look like most I've known who are—

well, slow thinkers. He doesn't sound like it either, but I admit, he is different."

"I know. From what Holly told me, I believe it is from a difficult birthing. Those things happen."

"But that won't convince him?"

"Not yet."

"Well, I can put some in your pack with the cigarettes that obviously Jesse wants." She smiled. "And the other thing?"

"Do you know Jason Tibbets?"

"The banker?"

"I understand that is what he does."

"Yes, he is a rather important person in Tucson."

"He owns property northwest of Tucson. It's part of the XY ranch. The manager there says that some parts are about to be sold off."

"And?"

"The one I am interested in is on the north side of Malpais Hill. I guess about twenty miles northwest of here. Do you have paper and pencil?"

Connie handed it to her.

"I am guessing, but from what Jesse told me, it goes onto Malpais Hill to probably 2500 some feet in elevation. The land lays this way." She drew the rectangle as she was guessing it would be. "It might be a hundred or hundred and sixty acres. It is the bottom border of the XY, but with the home on it, an adobe, corral, shed, I suspect it will be a separate plat-- possibly never joined with it officially. It has two small, apparently year round springs on it."

"Interesting." Connie bent over the paper looking at it as Lily added notations for north and south.

"I am hoping to buy it."

"Why?"

"It's where I'd like to make my home. In Tucson, I have a lawyer, James Angus. His office is across from the courthouse. I was wondering if tomorrow you might be able to tell him about my desire, and that he needs to find its legal location and then ask him to talk to Jason Tibbets about a reasonable offer on it. Complicating it is that for now, it has to be an anonymous buyer. This can't be public knowledge."

"Because it might bring these people who did this to Jesse out there?"

"It's a logical concern. Yet, I worry that if I don't start the proceedings now, we could lose it. Jesse had heard that Mr. Tibbets is going to break up the ranch."

"From your description, that's a long way from people. You think you would like living that far out?" Connie asked. "It's very different from all you have known."

"Maybe it won't be for me. It's Jesse's home now, but as part of his pay for working at the XY. The ranch foreman has told him that he'll have to leave soon. I want him to keep it for as long as he wishes."

"I will do what you ask." Connie frowned then. "You know it was interesting about the marking on Jesse's arm. It wasn't just an X but there was another line with it."

Lily felt a chill. "You think maybe a Y?"

"Without one side of it, but yes, that's what it looked like."

That scared Lily. If this whole thing connected to the XY, then the adobe wouldn't be safe either. She wished any part of this made sense, but as it stood, it didn't. She could only think she wanted to make Jesse happy and see him safe. That currently wasn't looking easy to do. Given what he said about them questioning him about her whereabouts, maybe she wasn't safe either.

When Jesse opened his eyes, he jolted up. Sitting, it took him a moment to adjust to where he was and what had happened.

"You're safe," Lily said. He looked to see she was sitting in a chair and had been watching him.

"It's dark."

"Barely. How do you feel?"

He tried to assess that. His head hurt. His back. His arm. His jaw. He badly wanted a cigarette. "All right," he lied. "Lily, you have seen what they do, how dangerous this is. I think you should get on a train and head for California."

"How would that make me safer?"

He let out a breath wishing he could say it would.

"I am safest with you." She came to sit on the bed. "You are so bruised." She brushed her finger lightly over his cheek.

"They go away."

"I guess." She reached over and kissed his lips lightly. "Did that hurt?"

He managed a smile. "Some, but it was worth it."

"Do you really feel you are up to riding?"

"I have to be. This won't be safe for long. They will be looking for me, and if Jamison talks or that other man, they saw you and Charlie."

"All right. We have the supplies, divided between our horses and Charlie's mule. How do we keep these men from seeing us though once we leave?"

"I'm thinking." He got on his feet and felt steady enough. "Let's talk in the kitchen. Is Charlie there?"

"He was, but first..." She pulled his head down for another light kiss.

He smiled. "I should talk to Del about another item."

"They're with your cigarettes," she said with a broad grin.

"Good girl."

In the kitchen, Charlie was sitting at the table drinking some of Connie's tea. "She packed me up some," he said. "Relaxing, she said, and it is."

"She do a reading for you?" Jesse asked as he sat at the chair across from him.

"She said you can do it as good as her," Charlie said with a tooth-less smile.

Jesse looked up at Connie who was standing by the stove. "Well," she said, "you could if you wanted, couldn't you?"

"Maybe."

"You talk to the other side?" Lily asked sitting on his right. "You didn't add that to your childhood experiences."

"I don't do it on purpose."

"There's a difference?" Lily asked with a smile.

"Can we talk about this another time?"

"We leaving soon?" Charlie asked.

"It's best. Did you have an idea for how we do it?"

"And avoid getting shot?" the old-timer asked as he sipped the tea.

"Definitely avoid getting shot," Lily said.

"Then I ain't got no ideas. How many men you figger were there at the cottage?"

Jesse had been wondering about that himself. When the door to the store opened, he jerked around, but it was Del. "Closed up for the night."

"You should eat," Connie said. "I fixed a chili. You like that?"

They all did and soon were eating what was a delicious and very hot chili. Just like Jesse liked it. "We should have added red beans to the list," he said as he finished.

"I did," Charlie said. "Bacon too. Love bacon."

"Rock candy too," Lily said. "Charlie likes it."

"My plan then," Jesse said, "is that Charlie takes Bear and heads out first, could even go right through town like nothing is going on or of interest. If they are expecting a man on a mule, they won't be the dog. Bear won't like it, but he'll do it. Then the three of you cut over at Picture Rocks."

"I can do that," Charlie said. "Where do we meet up? At the adobe?"

"No, before we get there. We'll wait until you have time to get out and then Lily and I will head south, circle around and go over Gate's Pass."

"In the dark?" Charlie asked.

"How it has to be."

"You been over it?"

"A few times. Once with Ollie and picking up horses in Avra Valley. It is safe enough if we go slow. They won't expect anybody going that way at night."

"No, they won't. It's a good place for accidents even in the daytime," Del said.

"Why?" Lily asked concern in her voice.

"It's steep, can be bad if a man isn't watching himself, but Jesse is right. It isn't a bad route. I've taken a wagon down it," Del said. "Tom Gates built it as a way through the Tucson Mountains. Good old Tom."

"I wouldn't put you at risk," Jesse said putting his hand on hers. "I am afraid though if you go with Charlie, you are more apt to draw attention, even with your brim pulled low. There is no way I can go through town without being seen—just too big."

"I still worry you aren't in any condition to do this."

"We can't wait here. We don't know how many are in on this." He looked at Charlie. "In answer to your earlier question, I heard six different voices at the house. Before they put on the blindfold, I only saw Evans, Jamison, and a man I never met, but he was a tough. At least one tried to disguise his voice, which means I should know him. I'll figure it out eventually." He thought then of the soft voice. The one who actually appeared in charge. He should know that voice too. "Billy had five men riding with him. Patrick has a brother, Rupert. He seems likely especially now that we know Patrick is involved. That would make it nine, if no more get hired." Why would anyone need nine? He didn't think Patrick Jamison was of much account in a fight though and maybe not the soft voiced man.

"All right, we leave now?" Charlie asked.

"It's best."

"Where I gonna wait for you?"

"Just beyond Picture Rocks, where it levels off. We'll wait to go to the adobe until the sun gives us enough light to be sure nobody is trailing us."

Charlie nodded. "Sounds as good as good can be. When do I leave?"

"Sooner the better."

"You still don't look well," Lily said watching Jesse with concern. "You sure we can't talk to the sheriff about this?"

"Trust me on this. I won't look any better if we stay." Smiling was getting easier.

Finally, she nodded and agreed. He only hoped he was right.

CHAPTER 18

With the moon rising, going south was easy and circling around to come to Gate's Pass from the hills below went without problems. Lily saw how Jesse watched the few people on the road. To her, no one appeared to have any interest in either of them.

When they reached the entry to the pass, he pointed to the cut, as he brought his horse to a halt. "We'll wait here just a bit to be sure nobody is moving around up there."

"Like who?"

"Like a lookout. I don't think they will be, not with the wind like it is, but better safe than sorry. I'd have been better off if I had taken my own advice."

In the moonlight, she saw his smile and tried to assess how he was in truth doing. He had held himself tall in the saddle, but she knew by now that his grit would do that even if he was suffering.

"And on the other side?"

"When we get the other side of Tucson Mountains, we head north, again watching for movement. You still have your gun?" She patted her side. "Good. About eight miles up, we should come across Charlie. Watch for movement and tell me if you see any." He loosened his revolver in its holster.

"You do expect trouble?"

She saw his smile. "With a storm brewing south of us, no. They are city boys, the ones I know. The one Charlie hit will be nursing a headache. I know about that. The others will be mad at what happened when they lost their pigeon. They're likely sleeping off a hangover about now."

"Storm?" She looked to the south, and it did appear to have sucked the energy out of the sky making it blacker than black.

"If it looks bad, with lightning, we'll hole up, but I don't think so. Most of those storms come later in the day. Still, keep an eye that way too."

She smiled again. "I can do that."

"You're becoming something of an owlhoot yourself."

"What's an owlhoot?"

"Somebody riding the outlaw trail."

"And I'm doing that because I'm with you?"

"You did use a gun to save me."

She laughed. "If Holly could only see me now."

"Would she be upset or glad?"

"Surprised, I think." She laughed again. "But what choice did I have if I wanted to keep up with you, you big galoot."

"Charlie teach you that word?" He was smiling.

"He did." She wished she could touch him and felt shocked when he reached out and pulled her from her saddle and into his arms.

"Jesse, don't hurt yourself," she cautioned while she felt joy at him holding her in those very muscular arms.

"You sure you got those condoms?" he asked as he nuzzled her neck.

"Connie assured me they are in with your cigarettes."

"Good. In a few hours, we might need them." He laughed and lifted her back onto her horse, which had stood patiently through the silliness of humans. His doing it had reassured her that he was stronger than she had feared. "As we go down," he said, "trust your horse. She's not a stumble-foot."

Since she had rarely been out of Tucson, Gates Pass was new to her as it wound through big boulders, with a wash on one side and huge rocks all around the road. She concentrated on following Jesse and not worrying about where this was ending up. Now and then, he would stop and listen. Once he got off his horse, handed her the reins, and walked ahead. "Rattler on the road," he said when he remounted.

"Did you kill it?"

He shook his head. "Just kicked it off. I didn't want it rattling and scaring Jethro."

After what seemed another half an hour, they came to where the mountain broke off and ahead lay a huge valley, visible even in the moonlight. There appeared not a light in sight. "Avra Valley," he said as he nudged his gelding ahead and they began the descent. "Lean back in the saddle a little," was the only thing he said as they went down. That did seem to help and slowly she felt more at ease that Jethro knew what he was doing.

Almost to the bottom, Jesse again stopped his horse and put his hand up. "Rider coming up," he said. "Pull your hat brim down and don't look at him."

They had taken the inside of the road, and the rider approached without seeming much interested. He kept to the outside. When the rider had passed, Jesse dismounted and watched him ride on. When the rider hesitated and looked back, Jesse handed his reins to Lily and loped up the road to where the man waited. She got out her gun and watched-- concerned now for what Jesse was doing as he talked to the man.

When he came back, he said, "I knew him from working with Ollie. I asked if he saw anyone as he was riding up. He said not. He's not the kind to talk to Evans. I think we're in the clear."

After they reached level ground, he picked up the pace to a slow trot. "You okay?" he asked once, and she nodded. She wasn't the one who had been beaten.

An hour later, they were heading north on the main road, riding between the huge saguaros. A wagon and then a horseman passed them, but Jesse didn't appear concerned, so neither would she be. The dark storm passed over with only blowing dust as evidence. She pulled her hat down to protect her eyes, but since they weren't heading into it, it wasn't a problem at least as long as she pulled her brim down far enough to avoid losing the hat.

"Wondered if ya was goin' to make it?" Charlie said as he rode Sarie out of one of the arroyos with Bear turning circles at his excitement in seeing Jesse and Lily.

"See anything to worry you?" Jesse asked halting their horses to talk.

"Nope. Nobody paid me no mind. I didn't though go past the cottage. Wonder if they are using that now for theirs."

"I hope not," Lily said hating that idea. She wasn't sure she'd want to live in the Rose Cottage ever again, but she hated how it had been defiled.

After Jesse had decided they were not being followed, they edged easterly to avoid mine traffic, waiting to cross Avra Valley Road when there were no wagons or riders. From there they took an arroyo and then another dirt road. She was totally lost but counted on the two of them not being. Bear eagerly ran ahead, chased a rabbit or two, and always came right back when Jesse called.

By the time the adobe came into view, the sun was rising with a gentle glow to the east. Lily felt a sense of relief and homecoming. She had come to love the Rose Cottage but nothing meant to her what this simple adobe did.

Jesse had them stop before they entered the clearing. "I'll go in first. If it's safe, you two follow."

She didn't like that but had little choice. She made sure her gun was easy to reach. When he waved them on in, she felt her second surge of relief.

"Glad the little mare is okay," Charlie said as she whinnied to them. They went first to the adobe where Jesse was already untying the packs on the back of his horse. When their supplies were on the table, Charlie and Jesse took the horses down to the corral while she stowed the goods.

Considering she'd had two nights with hardly any sleep, Lily felt exhausted and yet in a strange sense exhilarated. She only hoped that James Angus could secure this property for her. If he did, then she'd explain it all to Jesse. There was that secret and another-- the fact that their marriage contract hadn't been all he had told her it should be. With time, she was sure he'd agree what she had done was wisest. She had to stay positive about this. He didn't think about things as she did but given time, he could reason through anything.

Feeding sticks into the oven, she got a fire going and put on water for tea. They had been resupplied with some wonderful teas from Connie. She put the condoms in the cabinet alongside their bed. His cigarettes she put there also with one pack in the cupboard protected from the wind, which was dwindling but still blowing her hair around.

Jesse and Charlie came up from the corrals after taking the horses and mule to the overflow to drink and then securing them in an area that had grass growing from the recent rains. In the distance, she saw clouds building up.

"Will this one give us rain?" she asked Jesse as he sat at the bench by the adobe and lit a cigarette.

He looked to the south, and shook his head. "Not enough clouds in it for much." She saw for the first time how drained he looked. His bruises had turned a darker color.

"You need to lie down," she said.

He shook his head. "I am beyond tired right now."

Charlie poured himself and her some of the tea when Jesse turned it down. He moved to sit across the table from her.

"That Connie gal is something else. Never had tea I could stomach but this, wal, it's fine."

"She said it helps a person sleep too," Lily said, "not that I will need help. Should I fix us some breakfast?"

"Not for me," Charlie said. "I'm still enjoying the aftermath of that chili." He grinned. "I'm going to just nap with Sarie." He finished off his tea. "See you two later maybe about supper time." With that, he was gone.

"He must be exhausted. He's old, and he's gone through all that we have," she said as she watched him walk off.

He sucked in the smoke and let it out. "I'm sorry."

She looked up at him with shock. "Why would you say that? You didn't do it on purpose."

He shook his head and looked past her to the clouds. "I was stupid and let it happen.

She got up and walked to him, taking his head in her hand and turning it up to where their gazes met. "Nobody expects something to happen like this." She touched his bruises with a fingertip.

"But I did, and I still let it happen."

"Jesse, quit blaming yourself for being you."

"I'm doing that?"

"Oh, my love, you are. You are looking at what anyone could do and trying to think it goes back to your disability. Yes, you might take longer to think something through than someone else, but you can do it. You do it all the time."

"I wish I could see it like you do."

"You will. It just doesn't happen as fast for you. You know people, who think things through fast, they often make many mistakes rushing to conclusions. You know better than to do that. What happened at the house was because of bad people with wrong minded thinking."

She could see him trying to think it through. If he kept trying, he'd get one of his headaches. "Jesse," she said, pulling on his hands until he stood, "I need to sleep and so do you."

"But they might come."

"They might, but will you be better able to deal with it if you are exhausted?"

"No."

"Then." She led him into the adobe. Once inside, she tugged his shirt from his pants. "Let's both sleep. Just sleep. And later, the condoms are in the cabinet." She smiled as she pointed to it as she unbuckled his gun belt and put it on the trunk at the bottom of their bed.

He smiled then as he shrugged out of his shirt, then sat on the bed to take off his boots. She was right, when they woke, would be time enough to figure out what they did next.

Jesse woke in what he knew had to be late afternoon by the heat and where the sun was. He could hear Charlie bustling around the outdoor kitchen. Putting on his pants and boots, he buckled on his gun but left off his shirt. He wasn't sure when he'd finally feel he could stop wearing that blasted gun. For now, he needed its security.

He looked back then at her sleeping curled on her side, wearing only pantalets. His body swelled with desire, but he wouldn't wake her. She looked so slender and young. It was hard for him to believe this delicate rose was the one who had managed to get him out of the pit he'd let himself fall into.

Outside, Charlie was humming a little, Bear watching him for any possible treats to drop. "How ya feelin'?" the old-timer asked.

"Like I got run over by a herd of cattle."

Charlie handed him a whiskey. "I see ya got whipped." Like he needed a reminder. "But what's that on yore arm?"

He remembered being branded, remembered the rough words that had come with it. *Ever wondered how cattle feel when they get branded?* He hadn't looked at it. Holding his arm out for the first time, he saw the X with a slash behind it. He barely noticed when Charlie began applying a kind of salve to the burns.

"Connie said she thought it was meant to be an XY—like this ranch," Lily said coming out from the adobe. She was wearing a simple dress that he'd never seen, kind of a brown pattern, the color of her hair. He guessed she had bought at Sicillas.

He thought then about the disguised voice. Could it be? Then he knew. "Rasmussen. He was the one trying to change his voice."

"Yore boss?" Charlie asked.

Jesse let out a breath, chugged the whiskey and went for a cigarette, which he lit before answering. "He was."

"What kind of thing is this that we're facing?" Lily asked as she sat beside him.

"Nothing that has made sense from the start," Jesse said as he smoked and tried to bring his muddled thoughts together. "What brought Billy Evans here? Revenge doesn't work-- not on my pa or his. For men like him, it's about two things—hurting someone or making money. When he was questioning me, he asked about Pa but mostly it was you."

"But why me?"

He shook his head. "He didn't say. He was more interested in causing me pain than getting answers. There is though one possibility —money."

"I would pay to be safe?"

"Or your sister would to get you back."

He wondered then if he'd made a second mistake when he didn't go to the sheriff and report what had been done to him. No man liked to see himself as a victim, but it went deeper than that to all those years in an outlaw family and his own disability. Yes, he could deal with what he expected, but questioning, angry shouts all would cause him to lose his ability to explain or even reason out answers. What if they knew what he was? They locked halfwits, like himself, in cages. He must stay away from those who had the power to take his freedom. To him, the law had never been a possible rescue but a trap. If it got hold of him, it'd never let him go. The thing was, more than his life was at stake.

"Why'd Rasmussen wanta brand ya though?" Charlie asked as he flipped over whatever he had in the fry pan. "Seems like it'd tie it back to him onct ya saw what it was."

"He didn't figure I'd be around for it to matter." Maybe Jamison hadn't known that but the others had. They would have tortured him until he broke, told them what they wanted to hear, then they'd have taken him out onto the desert, slit his throat and buried him in an unmarked grave. Nobody would have found his body.

Lily put her hand on his shoulder, the comforting touch of a friend. Maybe she would no longer desire him realizing how his mental failings had led to physical ones. Then he remembered what she had said earlier. Maybe all she felt was pity. From the start, he had never believed a woman like her could love a man like him. She was a caring person, loving even to Bear. He was what Bear was to her.

When Charlie declared it ready, they ate the hash, which had been made from the smoked meat. It was chewy but with the addition of an egg, the new onions and fresh potatoes, not bad. A lot of pepper helped Jesse's appreciation even more. Sitting at the table, smoking, he tried again to reason through all that had happened. He was lost in a swirl of facts that didn't fit.

Lily rose and went back into the adobe. She came out with a towel. "Jesse," she said, "I badly need a bath. Will you come with me to be sure it's safe?"

He looked up and met her gaze. He couldn't mistake the message. It made no sense, but it was there. He went for his rifle and then followed her. "Keep an eye out," he said to Charlie. "Yell if someone comes."

"Yah expect that?"

"Eventually. If it was Rasmussen, he's always known where to find me. What he didn't know is that Lily is here. If Jamison told him she is the one who got me out of their trap, he knows now."

The thought scared him. Where could he keep her safe? She had become so precious to him. She had risked her own life to save him. He would do anything to protect her. What would do that?

At the spring, when she saw him walking toward her, she recognized the emotional burden he was carrying. He had to protect them all. He had failed in that. He blamed that on what he saw as the weakness of his mind. She had no idea how to help him, but she knew that having been a victim could lead to emotional consequences. How did she heal a lifetime of such moments in Jesse's life?

When he came to her, she reached for the buckle to his cartridge belt. She'd gotten good at that and laid it on the towel beside the condom. She didn't know if he saw any of it as he seemed in his own world. She would bring him back to hers, to theirs.

"Sit on the boulder," she said pointing to where she wanted him and he did it without comment. It took her only a moment to pull off his boots and socks and toss them by the towel. Then she moved to kneel between his legs. "Jesse, I love you. Do you know that?"

"I know you believe it now."

Instead of being angry or hurt as she once had been, she smiled. "You think me a shallow person?" she asked as she unbuttoned a button of his pants.

"No."

"But you must if you think I don't know my own mind where it comes to love. Did you know I was a little in love with you the moment I saw you?'

"No."

"Well, I was, but had to be sure and wanted to know what kind of man you were."

"Now you know. Stupid."

She shook her head. "I am tired of hearing that. You know you're not stupid. I know you're not. You are slow. I am tired though of telling you that too. I want to show you." She opened the next button running her fingers down the arrow of hair to where his reaction to her touch was obvious. In moments, she had his pants open enough that she could pull his erection from the opening. It stood proud, strong, but his eyes showed his reluctance to do anything about it.

She rose then and walked back to the towel. Whether he wanted to or not, his gaze followed her as she set about removing all of her clothing. When she was naked, she reached down for the condom. He had missed nothing of what she had done and was even more aroused if that was possible.

She returned to him and again knelt between his legs. "I've never used one of these. Have you?"

He looked down at the package. "I suppose there's only one way."

She reached up and claimed his lips with hers, pushing them apart to open his mouth and then thrust her tongue within. His response was immediate as his arms went around her. The kiss went on as she felt his hands move down her back, cupping her buttocks and bringing her tighter against him. She still held the condom when he dropped his hands. She opened its packaging, saw a soft ring with rubbery sheath, and carefully rolled it down over his shaft to the thick root where it fit snugly.

When he stood, his pants fell to the ground. He stepped out of them and carried her to the grass where he laid her down with seemingly one movement and entered her with the next. She groaned at the wonderful feeling as once again they found each other in the way she knew men and women had from the beginning of time.

An hour later, she lay in his arms. "This is no answer, you know," he said with his lips against her hair.

"Maybe not but it feels so good that I think we should do it again."

"How long do these things last?"

"I am not sure. Connie said a few times. I bought five."

"Confident weren't you?"

"About this. Yes. About everything else, not so much."

"I wish I felt confident."

"You were victimized, Jesse. That sucks security from anyone."

"I don't like thinking of myself that way."

"But you need to. I think in some ways you were victimized all your life by parents who didn't understand, who lived with fear, who couldn't see you for who you were when they were caught up in your few limitations."

He sat up. "It doesn't feel like a few right now. It feels like the only thing that matters. Muscle isn't much use if you don't know where to use it."

She smiled and sat up. "Jesse," she said, "do you have any idea how insightful what you just said is?"

He snorted.

"I mean it. Many people just go off without thinking, and muscle is all they use. I've been with you long enough to know you might take longer to get to a conclusion, but you do get there." Even when he was unhappy, she liked sitting next to him with them both nude. The sun was beginning to set, and its glow was on his skin and hers. The pool became almost a fairy tale setting.

She got to her knees, moved to where she was behind him, and began kissing each welt and abrasion from the whip. She was gentle with her kisses, but he still flinched. She knew it wasn't from the hurt that was physical. Then she went to the brand on his arm and kissed it. "The marks will go away," she said as she came to his face and kissed each bruise. "You have to let them go inside too. Don't let them win—not just those today but all the injuries you've had through the years."

He let out a sigh. "I will try not to."

She pulled him to the pool outlet. "Let's wash it all away."

CHAPTER 19

For Jesse, the next morning involved demanding work by the corrals. He, with Charlie's help, began extending the barrier he had earlier begun. It would enable horsemen to approach through what might appear an open gate but instead was a way to narrow an attacker's opportunity to charge the adobe. When it completed, he felt confident, that while it would not stop those approaching, it would slow them long enough to assess their intent. No matter what he was doing, digging in the dirt to set a post or adding railing, he watched for movement and always wore his Colt—with his rifle not far away.

By the time he walked back to the adobe, Lily had found a few dried desert flowers and put them in a container. The home was taking on the look of a place a woman lived. Jesse both liked that and feared it. This wasn't their home. Married or not, she wasn't his. Those little touches, even watching her paint, all made him feel he wanted it all to be his. The three of them ate without exchanging words, before going back to their work.

Setting a new post, Jesse didn't want to remember when he had been beaten, but his mind went there repeatedly. He used it as a way to retrieve a missing fact that would help him put the whole thing together. The more he thought on it, the more convinced he became that although Rasmussen had been with Evans, both enjoying hurting him, the soft voice, the one he'd only heard as a hiss, that man likely was the boss. Who was it? Someone in town? Someone whose voice he had heard and would recognize? Was that man the reason for the blindfold?

"Looks like it's gonna be a big one," Charlie said, pointing to the south. Dark clouds were building.

Jesse looked up. "And coming this way."

"Regular Fourth of July celebration." The old man chuckled as they saw the flash and then crack of the thunder.

Since Fourth of July had meant nothing to Jesse ever, he just nodded. "Tonight we will put the horses and Sarie in the lean-to. If it hits like it looks, I don't want any of them under the cottonwoods."

"Good idea. How about puttin' Sarie in the adobe?"

Jesse looked over to be sure he was joking and saw the sly look. "Only if she sleeps in your bunk."

Charlie cackled. "I'll sleep in the lean-to with 'em. Give you and the missus a little celebratin' yourselves."

"Not necessary."

"Tell her that." Charlie nudged with his chin to where Lily was back to painting. If where she was looking meant anything, she had been painting them at their corral.

"You said women never stick with anyone or thing." He didn't know why he said that. Maybe because he wanted to believe it wasn't so.

"Yeah, I thought that. But I hadn't met Lily then." Charlie's smile was softer than Jesse had ever seen it. "Yah, know," the old timer said, "I never had no family."

"Except when you were a child."

Charlie snorted. "I lied about that when Lily asked me. I didn't want to tell the truth. I was shoved from home to home from as early as I 'member. Friends, maybe some even family. I don't know-- except nobody wanted me there. I was an ugly little cuss, but mostly it was they didn't have, none of them to feed their kin, and I was in the way."

Jesse put down his shovel and turned to the old man. "You were orphaned?"

"One way or t'other. Dead or just didn't want me. Hell, I don't even know the names they either had. One of the homes that took me in called me by their name. I asked a time or two and got slapped for my trouble. I run away as early as I could."

Jesse didn't know what to say. Sorry seemed all wrong, yet what else was there? "I'm sorry. I didn't know."

"Didn't want nobody to know. I shouldn't have lied to her. She deserved better than that. She deserves the best there is. I will tell ya this, son, turnin' away from folks, pretendin' ya don't want them might seem easier than the other side of the coin—getting tossed out on your ear, but maybe it keeps ya from ever knowing family at all." His knowing gaze met Jesse's.

"You think that's what I'm doing?"

"Where it comes to her. She's the motherlode, son. Pure gold. I don't wanta see ya lose her."

"I know that about her." It had never been about her.

By the time, Jesse saw the storm coming close enough to see the bolts of lightning hitting within ten miles, he told Charlie they were closing up for the day. They got the mare, geldings, and mule and put them in the shed. "Won't be good for sleeping in there tonight," Jesse said as the two ran for the adobe, with pounding rain and wind.

Lily had put away her paints and was moving a pan to the table inside where she had already moved plates and utensils. "I think hot though it might be, we can't eat outside," she said as a four-pronged bolt hit what sounded like only a few miles from them.

"All right." Jesse knew lightning could hit and travel along the ground a distance. If it got struck, the adobe wasn't that safe either, but if she felt better for it, it was fine with him. Whatever he could do for her, he would.

"Don't ask me what it is," she said with a smile. "I just put together half that chicken we brought from Sicillas, rice, an onion, egg and not sure what else."

"You cook much, Lily?" Charlie asked as he scooped out a helping for himself.

"In the past just breakfast. We do have that now thanks to the town. While they last anyway." She looked then at Jesse. "You think you could build a sturdy chicken coop? We could have fresh eggs. I was thinking maybe a goat for milk. Rose said it makes good cheese too."

He looked at her as though he had no idea what she had just said.

"Be good to start drying adobe bricks too," Charlie said. "Gonna need more rooms on here."

"You two are dreaming," Jesse said finally understanding their hopes. He took his own helping of her creation. He smiled with his first bite. "Did you know you have to boil rice first to use it or else cook it a long time?" he asked.

She took her own serving. "Oh... I guess that is kind of tough."

Charlie chortled. "Tastes good to me."

"Oh, I will be eating it," Jesse said, "just hope they don't swell up in my stomach later."

"I should have brought a cookbook." She looked with disappointment at the food on her plate which all would have been tasty had the rice been cooked.

"I can fix this," Charlie said and scooped all their plates back into the pan and went back out into the now driving rain.

Jesse went out with him, not sure what he hoped to accomplish. If Charlie got hit by lightning under the ramada roof, he wouldn't be much help. He guessed he was hoping their combined luck might keep the lightning away as it was now striking all around them. He watched as Charlie added water to the pot and put it back on to boil.

He lit a cigarette looking back at where Lily was sitting on the bench. Before the rice had been cooked, the lightning was mostly hitting across the valley, most likely the Tortolitas. In an hour, the animals could go out of the shed.

Charlie brought the pot back inside. "Don't feel bad, Lily," he said as they again all dished up. "Ya tried. Ain't that the important part?"

"I'd feel better to try and succeed," she said smiling sheepishly. This time though the dinner tasted quite good, and they ate it all. As Lily insisted on cleaning up, Charlie and Jesse sat on the bench and watched the sky as it slowly calmed down into a wonder of intense purple highlighted clouds with sun streaking through.

"You smell smoke?" Charlie asked.

Jesse knew his sense of smell hadn't been as good since he had begun smoking so much. He looked around to see if he saw it. The wind was blowing mostly straight north, most likely if there was a lightning caused fire, it would miss them. Still...

"I think it's over there," he said wetting down a burlap sack, telling Bear to stay, before he grabbed a shovel and took off at a run.

"What is it?" Lily asked from where she was washing the tin plates, as Charlie got his own sack.

"Fire. That last lightnin' bolt might've hit that dead ironwood by the hill yonder. Right spot for it anyways." He took off following Jesse. Before he got out of sight, he said, "Grab your rifle, princess, and watch over the place. We'll be back."

Lily debated following them, but that would be foolish. She'd be in the way with no idea how to fight a fire. She worried that they would be caught in flames and hurt or worse. As she put away the plates, she gave Bear the leftovers which he lapped up. Then she sat with him watching the distant hills for any sign of flames, smoke, or an additional problem.

Much as she loved the adobe and watching the sun go down, without Jesse there, she felt the joy disappear. The adobe was about him. It was them together and more than them-- Bear, Charlie, the horses and Sarie. It was all of them.

Her day of painting had been sublime. She had seen Charlie and Jesse working together, half the time Jesse had his shirt off and sweat was rolling off his back as they extended the corral. The image of the skinny, old-timer and the strong man in his prime had been too much to pass up. She had laid in the colors quickly and then tried to capture the basic shapes. She hoped she could do the rest from memory, as she doubted she could get them to pose sinking postholes.

Perhaps a transcendent day would end in a tragedy. Was that the way it was in life? No, because she'd had a wonderful day, it didn't mean bad had to follow. They would soon return, and all would be well.

It was just after the sun had fully gone down, when she heard them coming, and they were laughing. The moon, playing hide and seek with clouds racing by overhead, lit them enough to see both were gritty with soot and happier than she had seen either.

"You got it out?" she asked as Bear raced forward to greet them.

"Lightnin' had hit the dried grass, and good thing we went," Charlie said. "Threw sand over it and it's out. So much for hittin' the highest thing. That old ironwood was jest laughin' at us."

"We need to wash up," Jesse said and headed for the spring with Charlie and Bear right behind them.

Half an hour later, they were back and both looking cooler than she felt. She smiled though as they seemed happy, and Jesse was the most at ease she had seen him.

"You neither one got burned?" she asked, unsure if they'd volunteer it if they had.

Jesse held up his left hand. "A little singed. But it's nothing."

She lit the lantern. "Let me see."

He held it where the light shone on it. It had a blister rising. "I think some of Connie's salve is in order," she said as she reached into the outdoor cupboard.

"No need."

She didn't take no for an answer and grabbed his hand, rubbing the ointment over it. "Does it hurt?"

"Less than it did."

Charlie poured them two whiskeys. She said, "I'd like one too this time."

Charlie poured a third and handed it to her. "You had much of this?" he asked with a sly grin.

"Not until I began hanging around you two."

"So, we're a bad influence?" Jesse asked. His smile was crooked as he lit a cigarette and watched her take the first sip with the same grimace she'd had the first time she'd tried it with him.

"It's fine," she said when she could manage her voice.

He took his in a gulp and held the glass out for Charlie when he refilled his.

Charlie looked over at Lily who was still nursing hers. "I gotta confession to make."

"All right." She didn't like the sounds of that.

"I lied to ya about leaving my family. I never had no family. I was with this one or that but not nobody who wanted me."

"Why didn't you just tell me that?"

"Don't know. I was ashamed of it, I reckon. Figured nobody wanting me said something about me. I never told nobody afore. But then, I told Jesse today. It just seemed ya didn't deserve me lyin' to ya that way."

"I am sorry for your childhood, Charlie. You have a family now though."

He looked over at her as though not understanding and then he got it. "You?"

"And Jesse. We're your family."

He smiled then. "Gonna adopt me?" He chuckled.

"We could. Do you believe in adoption, Jesse?" she asked smiling at him.

"Maybe sometimes the best idea."

She understood his meaning, but she ignored it. She'd argue out having children someday, if he decided to stay with her. This wasn't the day for the debate. She felt a warmth though toward Charlie, and the losses he'd experienced. "Charlie," she said, glad the darkness was hiding her tears, "do you realize that all of us here had less than perfect childhoods. My mother was addicted to opium. My father saw me as his servant. Jesse's father was an outlaw and his brother a murderer of their mother. You didn't know your parents. Maybe God wants us brought together now to form our own family."

"You believe in God?" Jesse asked and she heard the doubt in his voice.

"Do you?"

"No."

"I believe in something good in this world," she said. "I believe it wants good to succeed. Is that God?"

"And the bad too?" he asked taking a long draw on a cigarette.

She wished she hadn't brought any of it up.

CHAPTER 20

"And now what do we do?" Rupert asked Evans, who was smoking a cigar. Patrick watched them feeling as though he was a fox with his paw in a trap. He couldn't see a way out and almost felt desperate enough to chew it off. He looked around the Pedrales, but no one seemed to be paying them attention. He wondered if he knew anyone who would give him a loan? Just enough money to get out of town.

"We? We, suddenly it's we? Haven't you been all over the place for what you want to do?" Evans had that perpetual smirk that so annoyed Patrick. "I'll tell you what *we* do. We wait for orders."

"I don't like orders," Rupert said.

"But you take them."

"For now."

"Rup, you take them because you ain't never earned the right to give them."

"And it's working out so well."

Again, Patrick looked around the bar to assure himself no one was listening to the conversation. He did not want to be sitting here with these men, but he had also had an order he could not ignore. How had he let this happen? He'd never seen a man brutalized and endure what had been inflicted upon Taggert. He had been an accessory to it happening. And Lily. Poor Lily. What would they do to Lily to get their way?

Rupert was glowering. "I have realized I've been a dupe. I brought you here—I thought but had no idea why, did I?"

"Tools don't need to know."

"If I don't find out the rest of it soon, I'm gone. This isn't working out to make sense."

"What part don't you like?" Evans asked grinning like a hyena.

"All parts. When I start into something, I have a plan. I don't have a boss, where the orders are given by phone, and who I've only seen that one time. I'd like to know what he hopes to get out of this."

"He'll tell you if he wants you to know."

"I wish I'd never agreed to any part of it. The girl saw Pat. That means she can go to the law. They might ignore somebody like Taggert but they won't her. The law talks to power."

"When power can talk or has power."

"What does that mean?"

Evans chuckled. "You get into things a lot without thinking them through?"

When Rupert didn't answer, Evans turned to Patrick. "How about you, Fancy Pants, you dive in like your brother?"

"I did not knowingly get into this. I wish I never had." If he was blessed to survive it, he never would again. He'd paint and sell them on street corners if that's what it took. What a fool he had been.

"Good news for you both then. We are meeting him tonight for final plans."

"Where?"

"Since you're going with me, you don't need to know." He looked at Patrick. "You ride, Fancy Pants?"

"How far away is this place we meet?"

"Since you're going with me, you don't need to know. Let's just say it's safe, and we will get our instructions to finish this."

"You sure I need to go?" Patrick asked wincing when Evans nodded. "It all goes down tomorrow. Tonight, you do have to ride. "

Great. He'd have to get on a horse. He hated horses. Maybe this was only to take them out of town and kill them. He doubted his derringer would be much help if it came down to that. He had never fired a more powerful weapon. He didn't want ever to fire one in the future either.

He thought then about Jesse Taggert. In many ways, he admired the man. He had withstood more than he'd imagined any man could and through it never lost his dignity. Patrick had no such courage within himself. He could admire it in another. It wouldn't, of course, save Taggert's life.

His fear was Lily would be caught in it too. He doubted very much their peerless leader would care. Jesse would try to keep her safe, but he could not protect her against so many. The truth of it was-- Patrick respected none of the men he'd be riding with as much as he did Jesse Taggert—and that included his brother. Taggert might be considered slow-witted but whatever he'd been left with made him more a man than any he'd met.

~

When Lily woke, she was curled against Jesse's side, her hand on his chest. She realized his eyes were open and he'd been watching her. She ran her fingers lightly through his chest hair. "I never meant to make you unhappy," she whispered.

"You haven't."

"I have and endangered your life. To make it worse, I keep saying I won't pressure you and then I say what I did last night about us being a family with Charlie. I am sorry, Jesse. If when this is over, you want to go back to how it was for you before I came along, I won't hold you." Outside, she heard Charlie rustling around the oven and starting coffee.

"Why would you think I'd want that?"

"You haven't said you loved me. I talked you into marrying me, then taking me here."

He sat up and put his feet over the side of the bed, reaching for his cigarettes. The sun was just beginning to peek over the distant Tortolitas. "It's not about that," he said as he took the first drag on the cigarette.

"I think it is."

Before he could answer, if he even intended to, she heard Charlie yell. "Riders coming." Jesse pulled on his pants, boots, and belted on his gun. "Stay inside," he ordered as he headed for the door ordering Bear to stay with her.

Like hell, she thought as she hastily pulled on her shirt and pants before grabbing her gun. At the door, Bear beside her, she saw two riders and realized with relief... she hoped... that one of them was Jesse's father.

"What are you doing here?" Jesse asked gruffly the cigarette dangling from his lips.

Jeremiah was dismounting. "What makes you think it's not just a friendly family visit." He chuckled and then looked up at the adobe where Lily was standing barefooted in the doorway, her hair spread over her shoulders.

"My God, you and your sister look a hell of a lot alike," he said as he grinned. He looked back at Jesse. "Introduce me to my daughter-in-law, boy."

"Lily, as you probably guessed, this is my pa, Jeremiah Taggert. The other old scoundrel is Rance Evans."

Rance was off his horse and following Jeremiah to the porch with a broad grin. "Jumpin' Jehoshaphat, she is a beauty. No wonder ya swept her off her feet," he said as he and Jeremiah took turns giving Lily a hug. "Woman looks that good first thing in the morning' and a man's a lucky devil."

"You didn't answer my question," Jesse said, still in no mood to smile. "What are you doing here?"

"Offer us some coffee?" Jeremiah asked. "I don't have to ask who you are, do I? Must be Charlie Provo."

"I am-- though ain't met you that I recall."

"You did me though," Rance said. The three men shook hands. Charlie got the coffee pot and opened the cupboard for them to each take a cup. Lily went back inside and came out wearing her boots to see the four men sitting at the table and drinking coffee. Charlie had poured her a cup and she took it to sit on the opposite side of the table from Jesse. She wanted to touch him, but more she needed to see his face and understand what he was thinking where he'd not be saying it.

Jesse didn't touch the coffee but smoked as the others drank. When they had drained their cups, he said, "Now, why are you here?"

"Do you know who you are up against?" Jeremiah said.

"Billy Evans, Rupert Jamison, his brother Patrick, not that he counts a lot, Rasmussen who I worked for on the XY, and the man who runs the show, whose voice I couldn't place. Along with them, five others whose names I don't know."

Jeremiah grinned. "You got Rasmussen then. Good."

"I recognized his voice eventually when he... questioned me."

She saw on his face how much he hated saying that. She reached across the table to touch his hand, but he was only concentrating on his father.

"Rasmussen is Rasmus Wilson. That mean more to you?"

"No."

"He was the boss of the Fenders gang after the old man got killed off. Wilson previously had been operating with train and bank robberies along the border of Kansas and Missouri."

"He knew my Billy from there," Rance said.

"And most likely Rupert," Jeremiah added.

"And someone wanted the three of them here in Tucson?" Jesse asked.

"Yep."

"There is a reason then?"

"The trail gets crookeder than hell," Jeremiah said. "Remember who was foreman when you first worked for the XY?"

"Lester Adams."

"Died, right?"

"Broke his neck when thrown from a horse."

"He not a good horseman."

"As good as any I know, but those things happen."

"Convenient for Wilson wasn't it?"

"No accident?"

"Can't prove it. That's how it works with men like these... and the man they work for."

"Back to the reason."

Jeremiah shook his head. "It seems it's about the XY ranch and Lily."

She looked at him in shock. "What do I have to do with the ranch?"

"Money maybe. I don't know. The level where we got this information knows who but not why."

"Is any of this going to be helpful?" Jesse asked impatiently.

"Maybe some. What if not just one plan was going on here but two?"

"Go on."

"One plan coming from a gang put together for a deal but waiting around with not enough to do. The second came from the north."

"Brooks," Jesse said with no doubt in his voice. Lily stared at him and then back to his father. She had been afraid of Harold but then convinced herself she'd been foolish. Maybe not so much?

Jeremiah nodded. "Somebody wanted those three here and one more."

"Patrick?" Lily said still feeling shocked.

Jeremiah sighed and looked back at Lily. "What we been piecing together is Brooks thought he'd marry you—if need be, he'd scare you into marrying him by the toughs he brought in. If that wasn't enough, he had Patrick for a backup—your kind of soft man. He could control Patrick through his brother. Then you up and married Jesse, who he soon knew he couldn't control. Jesse ruined it for him in more than one way." He looked back at his son. "He hates you, boy. You blocked him and for a while he didn't know where Lily was."

"Patrick told."

"Nope, it was the other jasper, the one Charlie slammed over the head who saw a woman. Only one woman would be coming for Jesse. Not hard to figure out who she was." He grinned as he looked at her. "Good work by the way, gal. We didn't even know it happened before you pulled him out of it."

"How did you find out?"

Jeremiah's smile was mean. "One of Evans men thought he was nailing Rance here."

Both the old outlaws grinned.

"And he told you real friendly like?" Charlie said with a laugh.

"Eventually," Rance said.

"What good does knowing all this do unless you know what they plan next?" Jesse asked.

"Why do you think we're here?" Rance asked. "Jeremiah wasn't about to let his son get killed or end up in their hands again. Cruel bastards that they be." He stopped and looked at Lily. "Pardon my language, ma'am."

"No apologies needed. Bastards is fine by me." She looked at Charlie. "Present company excepted."

Charlie cackled.

"Sounded like Brooks is goin' a little nuts," Rance said. "He wanted the woman, her money, and the ranch. Now some of the ranch got bought out from under him."

"Tibbets sold this place?" Jesse asked. She saw from his face that it wasn't good news to him. She didn't yet know though if her offer had been the one accepted. Best to say nothing and tell him only when she had something firm to tell.

"Don't know what part. One more thing. Seems this Brooks ain't so flush as he pretends. He ain't been paying the crew, lot of talk, hot air, and not much dinero," Rance said. He gestured his thumb toward Jesse. "He's good at talkin' though and they are comin' for you."

"Why don't we go to the sheriff?" Lily asked realizing as she said that she was the only person at this table who believed in law and order.

Jeremiah smiled at her. "You are a real nice gal. Jesse here is a lucky man. You though don't know much about how the system works."

"How about the US Marshals if the sheriff is corrupt?"

"Didn't say he was," Rance said. "But he ain't got no reason to get into something that could cost him his life without proof. Marshals take time to bring into something out this far. And we ain't got no proof—except what a jasper said when he was falling down." He grinned.

"Jesse was beaten. He had bruises... and other injuries," she argued.

"Which he could've got in a fight," Jeremiah said.

"I think we all need breakfast," she said unable to find reasons for these men to change their view of the society in which they had lived. Hers had been different. Money had doubtless protected her. Was it now the threat to her life and love?

She went to the outdoor counter and began slicing bacon strips into a pan to set on the stove to fry. She was only aware, when she heard the movement and felt his energy, that Jesse had come to stand behind her. "It's hard for you," he acknowledged.

"It's like a foreign world." She bit her lip to stop from crying. She felt no fear for herself but for Jesse. The thought that he could be hurt terrified her.

"I don't disagree with you that maybe I should have gone to Adams."

She looked up then and met his concerned gaze. "He's the sheriff?"

He nodded. "I don't have a reason to think he's crooked. He was fair with me. The thing is I have spent my life staying away from the law."

She turned then and put her arms around his waist. She loved the feel of his muscular body against hers. "I trust you, Jesse. I trust your instincts."

"I wish I did." He tipped her chin up to give her a quick kiss.

"Maybe they'll just give it up now. I mean it's not easy like it might've originally seemed."

"Men like Brooks don't give up. They are too used to winning. Wilson and Evans like hurting people and the excitement of the fight."

"What might they do?"

"I wish I could tell you, baby, but I don't know."

She knew that he would stand between her and any danger. But even a powerful man could be taken down by a single bullet. Imagining Jesse lying dead nearly crippled her for going forth with any thinking. She had to protect him. But how? This had gone beyond anything she could imagine. Life didn't involve people wanting to shoot each other. It was about insults or emotional control. Jesse's world though had been so unlike hers. Could they really bring these two different worlds together? She would do anything she could to make it happen. Was he of the same mind?

Rance and Jeremiah set their bedrolls down by the shed. "You planning to stay?" Jesse asked his father as the older man came over to watch him setting another post.

"Sure not going off 'til this is settled."

"Then get to work." He smiled and handed his father a hammer. "These railings need to be put in place.

"For the horses?" his pa asked picking up a board.

"Later. For now, it's a way to slow down who enters and how."

He nodded approvingly. "Good idea."

"Did you wire or call Vince?"

"I ended up thinking better of it. I didn't want to lose both my sons."

"You'd still have Cole."

"Yeah."

"Pa, you never gave any of us a chance."

"Cole just seems to have no gumption."

"Or he had the most. Vince left. I got jobs that took me away. Only Cole stayed and did the best he could with a raw deal."

"Never thought of that."

When to announce lunch, Lily used the triangular dinner bell for the first time, Jesse smiled as he grabbed his shirt from a post and headed up. He felt pleased with the fence they'd created. It would not block entry but slow it to one or two riders at a time. When this mess was settled, it could be used to keep the horses from roaming too far and yet enable their eating grasses when it was available. At that point, he planned to fence off the spring leaving the overflow for the animals.

When he realized what he was doing, he sucked in a breath. He could not afford to think about this home being his. He'd be long gone soon enough. Don't get used to anything. That way was safest. If this was the part of the ranch already sold, as his father seemed to indicate, then the new owner would force them out. He would not live in a town. He knew no place he could take her with him. It would likely be the end for him with Lily.

Lily and Charlie had sliced bread, the last of the chicken and put that with fresh vegetables on a platter. They could each put together their own lunch. Jesse reached into the sack cooler for the beers he'd stashed and handed them to those so inclined.

With the heat building up, Rance, Charlie and Jeremiah were not enthusiastic about working through the afternoon.

Sipping the last of his beer, Jeremiah asked, "When you think they'd be here if they're coming today?" He was looking at Jesse.

"It depends on from where they come. If it's ranch headquarters, it's about eight miles from here. They could've already been if they were coming."

"Unless they wanta catch us nappin'," Charlie said with a yawn. Even Bear looked unenthusiastic as he lay under the table.

"What's the plan if they do come?" Lily asked sipping a tepid tea she had made using the sun.

"You stay in the adobe with Bear. That's my first plan," Jesse said.

She gave him a look. "You taught me how to use the gun. Why'd you do that if you didn't want me to help?"

"So you could protect yourself if I wasn't there," he said shooting her look right back at her.

The spring had been the last time they had made love, and he was beginning to feel edgy as much for sexual frustration as from concern over when Brooks could send his men after them. He realized how used he had become to sleeping with her, to having her nearby. It was another thought, which gave him no pleasure.

"Other than us all in agreement Lily needs to stay out of the way of flying bullets," Charlie said giving her one of his grins but then turning a somber look to Jesse. "What is the plan?"

"If we are right, they will come from the northeast and we'll hear them about five minutes before they get here. They will have to go through the fence one or two at a time. Pa, you be by the shed. Rance, on the other side, by that pile of wood. Rifles ready. I'll stand here watching as they ride up. Then we'll have to play it by ear."

"What about the animals in the corral?" Charlie asked. "I don't like the idee of Sarie being where bullets might hurt her."

"You want to take them down toward the spring now? Double rope them like we did before so they don't wander far."

Charlie nodded. They helped him put ropes on the horses, then despite the heat, he took off at a sprightly pace to get them away from the potential of gunfire.

"Why do you stand out front to talk to them?" Lily asked. "I don't like that part."

"Because we can't just start shooting people. If they turn unfriendly, I'll duck behind the table."

"Table isn't much protection," Jeremiah said. "Use the adobe."

"And draw fire to Lily and Bear. No thanks." Jesse lit a cigarette.

"How about we put together a stronger barricade for up here," Jeremiah said looking around for what materials might work. It was then they heard horses.

CHAPTER 21

L ily ran for her gun. Before she could come back outside, Jesse
stopped her and handed her the Remington. "Stay in and keep
Bear with you, or so help me to God, I'll tie both of you to the bed."
The cold expression on his face left her no doubt he meant it. Reluctantly, she nodded. Jesse turned to his dog. "Stay with Lily. Protect
her." When Bear started to come back out, Jesse's voice was more
forceful. "Stay." The dog went back to Lily's side.

She watched then as Jeremiah ran for the shed and Rance the other
side of the cleared space. She hoped Charlie would stay away until
this was settled. She felt fear at what that might mean but checked her
revolver to be sure it was loaded. Then she picked up the rifle. It
would be better if they didn't come close. She had only had the one
session with Jesse but felt confident she could point it where she
wanted. Pulling the trigger on a living person was another question.

"Stop right there," she heard Jesse yell, cigarette dangling from his
lips, as the first riders came to the fence and stopped, spreading out
along it. She counted eight. Patrick wasn't one of them.

"That's plumb unfriendly," a rough voice yelled back.

"Rasmussen, what do you want?" Jesse asked his rifle cradled in
his arms. He was out there all alone and looked so vulnerable. She
wished he had a barrier between him and any bullets that were likely
to be fired.

"To remove you from this property. You are being evicted, you
might say." The man chuckled as he leaned forward on his saddle.

"Was that what it was about last time I saw you, Wilson?" Jesse asked shifting a bit so his rifle was now pointing down but his finger was on the trigger.

"Wilson? Who's that?" the man asked with another laugh. He clearly was enjoying this.

"The name that will go on your marker."

"I ain't seeing you get a marker," Evans said chortling at his supposed humor. "Let the javelin have you."

Jesse ignored him as he looked down the line of men. "Jamison. Seems I remember you from Utah. You sure this is where you want to be?"

"The odds seem good to me," Jamison said.

"Where's your brother? He decide this wasn't a healthy place to be?"

"What brother? I don't have a brother."

She saw Jesse's cold smile. "Turn and ride out of here. Bring a sheriff back if you want this to be official. As it stands, I consider your visit real unfriendly."

"You do, do you, dummy," Wilson said. "Not like I'll take orders from the likes of you."

"How about me?" Jeremiah asked from the shed.

"And Billy, you really wanta die here?" Rance asked from the woodpile.

Now the riders looked around and seemed less certain, all but Wilson and the one she knew had to be Billy Evans. Wilson edged his mount to where it was more directly facing Jesse. "I never liked you, stupid," he said.

To Lily's shock, Jesse laughed. "Was that supposed to be my problem?"

The gunfire erupted so suddenly she nearly screamed. Wilson had pulled his gun and fired at Jesse as he was bringing his up. She saw him take a step back, unsure if he'd been hit, but he fired his rifle from his hip, and Wilson fell from his saddle.

Explosive sounds and screams filled the next few seconds, followed by an almost eerie quiet with only gun smoke filling the air. Three were on their horses, their hands in the air. Two besides Wilson had fallen to lie still on the ground. In the chaos, two had apparently ridden off.

"Use your fingers to throw your guns away, and then get off your horses," Jesse ordered. Rifle in hand, he walked down to where the men on horseback looked bewildered at how quickly it all had happened. Jeremiah and Rance likewise came out from their shelters. She realized for the first time that Charlie had entered into the shooting as he rose from his knees and joined the others.

She ran down in time to hear Wilson look up at Jesse and then the old men. His grin was as much grimace as smile. "Beat by a dummy and three old men," he managed before his eyes went dead. Even though Jesse felt for a pulse, she was sure the man had died.

When Jesse rose, he looked at the ones with their hands in the air. "Jamison," he said, "you've been a fool and could end up in Yuma for the rest of your life."

"We just came to evict you," Jamison said with a sick expression on his face. Although she had never met him, she could see Patrick in his features.

"Legal like was it?" Jeremiah asked. "Got the papers to prove it?" Jamison looked away. "Rup, you've been duped unless you are the one behind all this."

"I got nothing to say." He didn't sound confident.

Rance rose from his son's body. In his hand was a roll of bills that he'd pulled from his pocket. "this what was worth dying for?" He sighed as he looked back at Billy's body. "Plumb waste."

"You testify what you know of this," Jeremiah said looking at the three men, "and you will get off light. It's how the law works. O' course, only the first man gets the deal."

"We could just kill 'em all," Rance said with a smirk. "Bury 'em out here and who's gonna know."

Lily felt shocked at his words until it was swallowed by fear as she realized there was blood on Jesse's shirt. "You were hit," she said as she rushed to him pulling his shirt from his pants to see an ugly gouge along his left side.

"It's nothing," he said as he barely glanced at the wound. "Tie these up. Put their horses in the corral. Then we can decide what we do with them." He didn't resist as she tugged on his hand to bring him back to the table and push him to sit.

She pulled off his shirt tsking over the wound. She went for the whiskey. When she held it up, he nodded but didn't seem to care what she did with a wound he clearly regarded as of no account. He hissed as it hit the bloody gouge, and took the bottle from her to swallow a slug before handing it back.

Jeremiah had come up and watched as she applied an unguent

over the gouge. "It's fine," Jesse argued, but she was the more determined, and he didn't resist as she applied a gauze pad over the deepest cut before taping it in place. She was aware she was moaning, and he wasn't.

Bear had gone down to examine the damage but came back to sit next to Jesse for his own security. She had worried he might run off with all the noise and blood, but he seemed as committed to Jesse as clearly Jesse was to him.

She only realized how much she had been shaking when Jesse put his arm around her and drew her to sit on his good side. He was looking at his father but said nothing as he lit another cigarette.

"What do you think we should do?" Jeremiah finally asked, lighting a cigar and looking at Jesse. She saw the shock on Jesse's face at his father asking his advice. Then she saw his mouth tighten as he considered the words and tried to come up with an answer.

"Only one thing to do," he said finally. "Take these jaspers into the sheriff along with the bodies."

Lily felt shocked and saw the same look on Jeremiah's face and Rance's, who had come to listen.

"And you end up in Yuma or worse," Jeremiah said.

"There's worse than Yuma?" Rance asked with a snort.

Jeremiah had whitened more than during the gun battle. "There is for Jesse. They have these jackets, that the arms go in, they wrap them around tight to a person's side, then fasten them to the back, and it totally makes even a strong man like Jesse helpless. They lock them away where nobody can talk to them. They scream there, but nobody hears. Nobody believes a word they say. Family can't... get to them. They are judged insane, and nobody cares what happens to them. They never get another free day."

Lily felt livid and even more so when she saw how Jesse had gone silent. "That talk is what is insane, Mr. Taggert. Jesse isn't crazy. He's perfectly normal and smarter than most sitting here at this table." She gave Jeremiah a look that caused him to turn away. "You have fed him this threat since he was a child. Fear talk. There is no way anyone would do that to Jesse. They'd have no reason."

"Men died here today. Somebody be different, and they don't need reason," Jeremiah said his own fear showing.

"Why would you think that is true of Jesse?" She struggled not to scream out her rage. This man had done all he could to handicap Jesse when he'd had no reason. It was time to fight back. She had to remind herself he was Jesse's father. He probably did love him, but his fear mongering could destroy him. She had just seen Jesse handle a dangerous situation with more wisdom than anyone she'd ever known. How dare someone call him insane?

"He couldn't read. He was slow to talk and then not much. Even now. Look at him. He couldn't defend himself if somebody took him to court. He'd never be able to answer in time. They'd have him in one of them... straitjackets. That's the word for it."

"Mr. Taggert," she said as she put her arm around Jesse, felt the stiffness of his muscles, finally understood all he'd endured in his life. "Who do you know where that happened?"

"It runs in our family," Jeremiah said. "And it gets worse."

"Tell me who. Let's confront this."

"I think it's time for the whiskey," Charlie said getting out the bottle and glasses. He put one by Lily this time without her asking. She knew she would need it.

"My father," Jeremiah said finally. "He went crazy and it's why his brother killed him. Jericho had no choice."

"Crazy in what way?"

"Rotten angry, willing to tear into anybody, even his children, his wife. He was like Asa."

"So, Asa was insane?"

"I believe he was."

"But Jesse is nothing like him."

"Well, not in some ways, but he's slow. You have to know that. I don't know why you married him, but you know he can't respond like others."

"You mean like he did just now?" She was unsure how Jesse was taking this. She needed to protect him from these words. She just didn't know how.

"He handled that good. I admit."

"Mr. Taggert, I think you have lived with fear all your life and maybe because of your father and then Asa, but Jesse isn't like them. Jesse is fine and good. He's loving and concerned for others, for animals, for anything that needs his help. Surely you see that."

"Lily, it isn't any use," Jesse said rising from the table.

She put her arms up around his neck. "You are the best man I ever knew, Jesse Taggert, and if you don't believe it, you need to start."

"I admit he was good with animals from the time he was a toddler. He'd go right up to the meanest bull, and the animal would be licking his face."

"Because they had more ability to see who he was than humans," she said still infuriated but better understanding the handicap under which Jesse's father had operated all his life.

Jesse let out a breath and walked to the cabinet where he pulled out a cigarette and lit it. She knew he had hated every word they'd all said. He didn't like confronting or having others confront what he saw as his weaknesses. She also knew he needed to stop believing the lie. His weaknesses were actually his strength.

"Maybe I been wrong," Jeremiah said in the long silence. She doubted he believed it.

"Jesse, can we talk," she asked as she took his hand and brought it to her lips kissing it softly and tenderly. She loved him so much that she felt it flowed out of her as though in waves.

"About what?"

"Some things I think need saying."

"All right." He looked toward the prisoners and then back at his father. "You keep an eye on things."

His father, finally looking chagrined, nodded.

Walking down the path to the spring, Jesse followed Lily feeling numb. The insults that Rasmussen had thrown at him had been no surprise but followed up by what his father had said, he felt frozen. He did not know what Lily expected or wanted. Maybe now a divorce. He wouldn't blame her. She had defended him, but he had barely been able to follow what she had said. The words had jumbled together and now a headache was beginning, which would lead to blinding pain, making thinking even harder.

He only realized when they got to the spring that Charlie had followed. 'I'll take the horses and Sarie back," he said and grabbed ropes leading them back to the corrals.

When they were alone, she pulled him to the boulder where he'd sat the last time they made love. That wouldn't be happening, maybe not ever again. He felt cold inside.

"Jesse," she said as she pushed his legs together and sat on his lap. "You are my husband, are you not?"

"For now."

"Have you ever trusted me?"

"I trust you now." He wanted to rub his forehead but resisted the temptation. Between his head and his side, he couldn't decide what hurt most.

She took his head in her hands. "Look at me."

"I am."

"No, I mean really look at me. Do you remember what we said that day when we married?"

With his head beginning to pound, he had a hard time remembering anything. "I think so."

"You have a headache?" she asked. "I didn't understand. One of your headaches?"

"Yeah. It'll pass."

She rose. "Wait here." She ran back down the path, and he was left alone trying to get a handle on what had happened. He'd killed a man again. Two. After he'd shot Wilson, he'd quickly turned his gun on Evans knowing he'd be the other most dangerous. He had to take him out and didn't want his own father to have to do it. By that time, he saw the bodies falling, hands going up and men riding off. He had stood for a moment in shock at the violence that had overtaken his adobe. Would the energy of it ever leave this place? Not that it mattered.

That morning he'd been thinking about things that would make it more of a home. It was never going to be his home. He had to get a handle on that. He rubbed his forehead but nothing eased the agony of his head splitting open.

He was only dimly aware when Lily had returned. She brought a cup of water and handed him two aspirin. While he swallowed them and half the glass of water, she spread a quilt on the grass. She beckoned to him. "Come here. You need to lie down."

"I should go back."

"We have to talk."

"All right." He lay down.

She lifted his head and rested it on her lap. She ran her fingers over his temple, massaging and then working on his neck.

"I thought you wanted to talk," he said as he felt the tension beginning to leave his muscles.

"Eventually." She opened the top buttons on his shirt and ran her strong fingers down his shoulders. As much as it helped his physical pain, the emotional was worse.

"I have to get to town," he said but made no attempt to rise

"I know. Eventually." She continued with her soothing motions using her fingers lightly to close his lids. "Sleep for a bit. Nothing is going to need to be done right away."

"It feels good, baby, but it does have to be done now." He sat up reluctant to let go of her touch. He turned to look at her and tried to find the words. They weren't coming.

"Jesse," she said, "we've had this discussion before. You are not stupid. Your father obviously has experience with mental illness, but not what you have. Do you understand that?"

"I hear you." He stared at the grass at the edge of the quilt. It was beginning to dry up with July's harsh heat. He felt a little like that grass. Dry inside and no way to find life in himself.

She reached inside her shirt and pulled out a chain. "Remember this?" she asked holding up the ring.

"Yes."

"I want you to put it on my finger again but this time intending it to stay there. No more secret marriage. No more tomorrow I might go, or you might. I want it to be forever like we said that day."

He stared at the ring. "We aren't a match, baby."

She dropped the chain back between her breasts, got to her knees, reached out, and took hold of his head turning it until he was looking into her eyes. "Jesse, you know animals, don't you?"

"Yes."

"Look into my eyes and tell me what you see there."

With no more words, she didn't let go, forcing their gazes to meet. At first, he didn't understand and then he saw it. There was love there and understanding but more than that... respect. The thing she had wanted from him. She did trust him. More than he trusted himself. "You shouldn't," he said. "I'll let you down when you most need me. I won't be able to think through all that you need."

"That's what you've told yourself, but it's not true. Jesse, you are my mate. I don't want another. I will never want another. You have to trust this in both of us. You love me, don't you? No pretending between us. You do love me. Tell me."

He shook his head but never took his eyes from hers. "From that first day, the first time I saw you," he said. "Even before we met."

"Before?" She twisted her head with a questioning look.

"I saw you on the street... before Ollie and Rose's home that time."

She smiled then. "So it's why you didn't want to meet me."

He nodded.

"You fought what you felt."

"Yes."

"It's time to quit fighting it. We are a mated pair. We are going to stay a mated pair until the day we die and maybe beyond. I want you to put that ring on my finger and I want you to trust in us."

He let out a breath and stared at the pool instead of answering. Finally, he said, "This isn't over with Brooks."

"I understand, but we can face it together now. You took out half his gang today. He would have to find more. You won't give him that time, will you?"

"No."

"I will go to town with you. And there is something more that you should know."

He managed a smile. His head still hurt, but he could bear it. He wanted to believe she loved him. He needed it more than breathing. "What else?" he asked.

"That day, the contract we signed when we got married."

"You want to tear it up?"

"We don't need to. I just want you to know what it said."

"I didn't care. I just didn't want what was yours not to stay that way."

"There is no me alone anymore, Jesse. Everything I have, my body, my soul, and yes, all my money and property, it's all yours now too."

He exhaled a breath. "What are you talking about?"

"The agreement said what was mine would also be yours. If though I die after you, then it reverts to my sister, not your family."

"We agreed..."

She put her fingers over his lips. "We could not start a marriage that way."

"I didn't think you wanted a marriage."

"I wanted you. Anyway I could get you." She smiled. "I still want you. I did not want that money ever being a barrier between us. It had to be both of ours if we had any chance. You are a wealthy man, Jesse Taggert—whether you want it or not. That's how much I trusted you that day before we said the words. Can you start to trust me now?"

"God." He put his hands over his face.

"Does your head hurt again?" she asked moving quickly to stroke his neck again.

"My heart." He dropped his hands and pulled her around until she was in his arms. "Give me that ring." She smiled widely as she reached for the chain, unfastened the clasp, and handed it to him. "I thee wed," he said as he slid it on her finger.

"Forever," she whispered as he claimed her lips with his.

He wasn't sure how long forever would last. Brooks was still out there, but he'd never known more love than with her right then. He could die happy if that's what came next. First, he'd make sure she was safe.

CHAPTER 22

Loading up the prisoners and dead bodies took an hour with Jeremiah arguing against it the whole time. "We could just bury 'em all out here," Rance said agreeing with his old compadre.

"We do this right. They came here to attack us. We defended ourselves," Jesse said smoking as he worked.

"Two old outlaws, a simpleton, a cheating miner—what could go wrong?" Jeremiah protested.

"Pa, you call me simple one more time, and I'll knock you on your ass. And you two are reformed. But don't go with me if you don't want. We can say goodbye right here."

"I'll go all right. If that sheriff gives you any trouble, I'll shoot him and take off."

"You aren't too reformed are you?" Jesse said as he tied the last knot over the last corpse on its horse. He also put a line on the mare. There'd be supplies to bring back.

He looked then at Charlie who was sitting on the outdoor table. "You look after things and take care of Bear and Lily."

Charlie grinned. "How am I supposed to do that?"

Jesse turned to look and saw Lily on Jethro. "I am going," she said. He saw it on her face that there'd be no arguing with her.

"To the sheriff," he said, "and then to Ollie and Rose's until this is settled."

He saw she didn't like it, but she nodded.

Jeremiah chuckled. "Guess you got yourself quite a woman there, son. I like her."

Several hours later, they had ridden directly into town and straight to the sheriff's office. On the way, Jamison said, "Mr. Taggert, I'd like to talk to you."

Jesse slowed Judas and came alongside his horse. "And?"

"I would like to make a deal."

"The sheriff and your lawyer can do that. You think you know enough to be worthwhile?"

"I know Brooks was behind it. So you better keep me alive to testify." He smirked. "Wilson was his man locally. I was asked to bring in Evans. I should have listened to Patrick and stayed out of the whole thing."

"Where's your brother?"

"He went out to the ranch with us, but after we heard Brooks talk, he got me aside and said this whole thing was crazy. He wasn't going on with it."

"And?"

"I helped him drop back, and he rode back to Tucson. I don't know where he is now, but he never did anything more than watch over you that time. He didn't like any part of it. I've been paying for his education his art career. He owed me. I pressured him into helping me. I don't think he did anything he should go to prison for."

"Guess that will be up to the judge and sheriff. So he heard Brooks set this up also?"

Jamison nodded. "I just hope he stayed away from him. I think Brooks is more dangerous than others might believe. He orders killings but... there's been more to it. Don't ever turn your back on him."

Jesse had already figured that.

"One more thing. Wilson has a warrant out on him. It's why he changed his name. The charges are in Kansas and not all that old either."

"I'll tell the sheriff that I never saw you pull your gun out at the adobe." Jesse smiled. "Which is why you're still alive."

Jamison managed a sick smile. "I thought it might work that way."

By the time they had reached Sheriff Adam's office, they had acquired a following. Jesse dismounted and helped Lily down. Sheriff Adams came out, looked at the bodies draped over horses, the riders bound, and then up at Jesse. "You've been busy."

"Can you put these three in a cell, and we talk?"

"Oh you can believe we can talk," Adams said as Jeremiah and Rance helped get the men into the jail. The corpses they left on the horses.

An hour later, the whole story having been told, by four voices sometimes at once, and then repeated by Rupert Jamison, Adams sat back in his chair and lit his pipe. "I talked to Brooks after the Sykes shooting. He came back?"

"There are witnesses to say he did. Maybe never went that far."

"Looks like this time there is evidence."

"With so many seeing us come in, he may try to leave fast."

"I'll call the depot. Just a minute." When he came back, he said, "No trains go out until six tonight. We have time to find and question him."

"Unless he rents a buggy," Jeremiah suggested.

"I'll put the word out," Adams said. "I don't much care for grifters coming from out of town and causing my little town problems."

"I'll see if he's at the San Xavier," Jesse said as he lifted Lily from her chair. "You're near exhaustion, baby. You need to go to the Olivers."

"I would like to go with you."

He smiled. "Wasn't there something about obey in that thing?"

She laughed despite the tiredness in her eyes. "You going to enforce it."

"Try anyway." He looked then at his father. "Will you see my wife gets there?"

Jeremiah smiled. "With pleasure."

"I heard you two got hitched," Adams said. "Congratulations to you both."

Outside, Jesse lifted Lily onto the horse. "You will be careful," she said. "You haven't healed up the other wound. There better be no new holes in you."

"Yes, ma'am."

She bent then and kissed him. "I love you." He watched until she and Jeremiah disappeared.

When he mounted Judas, he found Rance Evans with him. "You going somewhere?" he asked.

"Yep. With you. I ain't about to see this varmint walk off. And I like that little gal of yores; so will do what I can to make sure you acquire no new holes."

Jesse gave off with a laugh. "That's all huh?"

"You are smarter than your pa says, ain't you?"

"Maybe."

"Wal, maybe I don't like what he did to get my son killed. Maybe I know ya killed Billy, so I didn't have to do it and figured I owe ya somethin'."

"It's not worth losing your life over it."

"I wasn't figgerin' to take it quite that far."

At the San Xavier, he told Rance to wait outside and make sure Brooks didn't leave. Inside, the desk clerk said yes that Mr. Brooks was still there. "Tell him someone needs to talk to him in the lobby," Jesse said as he stepped away from the desk and waited. It was a good ten minutes before Brooks came down. He looked around and then saw Jesse. He came over, carefully husbanding his features with a smile that showed none of what he might be feeling.

"I am surprised to see you," he said as he stopped in front of Jesse.

"Yeah, you would be."

"Did that have meaning, Mr. Taggert?"

"We both know it did."

"Are your things out of your room, Mr. Brooks?" the clerk asked from his desk.

"Checking out today, huh?" Jesse said.

"Business calls."

"You'll be talking to the sheriff first."

"I don't need a sheriff."

"Him and then a lawyer."

Brooks smirked. "You have nothing on me. You are nobody and less. Anything you might think you have will be blasted away by my good name."

"Maybe at one time."

"What does that mean?"

"There are more witnesses than one."

"You think so? Well they are all outlaws aren't they?"

"And you'd know that why?"

"Who else would make up lies against an upstanding citizen?"

"What about Patrick Jamison?"

Brooks smiled again. "What about him?"

"He one of those outlaws?"

"Was he with the ones who attacked you?"

"Did I say that happened?"

"I assumed it did with how you have acted and saying I need to talk to the sheriff." He was quick with his comeback.

"Your game is up, Brooks. Even though I don't know all of what your reasons were, I know enough. You are going to jail this time along with those you paid."

"You can't prove any of it."

"You will find out soon enough."

"I am going nowhere with you."

"Fine. The sheriff will be here soon enough." He had a concern then. "Where is Patrick Jamison?"

"Why would I know? He's not a friend of mine."

"But he was working for you, wasn't he?"

"Ridiculous. You really are a fool, aren't you? I can't begin to imagine why Lily married you. I am sure she will correct that mistake."

"That will be her business. Where is Jamison?"

"I just told you why should I know?"

"You're lying. Is he in your room?"

Brooks glared at him. "I am leaving. Good luck with your annulment."

Jesse let him get to the door where Rance was waiting. "You the bastard who got my son killed," he said with a snarl.

Brooks looked back then at Jesse. "This is all your fault. Why she would choose a man like you when she could have had me." He raised his voice then. "Wait, don't draw. Put your gun away!"

Jesse hadn't touched his gun, but he dodged to the side as he saw the derringer come into Brooks' hand. He felt the bullet hit his shoulder as he yanked out his own gun. It wasn't needed, as Rance shot first, and his shot went right into the middle of Brooks' forehead.

Adams was there by the last shot. "Guess he won't be using that ticket," he said as he knelt by Brooks' body. He looked then up at Jesse. "You got hit."

"Yeah, not going to make Lily happy." Being a derringer meant a smaller bullet, but it was still in the muscle and hurt like hell.

"You shoot him?" He asked rising.

Rance said, "Nah, I did it. He was about to kill my friend here. That derringer of his has two shots."

Adams smiled and nodded. "Good job then." He looked back at Jesse. "You're bleeding, son. You need to see Doc Hadley."

Reluctantly, he nodded. Rance stayed with him until he'd had the bullet dug out, antiseptic applied and then a bandage. "Come back to get the dressing changed," Hadley said. "Who do I bill?"

He had to think about that and then he remembered. "Me. I'll take care of it." He wrote down the address of Lily's house. Actually, he was owed wages for the last month at the XY, but it was highly unlikely he'd be seeing any of that.

"You okay for riding?" Rance asked as they reached their horses.

"This is nothing. I mostly don't look forward to Lily riding me about it." He stopped and lit a cigarette. Then he realized he hadn't told the truth. He was very much looking forward to her riding him. He grinned as Rance lit a cigar.

"Yeah, life is rough," the old-timer said.

"I'm sorry about Billy. You were right. I did kill him to save you having to do it but also to save my own hide. He was one of the few, other than Wilson, who knew how to use a gun."

"My son was a fool. They might call you that for being slow sometimes, but son, you make good choices when you move."

"I try."

"You got lucky with that gal."

"I did. More than I deserved."

"No man deserves a good woman like her. Purely luck. Or so I tell myself since I never did find one. Billy's mother was a whore—professional and otherwise." He shook his head. "Maybe though I'd not know what to do with a good woman. Hope you do."

When Jesse looked up, he saw Patrick Jamison standing above him on the boardwalk. Surprisingly, he was holding a gun, pointed at Jesse's chest. "Where's my brother?"

"I thought you wanted to stay out of this," Jesse said.

"Where's Rupert?"

"And if you don't like the answer, you plan to use that?" Jesse asked as he walked straight for Jamison.

"I might. Did you kill him?"

Jesse stepped onto the boardwalk so that Patrick had to face him but wasn't able to also watch Rance.

"I'm going to kill you," Jamison said.

"You might kill a man in a fight, Patrick," Jesse said, "but I doubt you'd do it in cold blood." To be on the safe side, he kicked out with his boot and knocked the gun from the artist's hand. He saw the tears then in his eyes.

"Your brother is in jail," he said as Rance picked up the gun. "He's singing like a canary to get a lighter sentence which, since he didn't shoot his gun off when he was there, is likely."

"Why didn't you tell me that?" Patrick said wiping away the tears.

"You didn't ask nice."

Patrick then managed a smile. "I respect you, Mr. Taggert. I hate to have to say that, but you might be the only man besides my brother who I ever have. I am sorry for being part of what was happening."

"What was Brooks trying to do? It can't just be about Lily."

"No, he told us last night when I saw how horrible the whole thing was. He is some kind of commodities broker. He found out about renewed interest in the minerals in the Silver Bell area. Some men have been forming conglomerates to make larger mines. He wanted to get the land first and then sell it to them at a high price. The XY has several promising deposits. It was to be his start."

"So he tried to ruin the ranch to get it at a cheaper price."

"That was it." Patrick nodded. "I am sorry I ever got into it. I had my own stupid idea that Lily would be attracted to me and marry me. That would've solved my money problems, but she never saw me at all."

"Brooks wanted her too."

"I know. I have never been such a fool on anything. I'd leave town but no money. Sorry to have to hang around. I am sweeping out the Pedrales to earn train fare."

"I know you didn't like what was going on that day."

"It sickened me, but I was too weak to do anything to stop it."

"I can understand that. And even now with you holding that gun on me, you were upset about your brother. Sometimes a man gets into a hole, and it's hard to get out." Then he had a thought. "You ever do portraits like on order?"

Patrick's mouth dropped open. "I do commissions."

"Well, if you can do one of Lily, I think I could get you the money for train fare back east."

Patrick smiled. "I'd do her for free."

"No need."

"You think they'll arrest me too."

"As things stand, unlikely. Unless Rupert knows more than I do."

"I'll go talk to him." He turned and headed for the jail at a faster walk than one would expect as hot as it was.

"You took a risk there, son," Rance said as they both mounted and started their horses toward Olivers.

"The way he was shaking with that hogleg, he was as likely to shoot you as me-- or himself for that matter."

"You gonna tell your woman about this?"

"Only if she's riding me about the bullet hole." Jesse took a deep draw on his cigarette. It wasn't giving him his usual pleasure, and he thought maybe he'd have to quit. He missed being able to smell the scents of the desert. Did he really need cigarettes anymore?

"Good thinking. I said you weren't as dumb as some thought." Rance chuckled.

Jesse thought about that. Since Lily had come into his life, he had begun to wonder about that himself. Maybe he had just not been pushing himself enough. She provided all the challenge he needed to wake up.

By the time they got to the Oliver place, Jesse was feeling enough discomfort to decide a derringer did more damage than he had thought. Or else the doc digging out the bullet had. Either way he was relieved to dismount. Before he could turn to head up to the house, she had run down and thrown her arms around him.

"Whoa," he said with a groan as she came in contact with the thick bandage.

"You did get shot again." It wasn't a question as she stepped back.

"Derringer. They don't do as much damage."

"Who?"

"Brooks. He won't be bothering you again. And before you ask. I didn't kill him. Rance did."

Ollie took his horse. "You staying here tonight?"

"I guess."

"When we went down to Rose's old home to water, found a few rats there." Ollie's smile was crooked. "We moved 'em out. Maybe though you won't like the memories there. Lily told us what happened."

"I have good ones too. It's up to Lily where we stay tonight."

Jeremiah had come down to listen but said nothing.

"Before you got shot again," Lily said, "I just wanted to get back to the adobe. Now though you need a night's rest."

"You know we aren't likely to be able to keep it." He also though could think of nowhere he'd rather be with Charlie and Bear. He had the strength to make it but getting used to what he couldn't keep seemed a mistake.

"Maybe we could rent a wagon and you could ride in the back," Lily suggested still wearing that concerned look regarding his wound.

He smiled at that. "I am not hurt that much."

"Hell," Jeremiah said with a chuckle. "We'd ride along to pick him up if he fell off."

That annoyed Jesse. "I've never fallen of a horse and am not about to start, but..."

"Jesse," she said, "I have something to confess to you."

He didn't like the sounds of that nor of her concerned look. Maybe she had changed her mind after all about being his wife. He looked down and the gold ring was still in place.

Ollie said, "We'll let you two talk this out—why don't ya head over to the gazebo. Rose and I have good luck there. Come on Jeremiah and Rance. I got a good bottle of bourbon up at the house."

They walked to the gazebo and Jesse felt concern with the way she was acting. "All right," he said, as soon as they sat on one of its benches. "Let me have it."

"When we were at Sicillas, I sent a message to my lawyer."

So, she did want a divorce after all. "All right."

"And he set in motion our purchase of the adobe, its buildings, the springs-- there are apparently three of them. It amounts to one hundred and sixty acres."

"You what?" He found his mind closing down. This wasn't going where he'd expected, and he wondered if he was having a delusion. He'd heard some had those.

"I am going too fast. Sorry. I had our lawyer, the man you met the day we got married, make an offer to buy the adobe. Mr. Tibbets accepted it. I arranged the offer as an anonymous buyer but that will, of course, change when we transfer the funds and both sign the contract." She looked at him with a worried expression. "I should have talked to you first but wasn't sure it would go through. He's selling off several parcels separate from the ranch. We had to pay a little more because of rumors there might be minerals of value on some of it. Frankly, we are lucky we moved fast because apparently there are other buyers interested."

"One of them is dead."

"Harold?"

"It appears that was why he was wanting Wilson out there, why they wanted me off the land."

"Then I am glad I told our lawyer to not quibble over the price. It is still quite affordable. It's such a wonderful place and from what I saw of the plat map that Mr. Angus brought up after I called him, it includes that old ruin and those petroglyphs. Maybe Holly would do a dig there."

He took some deep breaths trying to make sense of this. "You own the adobe."

"We will, at least as soon as we pay the rest of the money owed and sign the contract. There are a few legal steps, but the land will soon be ours. He accepted the deposit and signed the original purchase offer. James says it is just a matter of time now."

"You honestly want to live out there?"

"More than anything—well, except for you. I do want to change a few things.

"Like?"

"We will need a few more rooms with there being three of us."

"Three?"

"Charlie, you and me. I would like you to build a good solid chicken house. I seriously love eggs—and chicken." She smiled with a little more confidence.

"You want to stay married to me?"

"Haven't I convinced you of that by now?"

"Even if we can't have children?"

"Nobody knows about that for sure, Jesse. I mean maybe I couldn't, but someday, if we are blessed, I'd love nothing more than to have your babies. You worry about it now, but you will see that it'll be all right."

"You have a lot of confidence," he said with a small smile.

"I do... where it's us."

And then, he knew she was right. There was an *us*. He bent to kiss her lips ignoring the pain to his side and shoulder. He would make the adobe into a home. He had a family now. A bigger one than he had ever expected, made up of kin and friends. The word friends had a new meaning. It all was because of Lily. She had given him everything, more than he'd ever imagined possible. He smiled then. "So I think we better get something to eat and then go tell Charlie the good news."

She laughed. "Just don't you dare fall off your horse."

He snorted. "I have never fallen off one, but if I did." He laughed. "At least, now I have those I can trust to pick me back up."

Hours later, they had gone to the spring and spread a quilt to spend the night. He had made short work of her clothing, playing with her body, as he expertly knew how to do.

"You are a tease," she said beginning to unbutton his shirt and then push off his pants.

"Me? I'm a tease?"

"You are but so am I." She pushed him flat and began to use her own sensual skills to arouse him even further. "I love you so much, Jesse," she whispered as she nipped his ear lobe.

"And I love you." He smiled as he sucked in a breath at her next exploration of his body. "Verlebena," he said as he moved to come over her.

"Wait. What does that mean?" She pushed lightly against his chest to stop him.

"Vince told it to me. It's Apache. It means forever." With that he took her.

"Verlebena," she said with a cry of welcome.

EPILOGUE

April 1905 Tucson, Arizona

L ily rested her hands on her round ball of a belly as she took her sister through the expanding adobe to its newest addition. "I think we're a year away from an inside bathroom," Lily said, "which would be nice. One thing at a time though."

"I like this nursery," Holly said as she looked at the crib and dresser, the colorful art on the wall. "It's convenient to the master bedroom but won't be too hot in the summer with its windows facing north."

They walked back through the sprawling rooms. Room by room the original adobe had been expanded until it flowed with an almost organic shape with outdoor patios and gardens as part of its structure. For Lily the goal had been a home that easily moved from the desert to the rooms. She had shared that goal with Jesse. With Grace Cordova drawing the plans, he had made it happen.

They stopped in what classically might have been considered the parlor, except it didn't fit the usual pattern for one with its rustic qualities blended with comfort. It had an unusually high ceiling covered with large wood beams and between them ocotillo stacks. At one end of the large room was a floor to ceiling stone fireplace. Its two leather sofas were large enough not to be engulfed by the room. That room had been inspired by a visit to the Ryker ranch out in the San Rafael valley. In fact, Lily thought, every bit of the home had been inspired by various pieces of the desert she had come to love so much.

Over the fireplace was the Jamison portrait. Although Jesse had wanted Patrick to paint it of just her, he had pulled a trick on his client, and it was of them together. Jesse was standing above her, his eyes gazing skyward but with a protective hand on her shoulder. She sat on a garden chair like the one at the Rose Cottage except the background had been replaced by the desert she saw daily out her windows or when she went for a walk. Patrick had done a masterful job in making them not stand out as separate from each other or their environment. They were the desert.

"It's a wonderful painting," Holly said as the sisters looked up at it. "How is he doing?"

"When Rupert got out of prison two months ago, Patrick wrote to tell us that he would be there to pick him up. He said they will get a new start in California. I hope this one works better for them both."

Holly smiled. "Some people do change."

"True."

"For instance Jesse. He's not the same man at all since you and he married. I still remember the day we got off the train from our California trip. I saw you and was so happy and then there was Jesse beside you, his arm around your waist. I was literally floored, but Vince seemed less so. I never dreamed you'd fall in love with him."

"Why not?"

Holly laughed. "I don't know because now I can't imagine you not together."

"I don't ever want to imagine that."

"And this home is so you and him together."

"It does feel like it's part of the desert, doesn't it?" Lily said as they went into the kitchen where she poured boiling water into a teapot to steep the leaves she'd added earlier.

Going to the sink, she pumped more water to put on the stove to heat. One of the things she had appreciated, even more than the additions to the adobe, was when they had a well drilled and finally fresh water inside. The gas-fueled cook stove added to their comforts.

"I love adobe," Holly said pulling Lily's thoughts back to her sister. "I liked it in the rose cottage and the house Ollie built for Rose. Vince and I bought a nice frame home, but now I am thinking maybe we will build an adobe too. I mean with our family growing." She patted her own expanding girth. "It would make sense."

"If you came out this way, say bought that piece of land next to ours, we could share chickens and such. Maybe even expand our gardens to have you plant one thing and us another. I am still trying to convince Jesse we need either a cow or goat."

"I'd also love where we could sit down to tea without having to ride so far."

They had brought the buggy this time for convenience, and it made the journey take longer.

"The Reasoners bought the land two parcels over. This area could even have enough children someday for a school. They have three little ones." Lily poured their tea.

"Another plus." She sipped her tea. "Is this one of Connie's?"

"It is supposed to be good for the last part of a pregnancy."

"Will you have your baby in town at the rose cottage?"

"I would like to have her here." She smiled. "Doc saw no reason I can't."

"Ah and you know it's a she?"

"Of course not. Just a feeling."

"Jesse seems to be handling this one better than I expected."

Lily smiled. "Yes, now that he has stopped worrying that she will be born with his disability."

"Which in him shows up less and less. I do think it was made worse by his isolating himself so many years."

"Well, those years are past." She laughed. "If you move nearby, even if there isn't a school, we could teach our children together, each take a subject maybe."

"I've talked to him about it. Vince liked the idea but not the moving." She giggled. "He's pretty fond of the small ranch we have, and I think that he spent so many years always on the move, that he gets settled now, and doesn't want to change anything. He loves Jesse though; so it might happen yet."

Charlie came into the kitchen. "You ladies look like two flowers settin' there," he said as he reached into the ice box for a bottle of beer and came to sit with them. They did not have electricity yet but blocks of ice kept things cool until the hottest summer months.

When Lily heard the excited barking of Bear she got up and went to the window. The original adobe had become their kitchen, so it still overlooked the corrals and barns.

"Looks like Cole is here," she said as she watched two horsemen ride in and a tall man dismount.

Holly joined her on the veranda. "He looks good," she said smiling.

"He does. The most relaxed I've ever seen. I just wish he was closer and we could see more of him," Lily agreed.

"Do you wonder sometimes what he's been doing?"

"Jesse doesn't seem to know and yes, I wonder. Jesse just says he's fine which amazes me. Why isn't he more curious?"

"What we need is to get him married." The two giggled. "Do we know anyone?"

"You mean set him up?" Lily made a face of mock horror.

"I suppose that would be risky. Matchmaking often backfires. Still will he settle down on his own? With a wife, we'd know what he was up to. She'd want to be close to family and..."

"All right... I am thinking."

Holly closed her eyes as though drawing up an invisible list. "I did go to school with a few very impressive women—several of whom have not yet married... or are already divorced." She grinned.

"Divorced? I don't think we want a divorcee do we? I don't much like the idea of seeing Cole hurt."

"You think he'd like a woman like us?"

"Or might he prefer a fancy woman?" Lily watched Cole, who was moving his arms expressively as he explained something to his father who was the one who had ridden in with him.

"He's the thinker of the three. I doubt that... other than perhaps as a dalliance."

"He probably can get those on his own."

"I agree that he needs a wife. Then he'd want to be around us more. Maybe even move down this way and leave those cattle for somebody else to manage."

It was then that Lily noticed Charlie had been listening to them but not saying a word. When she looked back at him, he grinned. "I am seein' another side of you two and glad I put my faith in Sarie."

Lily laughed. "Watch out or we'll go matchmaking for you too."

He cackled. "Won't do ya no good. I am onto ya now. Ya know, it might be he's happy like me—being a bachelor," he added with a twinkle.

"Well, what we want and what is good for us can be two different things." Holly made a sanctimonious face.

Lily looked back at Holly. "I don't think I know a woman aggressive enough. I mean think what it took for us to hook a Taggert."

"Listening to you two, I'm thinkin' I oughta go down and warn the boy," Charlie said taking a slug from his beer.

"You wouldn't dare," Holly said laughing.

"I would but maybe be more fun seein' it play out."

The three looked down as Vince and Jesse joined the other two, hugging and laughing. Vince had a small boy in his arms, his and Holly's first son, Tyler. Joshua, Lily and Jesse's first child was right on his father's heels.

Once Josh had been born and was normal, Jesse's fears regarding his disability being passed onto a child began to disappear. As the boy had grown, talked early and often, been forceful, filled with determination, in his eagerness to learn each new life skill, Jesse lost his fear that the next one would be different.

"Not like it takes being married to be happy," Charlie said polishing off the beer. "Man can find a family other ways—don't have to want a wife." He winked at Lily.

"That's true but what we want and what is good for us are often two different things," Holly said adding back in that superior tone.

"Well, whatever the case, we don't tell Jesse and Vince," Lily said and she looked back at Charlie. "Promise."

"Nah, I won't ruin your fun."

"Especially since we have yet to think of a suitable victim... I mean bride," Holly said with another laugh.

Lily watched as Jesse laughed with Cole and Vince. Then he looked away from his brothers as though the invisible bond that they shared had again pulled him to her. He smiled with that glint in his eyes that told her he understood more than she might even wish.

As she watched the tall men walk up to the adobe, talking and laughing, Bear trailing behind two small boys who were giggling over something that likely only they would find funny, Lily's life felt very full. She rubbed her belly again. Well, almost full.

The End

Please leave a review and select more Rain Trueax books via the kinks at http://romanceswithanedge.blogspot.com/

ABOUT THE AUTHOR

Why Arizona ?

For fifty years, the Arizona Sonoran Desert has been one of the homes of my heart and soul. Although a small Oregon ranch held the rest of my heart, for years, I dreamed of owning a home on the desert, then one year the dream came true. After living in the house only a few days it told my husband and me its name—Casa Espiritu. It is a home to inspire creativity and spiritual connection to self and the other.

As with all dreams, it is not somewhere I constantly live, but for now, it is waiting when the time is right. In my little spirit home, I have seen dreams come true, written books, created art, loved, wept, experienced being.

From it, I have watched javelina, coyotes, bunnies, birds, bobcats, and most especially the families of quail. I have seen the lightning flash and felt the house rocked by thunder. I have watched the moon rise over Pusch Ridge and seen the sun go down behind the Tucson Mountains. From it, I have gone out to find interesting trails, desert pools, creeks, petroglyphs. I've watched the desert bloom, seen it snow. The house and how we found it might be magic even though it's a very plain house, except it doesn't feel plain when I fall asleep to the noisy calls of two owls from the ironwood trees right outside the bedroom window.

All this proximity to the natural desert, its denizens, and the historical remnants of many cultures has inspired six Arizona histor-ical romances and one contemporary. They become love stories to the desert as much as of the couples who populate the pages of the books.

November 5, 2015, I will be bringing out my next novel, *Lands of Fire*. I've had heroes and heroines escaping through the desert, set many of my stories in Tucson, to the south of it in the ranchlands near the border, or up in Central Arizona, but mostly my characters have visited the desert but not lived in it. For my sixth in this series, my hero does live on the desert and the descriptions of what he experiences there as well as my heroine's coming to learn about it make up a lot of the book. Writing about a region, which I love so much, the tall saguaros, the prickly ironwood, the hidden waterholes, the mountains, the canyons, was a joy.

As I write my books, I fall a little in love with every hero. If I don't, the story is going nowhere; but I will say the hero of *Lands of Fire* was particularly endearing. In Jesse Taggert's time he was regarded as slow-witted or by even crueler terms. Today, the politically correct term is mentally challenged. Jesse has retreated from people into the desert. He only trusts animals. As *Lands of Fire opens*, his life is about to be upturned. A woman is coming, who sees more in him than he does himself. She isn't about to give up on what she knows will make her life better, which includes Jesse and his desert.

Lands of Fire is about how we often find, when we are willing to look, that our limitations also are our strengths. It is the sixth Arizona historical. These books follow family and friends along a time in Arizona's history. Each stands alone with no cliffhangers. The romances begin in 1883 with *Arizona Sunset*, move forward with family and friends through *Tucson Moon, Arizona Dawn, Rose's Gift,* and *Echoes from the Past* until they reach 1902 and *Lands of Fire.* One more will be due out February 5, 2016 and whether that's the last is uncertain as the offspring of these characters are growing up and the country is working its way to WWI and a lot of major cultural changes. If I do continue with them, the possibility is they will no longer be considered western historicals. I'll worry about that if another time and set of characters call out to have their stories told.

Thanks for reading Lands of Fire, *Rain*

other
rain trueax stories

Arizona Based
Desert Inferno
Arizona Sunset
Tucson Moon
Arizona Dawn
Rose's Gift

Echoes From The Past

Oregon Historicals
Round The Bend
Where Dreams Go

Northwest Contemporaries
Moon Dust
Evening Star
Bannister's Way
Second Chance
Hidden Pearl
Her Dark Angel
From Here To There
Montana Christmas
Luck of the Draw

Fantasy - Paranormal
Diablo Canyon Trilogy
Sky Daughter